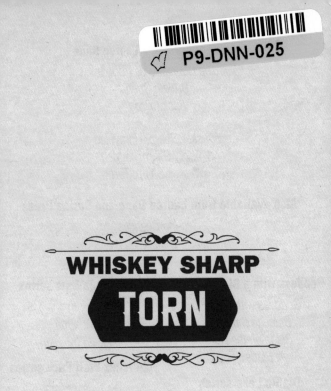

WHISKEY SHARP

TORN

L A U R E N
DANE

WHISKEY SHARP

TORN

HQN™

HQN™

ISBN-13: 978-0-373-79942-8

Recycling programs for this product may not exist in your area.

Whiskey Sharp: Torn

This edition published by arrangement with Harlequin Books S.A.

For questions and comments about the quality of this book, please contact us at CustomerService@Harlequin.com.

® and TM are trademarks of Harlequin Enterprises Limited or its corporate affiliates. Trademarks indicated with ® are registered in the United States Patent and Trademark Office, the Canadian Intellectual Property Office and in other countries.

www.HQNBooks.com

Printed in U.S.A.

May we all be fortunate enough
to be understood by those who love us.

Author Note

While Pioneer Square and SoDo are two very real neighborhoods in downtown Seattle, I've taken some liberties. Added some buildings, renamed a few, as it helped flesh out the characters and their stories. Still, Pioneer Square is every bit the former home to bootleggers and the criminal element partly responsible for the face of the city today.

CHAPTER ONE

Pointed west home beckons.
Waits for you like a lover.

NOT TOO MANY hours after getting off an airplane, Cora
approached Whiskey Sharp—a barbershop, and in
the evenings, a bar. The lazily swirling red-and-white
candy cane sign out front was illuminated and the interior lights cast a shine against the gold-toned flourish of the shop's title on the front glass doors.

Inside, it smelled of sandalwood and amber, two of
the more popular scents of the products used in hair
and beards. Music played loud enough to feel like an
embrace but it didn't drown out the low hum of conversation from the people knotted around the bar area.

Alexsei Petrov, Maybe's husband, but also Cora's
friend, owned and ran the place that had become another home for Cora. He saw her come in and smiled,
tipping his chin to where Maybe stood, working at
her station. Giving someone a shave by the looks of it.

Three months before, her friend's hair had been plat-
inum blonde, but currently the tips were a brilliant teal
blue that bled into a wash of purple.

It would have looked absurd on most people, but

Maybe managed to make it seem retro and futuristic at the same time when she coupled it with high-waisted gray pinstripe pants and a crisp white button-down shirt.

Rachel stood, her hip resting against the table, a smile on her face reserved for the client who Cora now recognized as Rachel's man, Vic, sitting in Maybe's chair getting that shave.

The weight of the familiar was lovely and bloomed through her belly. This was another one of her places. Full of her people.

"You bitches are still the hottest chicks I know," she said as she approached.

Rachel looked over, her eyes widening in pleasure and recognition. "You're here!"

"I told you I'd come by," Cora said, swallowed up into a hug.

"I know but you're here now. Yay!" Maybe took over the next hug, smacking a kiss right onto her lips before stepping back.

Laughing, she got hugs from the wild bearded Russians, as Rachel and Maybe referred to their dudes.

"Everyone missed you. Not more than us, naturally, but still," Rachel said after Cora had been loved up on by all her friends. "Three months is way too long to go without seeing you."

"It's nice to be missed." She was pretty sure she'd just finished her last extended trip with her mother. Yes, it was travel for work and she liked to go to new places. But these long stints meant she had avoided getting a dog or a cat. It wasn't fair to have to leave them with someone for weeks and weeks. It also meant that aside from one long-distance relationship that had ended two years before, Cora hadn't really seen anyone seriously.

She wanted more roots. And a dog. And maybe someone to go on dates with.

She'd settle for a drink and some food as she hung out with her crew to start.

"Wren said she already invited you to dinner," Maybe called out as she began to clean her station up.

"She informed me one of their friends is cooking and that there'd be cake. So naturally I'm in."

Gregori—another wild bearded Russian—was Vic and Alexsei's cousin. He also happened to be a hugely successful artist Cora had known for years through the local art scene. He and his wife, Wren—an artist in her own right—lived in a loft space above Whiskey Sharp.

"There's always cake at their place. It's like a little bit of heaven right upstairs," Maybe said.

"It's like what *I* imagine heaven to be, that's for sure," Cora answered.

"If there's no cake, how can it be heaven?" Rachel said it like a sacred prayer and Cora agreed utterly.

"I can't wait to hear all about your time in London but Wren said she wanted to hear it too and so not to visit too much without her." Maybe hooked her arm through Cora's. "I want to hear it now, so let's get going. I'm also hungry."

"You know how she gets when she's hungry," Alexsei said with a smirk at the corners of his mouth. Maybe rolled her eyes, but smiled as she did it, so Cora knew she wasn't offended.

And he was right because Maybe was lovely and sweet, but *not* when she was hungry.

They all headed out and down the sidewalk half a block to the doors leading to the small lobby, where the residents of the lofts had their mailboxes and the elevator.

The scent of garlic and onions swirled around her senses as they got out on the right floor. Gregori and Wren's door was painted bright, shiny red and flew open before they were able to use the doorbell.

Wren, wearing a huge grin, rushed at Cora and hugged her tight. "Hi! Come have champagne and eat yummy food while you tell us all how the last three months were."

"I can do that. You look fantastic," Cora told her as they headed toward the kitchen area. "Marriage agrees with you."

Her friends had come back from an impromptu trip right before Cora had left for London only to announce they'd gotten married along the way. After several years of living together, it had been the right choice for their relationship.

"I look exactly the same except for the ring part and the way his mom gives me, and then my belly, a pointed look every time I see her," Wren said.

"Welcome to my world," Maybe said. "Irena has now taken to telling me about all the baby clothes she saw but didn't buy because she had no grandchildren to wear them. I tried to get her obsessing about Rachel's womb, but she's too wily."

"Mind your own womb. You've been with Alexsei longer than I've been with Vic. It's your time to shine, bitch," Rachel said with a laugh.

"I'm so messed up. I missed you all so much." Cora hugged each one tightly.

"You're the perfect kind of messed up," Rachel said, linking her arm through Cora's.

This was good. The best, happiest part of her life.

Her stomach growled as she sucked in the scents all around. "I need food."

"We've got that covered," Gregori called out to them. "Come, I'm pouring champagne."

"No need to call me twice when there's booze involved," Cora murmured to Rachel, who snickered.

Fairy lights and candles made the loft glow. Plus it was the perfect light and her skin would look way better than the jet lag currently responsible for dark circles under her eyes.

"It's all romantical in here and shit," Cora said, and then nearly swallowed all her spit when she caught sight of who was standing at the stove.

CHAPTER TWO

There is wild joy in recognition.
A leap of faith to let yourself be known.
An old magic.

WELL OVER SIX FEET of hot-ass ginger celebrity chef, former model and childhood poster boy for a cult—and
most notably one of her first really hard crushes—Beau
Petty had aged really, *really* well. He had the kind of
face that would only get better as he aged. At seventy-
five, he'd still be searingly hot because it wasn't just
that he was chiseled and taut and broad shouldered,
his attitude seemed to pump out confident alpha male.

He'd been gorgeous when she'd been sixteen and he
twenty-one or -two, but seventeen years later, he was
magnetic and intense on a whole new level. It made
her heart skip a little just looking at him.

Cora had to lock her knees when his gaze flicked
from Rachel over to her and his expression melted from
surprise into pleasure as he dried his hands on a towel
and headed toward her.

And then he hugged her and holy wow it was better
than a doughnut. He smelled good and was big and hard

and, wow, he was hugging her and when he stepped back he said her name. "Cora."

It seemed as if the word echoed through her, plucked her like a musical note.

Wow.

"It's really good to see you," he said as he stepped back, and she had to crane her neck to look up, and up, into his face.

"What an unexpected surprise," Cora told him.

"We have some catching up to do."

The lines around his eyes begged for a kiss.

"You guys know each other? I mean, duh. Obviously as you just said her name and there was a hug and stuff." Maybe smiled brightly, fishing for details in her cheerful, relentless way.

"First champagne and introductions, and then we will hear that story," Gregori said, interrupting Maybe's nosiness long enough to hand out glasses.

HE'D KNOWN BACK then that she'd had a crush on him, but she was still a kid. Then. Now? She still carried herself as if a secret song played in her head. But there was nothing girlish about her now.

Her hair—shades of brunette from milk chocolate to red wine—was captured back from her face in a ponytail, tied with a scarf that managed to look artsy and retro instead of silly. It only accentuated how big her eyes were, how high her cheekbones, the swell of her bottom lip that looked so juicy he wanted to bite it.

"Get started, if you're hungry." He indicated the long butcher-block counter where he'd set up some appetizers. "I was down at Pike Place earlier so the oysters are sweet and fresh. That's also where the octopus in the salad came from, caught today. Just a quick grill with lemon and olive oil and pickled red onions."

"Oh my god, really?" Cora cruised straight over and grabbed a plate.

A woman with an appreciation for food was sexy as hell.

"Update me on your life. What are you doing here in Seattle?" she asked, after eating two of the oysters and humming her satisfaction. "So good. This octopus is ridiculous. Is that jalapeño?"

"Good catch. Yes, in the olive oil I used to dress it."

"I like it. What else are you making? Not that this isn't really good, but I'm greedy."

Watching her enjoy his food was a carnal shot to his gut. It set him off balance enough that he focused on the food for a few beats.

"I'm working on a new cookbook so I'm trying out some seafood recipes. Scallop and crab cakes with a couscous salad," he said, pointing at the food.

"Yum! Ah, that's why you're in town?"

"I've been in Los Angeles for a long time." Feeling antsy. He had houses, but no home. "I felt a change would be good. A friend who owns a number of restaurants in the area has given me access to his kitchens so I can try my ideas out there, as well." He liked working around other chefs, found creative challenge in that atmosphere in a kitchen where the whole team loved to cook.

It was a good sort of competitive spirit. Pushed him

to up his game, to be better. Far healthier for his liver and heart than all the drugs and alcohol that'd fueled his early twenties.

"That's excellent," she said. "Sometimes a change in surroundings is what you need to hit the reset button. Congratulations on your success. Every time I see your face on a cookbook or on television it makes me smile."

He'd come a long way since he'd left the religious group many called a cult back when he was just seventeen. When he'd met Cora he'd only been out of Road to Glory for three years. Barely more than a legal adult. Modeling and wasting his money on drugs and private investigators, trying to find the children that had been stolen from him when the remaining cult members not yet arrested had gone on the run.

Seventeen years and it had been more than one lifetime. And he still hadn't found his sons, who were adults by that point. Wherever they were now, all Beau could do was hope they were all right.

He shoved it away, into that well-worn place he kept his past, and went back to her compliments. "Thanks. What are you up to these days? I know your mom is still working because I listen to her stuff a lot when I cook."

"She and I just got back from three months in London as she finished up a project."

Rachel wandered over to them to add her two cents. "*And* she pretty much runs the gallery. Plus she holds the tattoo shop together. *And* keeps Walda out of trouble, which is a full-time job. She writes poetry and takes amazing photographs. Oh, and she's an amazing knitter."

"I keep books for my sister from time to time. That's hardly holding the shop together," Cora said with affection clear in her tone.

"And the marketing. You set up the new network too. So, yeah, holding things together. It's what she does. How do you and Cora know one another?" Rachel repeated Maybe's earlier question more firmly, clearly taking his measure.

"At first glance you think it's Maybe who's the pushiest. But Rachel is way sneakier," Cora told him with a shrug. "Beau and I met when he and Walda lived in the same building in Santa Monica. I was fifteen or sixteen at the time. He was a model so Mom kept herself between us. As if he even noticed me when he was surrounded by gorgeous models."

He hadn't noticed Walda getting between him and Cora, but Cora had been correct that he hadn't seen her in that way. For a whole host of reasons, chiefly that she was simply too young.

Then. Not so much now.

"We were there a year so I had a tutor, who, if I recall correctly, Beau *definitely* noticed." Cora snickered.

Beau hadn't learned algebra until he was an adult. Hadn't read a single classic literary novel until he was twenty-one. Education was a tool, something to dig yourself out of a bad spot—especially if you didn't have the face and fortune to be a model while you got your education—so he was glad Walda snapped to it when it came to being sure her daughter got what she needed.

He honestly couldn't even remember the tutor, just the sweet kid who'd grown up well.

"Anyway, that's how we met, and in the intervening years he's been a supermodel and now a celebrity chef and cookbook author." Cora smiled at him. "Go you."

"How do you know Gregori?" Rachel asked once they'd settled in at the long table in the main room.

"Beau and I were young men with more money than sense in the art scene," Gregori said. "He was one of the first friends I made here in the US. We've been in contact on and off since. I had no idea of the connection between him and Cora."

"It was a pleasant surprise," Beau told them with a shrug. "I know many people. I'm friends with very few, so those I like to keep around."

"I didn't even know crab and scallop cakes were an actual thing. I vote yay," Cora said as she put another two on her plate.

In addition, there were brussels sprout leaves roasted with parmesan and walnuts, fruit and cheese with honey, wine, champagne and at the end, not just one cake, but two.

Not a lot satisfied Beau more than seeing people enjoy food he'd made. Cooking was his way of pleasing others. Of being worthy.

Even as fucked-up as he was, he'd managed to substitute out the most harmful ways of feeling worthy and pleasing others. His life was his own now. *No one* made his choices. He owed no one anything he didn't want to give.

A far cry from his days in Road to Glory, when every bit of his life had been chosen for him and the others in the group.

"You're having a very intense conversation in your head," Cora said quietly.

He shrugged. "Not really," he lied.

She sniffed, like she wanted him to know she saw right through him. Defensiveness rose in his gut, warring with fascination and no small amount of admiration that she would not only see the truth of it, but also let him know she got that he was evading.

But she let it go and he appreciated it a great deal.

A few hours in, Vic and Rachel peeled off. Gregori explained that Vic worked in a bakery, the same one that had provided some of the sweets they'd eaten that night, and had to be up by four-thirty.

He realized, as they cleaned up, that he didn't really want his time with Cora to end. Which was unusual. Unusual enough that he paid attention to it. She was a gorgeous, creative, interesting woman and an old friend. That was it. Probably.

Still, when she headed to the door, he followed. "Hey, where are you off to?"

"Home. I've been up well over twenty-four hours at this point and the travel has just sort of smacked me in the head. Now that my belly is full and I've been loved up on by my friends, I'm going to head back to my place and sleep for many hours."

"Where are you parked? Do you need a ride home?"

Wren asked Cora, and then Gregori sighed. Clearly *he'd* noticed the chemistry between Cora and Beau all night.

Cora hadn't seemed to hear Gregori's sigh as she replied, "I'm just parked right around the corner at the lot near Ink Sisters. I'm good. Thank you though." Cora hugged Wren, and then tiptoed up to do the same with Gregori.

"I'll walk with you," Beau said, grabbing his coat. "If that's cool with you."

Cora shrugged. "Sure. You don't have to. It's not that far."

"And then you can give him a ride," Gregori told her. "He's staying in a flat in the Bay Vista Tower so he's on your way home anyway."

Gregori gave him a very slight smile. Beau owed his friend a beer for that little suggestion that allowed him more time with her.

"Ah! Yes, that's totally on my way home. I can easily drop you off as a thanks for walking with me and defending my honor in case a drunken Pioneer Square reveler gives me any guff. Not that they would with an eleven-foot-tall dude, but you know what I mean," Cora said.

"There are perks to being tall. And I'd appreciate the ride as I walked over earlier today." And he'd get to be alone with her in the car, where he planned on asking her out.

He shouldn't. He usually kept himself clear of getting involved with a friend or anyone in his social circle that he might have to see regularly in the wake of something unpleasant.

But she felt like home to him in a way that he couldn't really put into words. And he really needed home after drifting for far too long.

CORA LIKED WALKING with Beau. When she stopped to peer more closely, and then photograph a wet leaf, he didn't get impatient. When she wanted to look in a window or pause to stare up at the lights, he paused too. He meandered like she did. Which was something she found herself charmed by.

Certainly there was no denying the way people tended to get out of their way as they came along. Even sauced-up patrons, who'd poured out of bars and onto the sidewalks, parted to let them pass. He was big. Sturdy and broad shouldered. As a short girl, it was pretty freaking nice, she had to admit.

So she told him. Or, well, she thought it out loud, and then just went with it because it was too late to do anything else.

He leaned closer and the heat of him seemed to brush against her skin. "It's a novel thing to imagine the world from your perspective," he said in a voice that wrapped around her and tugged.

What an unexpectedly wonderful compliment that was.

"Thank you. You have a great voice. I figure I should go ahead and tell you that." Flattered and a little flustered, Cora pointed at her car as they came upon the lot where she'd parked. "That's me."

Cora didn't think herself overly concerned with things. But this car—named Eldon—was her not-so-guilty pleasure.

A gift from her mother—because Cora never would have done it for herself and because Walda loved giving extravagant gifts. When it appealed to her anyway.

It was low-slung and sporty, and when she got in and closed the door, the world drifted away.

He came to a startled halt. "That?"

Cora was glad it was dark enough he couldn't see her blush. "Okay. I know. It's an extravagance. My mom decided I should have it. And I tried to turn it down or talk her into a less, uh, over-the-top choice. But she's Walda and she does what she wants."

"I'm jealous. I nearly bought a TT S last year."

Oh. Well, that was nice. Thanking him, she clicked the locks and he waited for her to get in before he followed suit.

"You're really tall and I was worried you'd have to bend like a pretzel to fit in the passenger seat. So I'm glad that didn't happen because you have those jeans on and I don't want you to have to cut off circulation or whatever."

Jesus, she just made a thinly veiled joke about his dick getting bent in an uncomfortable way. She'd been hanging out around the Dolans way too long.

He snorted a laugh. "I've never been as entertained by a conversation," he said as she pulled out of the lot.

"Oh. Well. Good because I'm entertaining that way so I'm delighted you can see the benefits. I'm glad you're in Seattle, Beau. I hope we'll see one another again before you leave. And wow, this whole segment of our conversation is really just me wandering all around. I'm normally better at this. Really."

"Still entertaining. Five stars," he said through laughter. "I'd love to see you again. Me and you. What does your kitchen look like?"

"Uh. It's a nice kitchen. I like to cook well enough. I decided to take the space from a third bedroom and make the kitchen and the master bigger. Gas stove."

He nodded and she felt a little relieved that she'd passed a test of some sort.

"Are you free tomorrow night? I'd like to make you dinner and catch up on the last seventeen years."

He just asked her out. She *hadn't* imagined the chemistry between them. This day was pretty fucking great so far.

"Totally free. I'll be home by six and I can handle the dessert."

"I'll be there by six-thirty with everything I need."

A wave of heat washed through her. There was no misunderstanding the way his voice had that husky undertone. That was perhaps—hopefully—an *I'll be putting my mouth on you at some point during this date* tone and she liked it. It left her drunk with delight.

She gave him her address as she found a space to slide into across the street from his building. "Okay. So. Um. I'll see you tomorrow night then."

He unbuckled himself, but before he got out, he leaned close and surprised her when he laid a kiss on her lips.

Just a casual kiss. Quick but not so fast he didn't slowly drag his teeth over her bottom lip as he pulled back.

"See you then."

Still tasting him, she watched as he jogged across the street, and then made his way into the building.

Cora wasn't entirely sure what she was getting herself into, but she liked it.

CHAPTER THREE

In a flurry of wind a red leaf skitters
Dances on the air
As summer dies
And autumn puts on her fiery crown.

"Why am I not surprised?" Cora asked.

Rachel and Maybe stood on her porch with a pink-and-white box holding her favorite doughnuts and bearing big grins as well as coffee.

She opened up. "Get in here before you let out all the warm air."

"You're not surprised because we're predictable and nosy. And because we come bearing coffee and doughnuts." Rachel kissed Cora's cheek before she put her things down and hung her coat in the front closet.

"We were sort of bummed to find out you're alone this morning," Maybe told her as she popped the lid off the doughnut box and carried it, along with her coffee, to the living room.

Cora snorted. "Don't you two have to be at work or something?"

"My first appointment isn't until one," Rachel said as she chose a chocolate-glazed.

"I'm sleeping with my boss," Maybe told her. "Makes it easier to take time off when I want to. So what's the deal with you and sexy chef guy? I know I wasn't imagining it. Especially when he just about shoved Wren out of the way when he got the chance to walk you to your car."

"He's making me dinner tonight." Cora sipped her coffee.

Rachel grabbed one of the throw blankets Cora kept everywhere and tucked it around herself before saying, "I Googled him this morning after Vic left for work. He pretended like he didn't know I was going to. We like to pretend I'm nicer than I really am. It's why we've stayed together for two years." Rachel continued after another bite of her doughnut, "But you know Beau's had quite the colorful life. I mean. Wow. Also the modeling shots alone might have made me pregnant."

Cora nearly choked on her coffee as she laughed. "Now imagine seeing that in person when you were sixteen."

"Dude, I'm absolutely convinced I'd have had no idea what to do with a guy like him when I was sixteen. All the tattoos and the piercings. Super hot."

"We saw the tasteful nudes. He's quite gifted. And a *natural* redhead." Maybe toasted Cora by holding her doughnut aloft a moment.

"You're going to have to Heimlich me if you make me laugh like this while I'm eating," Cora said between fits of giggles. "I missed you both. A lot."

"We missed you too. When you're done telling us about Beau, let's talk about you not leaving for so long again." Maybe reached out to squeeze Cora's leg a moment.

"He's got a complicated backstory, to say the least. It's not every day you meet someone who was raised in and later escaped from a cult. Still, there's something, I don't know, genuine about him. He's..." Cora raised her hands, not finding the right words for how she felt. "Aside from being gorgeous, he's interesting. It was easy being with him last night at Gregori and Wren's. And then after. He kissed me. Just a fast thing. Not a peck. No tongue, but he gave me some teeth when he broke the kiss. And he used the sex voice on me. It worked. I mean. Every part of me heard it, like a tuning fork."

"Zing." Rachel nodded her head and Maybe echoed the action. "You have zing. I have zing with Vic. Maybe's got it with Alexsei. Zing is good if it doesn't, you know, cloud your head because your *other* parts are too dazed. If you know what I mean."

Cora batted her lashes and leaned toward her friend. "No. What do you mean?"

Rachel started to reply before narrowing her gaze and flipping Cora off.

Laughing, Cora said, "It's been a while since I've been dazed with zing. It's not underrated." She hadn't had that sort of delicious sexual chemistry with someone in years and she hadn't realized until then how much she'd missed it.

"Seems to me your priorities are in the right order," Maybe told her. "Get some."

Rachel rolled her eyes before adding, "He could get

it, no lie. I mean, if I wasn't head over heels in love with Vic. Literally over the weekend. I need to start stretching before sex."

Cora and Maybe both burst into giggles. This too, *sisterhood*, was a sensation she'd missed. The ability to be totally who she was—bumps and scars and flaws aplenty—with these two women in her living room filled her with happiness. Made her more confident.

"Now I'm going to have that in my brain every time I see him. Which is often, in case you haven't noticed," Maybe managed to say.

Rachel just shrugged. "So you're going to let Beau get all up in your space. I also found out some details about his personal life. He's got a reputation. Or maybe had? Anyway, he likes the ladies. And a few gentlemen too. But not for very long. He used to be a favorite on all the gossip sites. Partied. A lot. But you know, some of those pictures from back in the day were with Gregori and we know he's changed. He's had the same core group of friends for years. Gregori and Ian Brewster, the restaurateur friend he mentioned, both live here in Seattle. Another lives somewhere in Europe. That shows something good about him, I think. He's loyal once he, uh, commits."

Cora clapped her hands over her ears for a moment, blushing hard. She shouldn't be gossiping about him! "Oh my god. I should have stopped you sooner but let's be honest, I wanted to hear it." She waved a hand, took a bite of her doughnut and thought awhile before she spoke again. "I knew about most of it. I've followed his career here and there over the years. I'm going to let him make me dinner. We'll catch up and have—hopefully—great conversation, and then if there's anything else—smooching, groping, what have you—that's all good. At some point he'll take his new recipes and that chiseled jaw away from Seattle. So why not enjoy what I can now? It's not like I want him to move in or be my boyfriend or whatever. I just want some fun and to hang out with an old friend. Hopefully have excellent sex. Also I'd like a dog, which isn't really about sexing up Beau, but more of a life goal thing. Not a big one because my little yard isn't really good for a big dog. Small and smart and not yappy. I don't like yappy dogs and the neighbors would complain."

"This conversation is moving at the speed of light. I'm here for it. And another doughnut. We need to start our walks again so I can have more than one doughnut without guilt," Maybe said, and then started to snicker. "Just kidding. I love having more than one doughnut and feel zero guilt about that. But I do love our walks too."

Rachel said, "Okay, now that you've told us about your romantic life, why don't you tell us the rest. Seeing you so happy about this Beau thing has underlined for me I've seen that Cora less and less over the last eighteen months or so. You've sounded less and less happy, more and more tired. Don't you think it's time to seriously rethink your job situation?"

They knew her so well. She hadn't even really had to say anything.

"I love to travel. A few weeks away is one thing, but three months and more? Too much. And, to be totally honest? It's a lot harder on my mother than it used to be. But she won't admit it and she doesn't have an off switch. So things go left and I have to clean up the mess. Then she gets mad at me because she's not forty anymore. More often than not what I do is make excuses for some terrible thing she's done to make someone cry and keeping her out of jail or worse. It makes me tired." And it wasn't what she wanted to do with the rest of her life. Being her mother's cleanup person wasn't a career she was interested in.

"Fair enough. She's a big personality. But you're not her keeper." Maybe used what was left of her doughnut to stab Cora's way and underline the point.

"Ha! I totally *am* her keeper. It's turned into a family joke. I'm the Walda whisperer, the keeper of the creative. It's fucking exhausting and I don't think it serves her. Not who she is now. Her career is different. The world is different. I'm different." Cora shrugged. "Anyway, I used to be content wandering the globe whenever and wherever she needed me. It was wonderful while it was wonderful. I've learned a lot. I've had a relationship with my mom that is totally unique and good. But it's also… *I'm* the mom most of the time."

"I think it's absolutely fair that you want to reevaluate the situation now. Yes, she's getting older, more frail. Especially in the last two or three years." Rachel paused, looked Cora square on. "Even if *none* of those things were true it's still okay. You're an adult. You get to make choices based on what *you* want. You get that, right? You want to build a life that'll take you into your future. You want to shift gears, sink roots and make a life that entails a different sort of work," Rachel said. "Do it."

"It should be all right for a while. She's done, except for promotion, which won't start for three or four months. And even then it shouldn't take her too far from home. I should encourage that." Cora grabbed her notebook and jotted a note down to do more radio and podcast interviews and to have them done in a local recording studio instead of traveling.

Rachel looked pointedly at the notebook before focusing on Cora again. "You're still taking a few weeks off though, right?"

"Well. I won't be traveling anywhere nonrecreational. In fact, I was thinking of leaf peeping and could probably include some birding. Perhaps cap it off with a stop at Samish Cheese? Something for everyone." Cora grinned at them.

"I'm in," Maybe said.

"Me too," Rachel said. "Now, getting back to the question, which was about you taking a few weeks off."

"Yes I am. From my mother. But I'll be at the gallery. There's a new installation coming up so I want to be there or who knows what they'll do?"

"So now you can finally quit being the Waldakeeper and shift to the gallery full-time. But you can still take a week or so. I mean, what did they do for the last three months without you there?" Maybe asked.

The gallery was her baby. Sort of. Cora had spent a lot of time and effort in creating a space that had a voice. A unique voice in a very rich local art scene. "Call me fourteen times a day?" She'd pretty much done the job over the phone and online anyway. But that? That'd felt like it should have. She'd *wanted* to be involved. It fed her creative hunger in a way few things did.

"Okay then," Rachel said. "Over the last several years you've mentioned here and there that you want to run the gallery full-time. Why not finally make that shift? Then someone *else* can handle your mom." Rachel's severe look had Cora's denials dying in her chest. "It's unfair that they'd expect you to keep on like this indefinitely. Oh sure, they all thank you for doing it— and they should—but none of them has stepped up to help you out. Not on this. Plenty of people can be your mom's personal assistant/manager/keeper. For the right kind of money," Rachel added at Cora's expression. "You're irreplaceable because no one will be as perfect as you. That's a given. But Walda's not the only diva in the world. We can help you find the right solution."

Maybe leaned over to squeeze Cora quickly. "You want to defend your family. But I promise you we aren't attacking them. We're your best friends and it is our god-given right to take your side. And to tell you the truth."

"So let's skip the part where you tell yourself you're selfish for wanting something for yourself. Who but you knows Walda works better when lightbulbs are this or that wattage? Or that she likes nutmeg in her coffee? And so what if you do? She's a grown woman, not a toddler. She can express her wishes to someone else. It's not like she's shy," Rachel said, deadpan.

No, Walda wasn't shy. But beneath all the feathers

and bright colors and whatever else she did, her mother wanted to be loved.

Of course Cora felt selfish. And guilty.

"It's on the list of things I'm thinking about," Cora told them both. "Thank you for caring about me enough to make me face this stuff. But I'm done with facing it for now. Let's talk about something else. Tell me what's been happening. How was your show last weekend?" she asked Maybe, who played drums in a punk rock band.

As Maybe excitedly filled her in, Cora leaned back, tucked herself under a blanket of her own and let being with her friends wash over her.

CHAPTER FOUR

That time you walked in
And the universe shifted…
I've been falling ever since.

OF ALL THE things from his childhood, Beau had come to terms with the way he'd been raised when it came to a usual lack of nervousness. He'd been a spokesperson, a face for Road to Glory from a very young age, which had given him a natural sense of ambition and ability. A gift of relating to people.

But as he wrestled the box with all the ingredients for dinner out of his trunk, he realized the butterflies in his belly were all about her.

It was fucking delicious.

He didn't even have to look at his phone for the number of her town house because once he entered the circular courtyard he knew immediately which porch was hers. It just had the most life around it. An overflowing planter on either side of the steps framed them artfully.

And on each step, words had been painted.

I am the light of a thousand stars
I am cosmic dust made human.

As he got to the top step, he caught sight of her through her front window. She stretched up to light candles dotted across a mantelpiece. He couldn't see anything but the grace in the movement, lost his other senses for a bit as his heartbeat seemed to thunder in time with the blood pounding in his cock.

He managed to hit the doorbell, and when she opened up to him, her smile lightened his nervousness. She looked at him like she knew him. And wanted to be with him anyway.

"Come in!" she said as she stepped aside to admit him. "You can put the stuff on the table." Cora indicated a stout, round table in the nook just to the left of the kitchen.

He managed not to rush, no matter how much he wanted to hug her. Beau even managed to get his coat off and slung over the back of one of the chairs before he said hello and pulled her into an embrace.

She hummed, low and pleased, and a shiver rode his spine.

"Good evening," he murmured as he brushed a quick kiss over her brow.

"You smell good. What are you cooking for me tonight?" she asked him as she started to poke through the crate.

"Thank you. You not only smell good, you look good." She wore a bright yellow sweater with faded blue jeans and thick socks. Cora looked like a fucking flower. Pretty and fresh and sexy all at once.

She blushed and he found it incredibly appealing.

"So I, uh, do you like pasta? I was thinking linguine

with clam sauce for the main. Some bruschetta with mushrooms and parsley and another with roasted and marinated red peppers and garlic."

"Yum! I like all those things. I have a feeling I'll be overeating. I grabbed some wine, red and white, and some Prosecco just for giggles. I wasn't sure what you'd be making and it's not like a bottle of wine won't find another use if I don't drink it tonight. Oh, and there's beer too.

"I didn't know what you'd be needing, so I just made sure the counters were extra clean," she said with a shrug. "Cooking stuff is in the cabinets and under the stovetop there." She pointed. "Use whatever you find. Ask if you don't see something."

"Perfect." He washed his hands while she poured them both a glass of red wine.

"I'm a rebel. I wear white after Labor day and drink red wine whenever I please." She toasted him, clinking her glass to his.

"I like a little rebellion. We can have white later with the pasta, if you like. Red would be fine, as well. Basically, anything you want because I aim to please." He tied on an apron and began to get to know her kitchen, setting the oven to get the bruschetta started.

She cleared her throat before speaking. "Can I help in any way or just watch you prepare a feast for me and fantasize about you kissing me?"

He didn't stop himself from bending down to kiss her. Intending it to be quick. But once she sighed softly, he couldn't keep it quick. Instead he backed her to the counter and settled in, tasting, teasing, sipping at her until his skin felt too tight.

Cora slid her tongue along his as she pressed herself closer, her hands at his waist, fingers hooked through the belt loops of his pants to hold him there.

She was sexy. Sweet and hot. Like nothing he'd experienced.

It rattled him enough to break the kiss, but in two breaths he had to go back for another kiss.

Because he needed it. Her taste was dark and rich and utterly irresistible. He wondered if the rest of her tasted as good.

With a groan, he pulled away when the oven preheat timer dinged.

Cora cocked her head, her smile gone feline and satisfied. "Well, okay then. You can find me available for kisses anytime." The slight slur of pleasure in her voice was a caress along the back of his neck.

"Now I'm ready to get back to work. You just sit there, keep my wineglass filled and be available for more kisses in case I can't get along until I have another."

"Right-o." She hopped up on one of the stools facing him across her kitchen island.

He sliced mushrooms thin as he tried not to stare at her mouth, but she made it difficult because she talked a lot, smiled a lot, laughed a lot.

It was really only the fear of slicing into his finger instead of the veggies and herbs that kept him from drooling over her like a cartoon dog.

That made him snort, catching her attention.

"Do I amuse you?" she asked, a teasing note in the words.

"Absolutely. So what did you do today? What have you been up to over the past seventeen years? You only hit the highlights last night."

"Today I had coffee and doughnuts here with Maybe and Rachel, and then I went into the gallery for a few hours."

"I need to stop by the gallery and check it out. I'm curious and always looking for something new. Up until now, my art guidance has come from Gregori. Fortunately, he knows my taste so he rarely steers me wrong."

Her eyes lit as she beamed at him. That's when her dimple came out and had him licking his lips for another taste of her.

"That's such a mistake to reveal to someone who runs a gallery." She sipped her wine. "I had a meeting with a new artist today. She's got a show coming up with us and I'm amazed at the stuff she does. We like to focus on regional artists, give them space and a voice. She came here with her family from Cambodia when she was an infant, so her stuff, which is mixed media, has this sense of roots and ownership of gender and identity that blows me away. She used to be a chemist for the state department of fisheries and one of her kids encouraged her to take early retirement and give her art more time. And she did. That was three years ago."

He liked the way she talked about art. A lot like he suspected he sounded when he talked about food. As she described the pieces she planned to put into the show, the passion for what she did seemed to flow from her.

"Sounds fantastic. I'll definitely cruise by the opening."

"Oh gosh, please do. Not only do I think you'd like her work, it's nice to be supported by your friends. The opening should be pretty fantastic, if I do say so myself. Which naturally I do because I'm speaking. Anyway, I throw a good party. I'll make sure you get an invite."

Her kitchen was well stocked but not overdone. The town house wasn't huge, like the condo he was in. But it was comfortable. She'd made excellent use of the space she did have.

It was warm and accessible, a lot like her, so that wasn't really a surprise.

He found all the tools he needed—which meant he could leave all the stuff he'd brought just in case in the trunk of his car. She kept his glass filled and did an excellent job of rubbing garlic on the bruschetta when he asked it of her.

By the time they settled in at her table, it was nearly eight, but he was warm from the wine and the exertion and though he'd snacked as he'd worked, he had quite the appetite for the pasta.

"Would you be weirded out if I took a picture of this? I mean it looks like art," she said.

Pride filled him. "Not at all. I'm flattered." And he was.

She went to grab her phone, took a few pictures

and then put it away again, giving him all her attention once more.

Mesmerizing.

After she ate and moaned with joy at whatever it was she tasted, his ego was about to explode. That and his dick. He was grateful his lap was hidden by the table.

"Tell me about the words on your porch steps," he said. "Where's the quote from?"

"Do you like it?"

He nodded. "Very much."

"It's mine. I've been writing snippets of poetry since I was a kid. That's part of a poem called 'Star Stuff.' I change it up from time to time. Paint new verses when it appeals to me."

"Lots of layers to you, Cora Silvera."

"Like an onion."

He stood and began to help her clear the table and clean the kitchen, over her protests that he'd cooked so she would clean up. It also enabled him to be close enough to brush against her as they moved around, wiping counters and filling the dishwasher.

"Come through to the other room for a while. Tell me how long you're going to be in Seattle." She took the bottle of white wine along with her into the living room, where he joined her, settling on her overstuffed couch.

"I'm here for…well, for the next while. At least a year. Likely more. Love the weather and all the stuff to do outdoors. My friends live here—including you. It's a food culture I really like. And I'm done with New York and LA. Not for visits—I still love both cities.

Both were great for my career. But it's time for something else. Seattle seems a good place to be somewhere to land. Finish this cookbook."

"Well, I'm glad to hear it. There's a cherry walnut cake for dessert but I'm pretty full," she said, voice lazy as she leaned against the cushions.

"We should do something else until we digest dinner." He took her hand, threading his fingers with hers, and tugged her toward him. "I can think of a few ways to spend some time."

"Yeah? I think maybe we have some of the same ideas on that."

"Let's compare notes."

Before he knew it, she was on his lap. And like he'd figured, she fit him.

Perfectly.

"Let me know when I get too heavy," she said, her lips so close to his, the heat of her made him a little light-headed.

"When that happens, I'll get on top. I like being on top."

With a laugh, she nipped his bottom lip, tugging it sharply. "I'm not surprised by that."

CHAPTER FIVE

The way your mouth skates over my throat
is burned into my skin.

A WAVE OF dizzy delight flowed through her as he
leaned her back against the arm of her couch, never
losing contact. It terrified her nearly as much as it excited her. In another person she might have found it
too much. But while intense, it met her own intensity.
Her own want of him.

He didn't flinch from what he wanted, instead, once
he was sure she was on board—which was scorching
hot in and of itself—he took it.

Nothing had *ever* seemed so sexy to her.

He didn't rush to her mouth, instead he sent hot,
openmouthed kisses from her temple down to the hollow beneath her ear.

It was… Well, whatever he was doing to her, it set
her aflame.

He seemed to radiate sensuality and every bit of
it was focused on her. Added to the sheer physical-
ity of him—that ruggedly handsome face with those
gorgeous eyes and the mouth she was currently very
fond of—it was as if the universe had detonated a sex

bomb right there on her couch. Sporting a seriously impressive erection if the ridge under her thigh was any indication.

Cora dug her fingers through his hair as he teased kisses down her throat. She wanted to take a big bite of him. Wanted to leave a mark.

He hadn't even touched her boob yet and she was this mad for him.

"I want to gobble you up," she said, shoving back at him, twisting a little to climb into his lap, facing him. In her position, he was less intimidating and more deliciously big and tall in a hot chef/lumbersexual way.

And…she could also confirm that the ridge against her thigh was indeed a very healthy hard-on.

Yay!

He groaned, pulling her closer until she groaned in return, grinding herself against him.

It wasn't quite a frenzy, but their chemistry seemed to sizzle and rise, humid with sex. Pumping her full of desire.

His hands slid to her waist, gripping and holding her against him as he rolled his hips.

At the very end of his movement upward, he dug in just a little harder, brushing against her clit just right, even through the denim.

She gasped as a burst of pleasure brought stars behind her eyelids.

And when she opened her eyes, it was to find him watching, naked greed for her on his features.

It was humbling. It was giddy wish fulfillment. And it was flat-out hot. Shivers of delight rode her skin as he reached up to grip her by the back of her neck and brought her to him for a kiss.

Heat roared from his fingertips up to her lips, where he slid his tongue over and then into her mouth, and got busy devastating her with deft nips, licks and kisses.

In all those fantasies she'd had back as a young woman she'd had *no* idea what he was truly capable of. Of what he was capable of evoking in her.

Hot damn.

He wanted her as much as she wanted him. More than that, there was something else, something extra between them, that only seemed to stoke the heat.

CORA DIDN'T WANT to stop whatever was happening. She wanted to ride it out with him. Wanted to jump into whatever storm they were making.

She sucked his bottom lip and pressed herself to him, grinding herself over his cock.

He moved to lean her back, pushing her coffee table out of the way with a foot until they landed on her rug.

"You with me?" he asked her, his voice full of briars and thorns.

"Yes!" She pulled him down to her to get at his mouth again. The slight burn on her neck his beard had left behind was something she felt to her toes and straight to her clit.

He broke from her mouth long enough to angle his free arm under her shoulders to bring her where he wanted, but also to give her some protection against the floor at her back.

Not that she'd have complained.

Cora squeezed her thighs together, needing a little more sensation. Orgasm had been building since before she'd even opened her door to find him on her porch. Before he'd made her a meal and kissed her into oblivion.

By that point, her whole body seemed to be an erogenous zone. He'd pushed every single one of her buttons, including a few she hadn't known she possessed.

He grumbled, "Mine." Before reaching down to cup her through her jeans. The heat of his hand—a strong, big hand—brought a shudder of pleasure and a thrust of her hips seeking more.

HE'D GIVE IT to her, but on his own schedule. He wanted to be sure she remembered this any time she thought of him. Wanted to burn himself into her skin, into her memory.

Cora never ceased to surprise him though. She reared up enough to get rid of her sweater and yanked at his until he got her meaning and tossed his off and to the side with hers.

Skin to skin, though she wore a pretty purple bra, still, the sensation was nearly overwhelming, bringing a hiss from his lips before he shifted down to kiss along her breastbone. He inhaled the soft, sensitive skin between her breasts, and then she dug her nails into his shoulders.

Urging him on.

"More," she said, underlining it.

The wave overtook them both once more, sucking him back to that place where there was only sensation and the relentless need to touch her, taste her, make her moan.

When she dragged those nails down the front of his pants, over his cock, he was the one who moaned, was the one who let go and gave over to whatever she wanted. In whatever way she wanted it.

He snarled a curse when she unzipped his jeans and slid her hand inside. First cupping him through his shorts and then—sweet Christ—she slipped inside, down the front and grabbed his cock at the root, sliding her grip upward before swirling her thumb over the slick of precome on the slit.

It was her snarl he wanted, and got when he slid the cup of her bra down and bent to lick and then graze the edge of his teeth over her nipple, delighting in the way it stood up.

She rewarded him with that desired snarl, and then adjusted to fist him from balls to the head a few more times.

Beau gripped his control as best he could, drowning in the feel of her against him, of the scent of sex in the air, the raw desire arcing between them.

Cora's rhythm dug roots into his balls, dragging him toward climax. No matter that it was her living room floor and they were both still clothed. Perhaps it was even hotter that it was so urgent and raw and necessary to do right then.

He moved so that he could slide a hand down her belly and then into her panties, the heat and then the wet of her against his fingers and palm.

He'd been so cocksure when he'd started this, sure

he'd finish her first, but it wasn't so certain as he tumbled even closer to coming when she reared up and dug her teeth into his biceps. Not enough to truly harm, but more than enough to turn him on past bearing.

He wanted her climax. Needed it. She wasn't holding back with his either. So it was a tangle of arms and legs, of mouths on skin and arching backs.

She made a sound then, a sucked-in surprise and then a moan so carnal he couldn't have stopped his orgasm no matter what. She came in a rush against his skin, a clasp of her inner muscles around his fingers that seemed to fit around his cock as he hit his own climax in a blinding rush.

SHE BURST OUT with a satisfied sigh, and then started to giggle. "I'm sorry," she told him, indicating the mess on her hand and his belly before rolling to her knees. "Let me get a towel."

He snorted, reaching out quickly to catch the dish towel she tossed his way.

She washed up before joining him again. "I can't remember the last time I did that on a date. I hope you liked it as much as I did. Because, wow."

It was his turn to clean up and hers to watch as he prowled to her kitchen to wash his hands and toss the towel in the laundry basket.

He'd just fed her a gourmet dinner, made her come and cleaned up after. As first dates went, it was pretty much the all-time winner.

The grin he flashed as he flopped down on the couch next to her eased the knot of anxiety in her gut.

"I totally enjoyed it. Though I do hope you understand I have more than just handjobs in my tool kit."

"Your tool kit is pretty impressive so far." She raised a shoulder and grabbed her wineglass, clinking it to his.

Once they both got everything zipped up and tucked back in, Cora brought out the dessert. They settled back on the cushions, tucked under a blanket, a fire going to keep the room warm.

"So tell me about your cookbook idea. If it's not a secret, I mean," she said.

He started to give her details about audience numbers and she waved a hand. "No. I mean, congratulations for those great numbers and it's very awesome you're using them to guide your next choices. But my real question is what drives this idea? Your face sells pots and pans and some very good pot holders and aprons. Naturally you're a brand. But I've eaten your food twice now and both times it's read and tasted like art to me. You're not just cooking, which takes skill obviously. You're creating. You approach the plate like a canvas."

Which was totally hot.

"Thank you. That's a very nice compliment. I've been fortunate in my career. I've had three shows on cable that have all been successful. My cookbooks do well. I have more than enough fame and money and success. So I'm grateful. But I was at a creative crossroads and I have the option to try something new. I've spent more and more time up here visiting Seattle and my friends. More time getting to know the ingredients, the seasons, what was available where. It ended up dovetailing with the fact that I needed to get out of Southern California."

"So what's the process? With a cookbook do you have the recipes already or do you develop them? How do they get tested?"

His surprised yet undeniably pleased smile warmed Cora's belly.

"Right now I'm in the development stage. I have a general idea of the theme and now it's organization. I'm thinking of doing whole meals with swap-out side dishes. I coordinate with my recipes so it has some direction. And then I cook a lot. Make people eat my food and give me their opinions."

Cora raised her hand. "I volunteer as taster. I mean, if you need anyone else in your focus group."

It was only at that moment that she realized she might be pushing him into a place he wasn't ready to go. Or a level of relationship he didn't care for.

She genuinely liked him, aside from the sexual and romantic attraction, and she hoped they could hang out more while he was in Seattle.

But he nodded, smile genuine. "We'll see how you feel when you get sick of my cooking."

She just looked at him, scoffing. "Yeah, it's such a bore to have a gorgeous man cook a gourmet meal for me. You must run up against that all the time."

He shrugged. "You know as well as I do, sometimes people aren't around you for you. They want your money or your fame or what you can do for them."

"I see it with my mom. But I'm the chick in the

background. Which is good. The people I need to know who I am, know who I am."

"It feels like I'm constantly under a microscope in LA and NYC. Here I can be left alone for the most part. It's nice, you know? To just shop for produce or get toilet paper without people coming up to me."

"I imagine it weighs on you. Having to constantly be on like that."

He stared at her carefully before responding. "You do, don't you?"

"What?"

"You do think about what it would be like for me. Most people, they just focus about all the perks, and I get it. But you realize there are costs for those perks."

Cora shrugged. "I probably wouldn't if I didn't grow up the way I have."

"That's a good way to look at it. So what are you doing Friday? Want to have dinner?"

Oh. He asked her out. It delighted her with the simple joy of it. "I'm going to the pumpkin patch so I can start all my Halloween decorating and there's an event at the gallery so I'll be there until about eleven. But I'm free after. Or before if you want to come to the pumpkin patch with me."

"Well, that's… I've never been to a pumpkin patch."

"Really?" she asked, incredulous. "I'm not sure… I mean, are you averse to Halloween entirely or are you indifferent?"

He gave her a raised brow. "You seem passionate on this point. It's terrifying and also sort of sexy and mysterious."

"Terrifying? Me? Ha! The truth is, I love Halloween. It's my jam. And I love decorating for it and for fall in general."

He cocked his head, looking fucking gorgeous doing it. Jeez. "I can believe it. I'm not averse to Halloween. Or pumpkins. In fact, I'm mulling over a few different fall soups so if they have cooking pumpkins there, I might go just for that. We didn't celebrate Halloween when I was growing up. And then when I wasn't with the group anymore, I was already an adult and sure, I went to parties at Halloween, mainly to ogle women in sexy costumes and drink too much."

"Mom is an immigrant so she never really got into Halloween because she didn't grow up with it. But my dad, being a first generation American, absolutely loves it. When we were kids, we'd go to the Halloween store the day after Halloween and buy all the stuff on sale. Our house is on a lot of land, but most of it is behind and to one side so we'd decorate the front yard with gravestones, giant fake spiders in the trees. Cauldrons and vampire bats. Spooky stuff in the windows. We were sort of in the country a little, at the edges of what's now a much larger city, so you had to drive to trick-or-treat in our neighborhood. But people did! If you came to our door you got scared, but it was all so fun. My dad dresses up every single year as Dracula. I'm not joking. It's adorable. So. Pumpkin patch? Do you have rain boots? It'll be muddy probably. I mean, it's just a big field."

"You seem excessively excited about the chance of mud."

Cora giggled. "It's a damned mess. So I don't take my lovely car but rather borrow a truck. It's a work truck so it won't be a crime if we get mud in the bed. Of the truck, I mean. I don't want mud in my sleeping bed. Because that would suck."

She was being way more random than usual. He made her nervous but more in a giddy way than a scared way.

Instead of panicked or annoyed, Beau appeared to at the very least be amused by her. His body language was easy, relaxed.

"Agreed on the mud in the truck versus the sheets distinction. I'm in. This sounds like an adventure."

She wasn't sure if that was purely a compliment, but it made her happy anyway.

CHAPTER SIX

A star seared its way through the icy black
of space as if it were fabric.
Becoming something else.

"Do you have rain boots? Or know where I can get
some?" Beau asked Ian the following day when he
came over.

His friend, who stood at the counter in his wet
dream of a kitchen, gave him a wary look. "Should
I ask why?"

"Cora tells me I might want them at the pumpkin
patch because it could be muddy." Beau grabbed a slice
of mango from the cutting board.

Ian gave Beau all his attention then, one of his eyebrows rising a moment. "Oh, *Cora* does. Well then."

"She's apparently wild about Halloween. I'm apparently wild about her. I'll make her a meal when we
get back."

And then he needed to find a way to be invited to
the gallery event. She'd brought it up to him in the first
place, which he had decided to take as an invitation. Of
a sort. He just needed to get that firmed up.

"That's a lot of togetherness in a short period of time

for you. This is the woman you knew back in the day in LA? The composer's kid?"

"She's only five years younger than I am." Beau rolled his eyes. "It's easy to be with her. God knows that's not always a thing. She's weird and thoughtful and funny and sexy as fuck." Beau leaned against the kitchen counter and looked out the windows over Elliott Bay, thinking about her laugh and the way she sounded when she came.

Need for her, to be around her more, made him greedy. It confused him but not enough to make him so wary he didn't pursue her.

"You're breaking your rule about not getting involved with people in your friend group. So does that mean she's not in your friend group so I keep my distance? Or, you're breaking your rule because she's different? In which case I *really* want to meet her."

Beau said, "She's unlike anyone else I've been attracted to. Like I said, it's easy to be with her and we have wild sexual chemistry. Off the fucking charts, for real." He shoved a hand through his hair as the remembered heat between them brushed against his skin.

"So you're up for the pumpkin patch because you want to get some? That's the tale as old as time there, dude." Ian snorted and indicated the cabinet near Beau's head as a way to invite him for a cup of coffee.

Beau grabbed himself a mug and after getting the coffee sugared up, he eased into a chair at Ian's breakfast nook just off the kitchen. "Like I said, mad chemistry. But there's something else about her. Like she's going on an adventure even if she's just going to get her mail. I can't say I ever really wanted to, but I find myself thinking maybe going to a pumpkin patch with Cora would be fun."

"You came up here to start a new chapter in your life. So it's not that strange really that you're attracted to someone who is also a new sort of chapter. And you know her, which alleviates all that suspicion that she might want something from you. Her mom is famous in the music and art communities. She gets the celebrity thing."

They shared a look, both of them having experienced people trying to use them for something. To get an endorsement, investment in this or that business, wanting to be on TV as a date at some big event. Ian had a divorce under his belt because of it.

As a result, Beau had a policy about not getting involved with anyone in his social group because if it was going to go wrong he could walk away unscathed and still protecting the strength of his private life. His closest friends were family. They'd seen him through some pretty dark times and no one was worth threatening that.

"I totally think the fact that she's familiar with the weirdness of our world is a big part of why I'm so comfortable around her. She doesn't want me for anything but my dick and maybe my cooking. I'm good with that."

At least while he tried to figure out just what it was about her that fascinated him so much. She was unexpected, but not an engine of chaos. Another thing he found interesting.

Ian shrugged. "Okay then. Yes, I have some mud boots you can use. I wear them when we go digging for clams and when I head out to the fields of any of the produce farms that supply my restaurants. They'll do."

"Thanks."

"Bring her around one of these nights to meet us all."

Cora and a bunch of foulmouthed chefs drinking and eating at one in the morning? Yeah, he could see her fitting in just fine.

JUST TWO DAYS later and the sky was blue-gray, the clouds dark with the rain threatening to fall on them any minute, and yet Cora nearly shone with her excitement when he showed up at her place Friday morning.

"Hi!" she told him with a huge grin, right before she launched herself into his arms for a hug.

Delight warmed him. No one greeted him like this, with such raw happiness.

She seemed to exude it. Give it off in waves. The more he experienced it, the more he craved it.

"Hi yourself." He squeezed her, smiling into her hair a moment before releasing her. "Do you treat everyone like this when you see them or am I just that lucky?"

"You're just that lucky. You could be again, later on if you're extra sweet to me today. Are you ready to go?"

"Hell yes. Let me put this inside before we go though." He held up a basket of food he'd put down to hug her.

"Oooh! What did you bring me?" Her eyes lit with interest.

"Supplies for a meal after we bring home all the pumpkins."

"You're going to feed me too?" She clapped her hands without a bit of sarcasm.

"It's the least I can do. Think of it as payment for introducing me to something new." And cooking for people was his way of taking care of them. Showing his love or concern, whatever.

"The least you could do would be fast food. Or a bag of chips or something. A talented chef cooking for me is really nice. Thank you."

He made quick work of unloading the food, putting things away and before too long, they were headed south in a landscaper's truck she'd borrowed, on their way to a pumpkin patch.

"How was the rest of your first week back home in Seattle?" he asked.

"I've been at the gallery a lot."

When an asshole cut her off, she smiled, sunny and sweet, enough to disarm the guy, and then she flipped him off before heading her own way.

"So, road rage with a little pizzazz?" he teased of her middle finger salute.

"Well, I'm a work in progress."

He snickered. "I can dig that. Tell me about the event we're going to tonight." He just slid that in there, his assumption they'd be attending together.

She gave him some world-class side-eye though, which had him leaning back with a satisfied smile on his face. In some nearly perverse way, he absolutely got off on the idea that she would be a person who didn't let him get away with things like pretending they already had a date without doing the work of asking.

"Would you like to come to the gallery tonight?" she asked, laughter in her voice. "Gregori will most likely be there with Wren. A few of the artists showing are friends of hers."

"I should offer you an out here. Some sort of self-deprecating bit about how you don't really have to ask me to go tonight. But I won't. I want to be there. And not because I'm in the market for art."

"You should always be in the market for art." She said it like a mantra.

"Clearly I have a lot to learn."

"Hmm," was all she said for a moment. "Seems to me you know a lot of useful things. So you're welcome to make me food, make me come and eat appetizers while looking at evocative artwork. But that's a lot of Cora in one day. Just an advance warning."

It would have been a lot of anyone in a day. Aside from a few very close friends, there wasn't anyone he liked to spend a lot of one-on-one time with.

But he'd already accepted she was different than most other people. His reaction to her most definitely was unusual.

"I like a lot of Cora in my day. Come to think of it, why aren't you at the gallery now? You strike me as the type who likes to manage closely to be sure things are perfect."

"That's the coolest way to be called a control freak ever." She laughed. "I was there most of yesterday and into the night, and then back first thing this morning. And now it'll marinate until later. If I hang out too much I start to pick my work apart, second-guess and redo stuff. Then everyone hates me and I do three times the work because, in the end, I go back to how I originally had it."

She pulled into a patch of dirt that'd been transformed into a lot where people parked their cars to head out into the wide fields of pumpkins just beyond. "This is still early days for this patch. In two weeks or so, there'll be ruts deep enough to make your teeth hurt when you drive over them."

"It's weird how cheerful this makes you."

"I like knowing I made a good choice when I'm lucky enough to make one. You come early and you get the best pumpkins and avoid the worst of the crowds and traffic. This lot is the one we went to when I was a kid. Family owned. It always smells like mulling spices and kettle corn."

And on that word salad, she hopped out of the truck, turning back to grab her camera. "It's a little muddy, but not too bad. You don't have to wear the boots if you don't want to."

BEING OUT THERE with the brilliant orange of pumpkins against the pale gold of the straw and hay bales all around, Cora let herself fully live in that precise moment. Happiness at being back home. Comfort in the familiar signs leading to the corn maze. The same goofy cutouts she and her siblings had stuck their faces in for the pictures their father had on his desk to that day. Butterflies and giddy delight in the birth of something new and delicious between her and Beau.

"So what's the process then? Do we just pick one?" He looked dubiously at the big, flat-bottomed wagon she grabbed.

"They're sold by the pound, so at the end we'll come back and put them on those big scales over there." She pointed. "As for *one*? Pah! I'm no amateur, Beau. I'll get as many as it pleases me. I have a nice-sized porch so naturally I'll need several for that. And whatever else that strikes my fancy. And my fancy is easily struck."

He just shook his head as he looked out over the wide fields beyond, full of pumpkins ready for the grabbing before he took the handle of the wagon. "I'll pull. Point me the way."

It was early enough on a weekday that the patch wasn't crowded at all, which didn't stop a few people from nearly falling over themselves as they stared at Beau. It wasn't even that they recognized him—at least not at first—but purely the fact that he was so beautiful.

Because he tried to ignore it, she did, as well. And it wasn't like she didn't totally understand everyone who gawked at him. She felt like gawking at him too.

"Is that weird for you?" Cora asked him as she began to think about just exactly what she wanted her porch to look like.

"Is what weird?"

"Being so handsome you literally make people halt in their tracks to stare at you."

His surprised laughter rang out and made her smile in response.

Seeing the pumpkins for herself, she began to build a theme. She headed toward a group of tall, narrow ones. "Look at these bumps all over. I love that. Then I need squat ones. So they can group together."

He bumped her aside with a hip and loaded the ones she pointed out onto the wagon. "Getting recognized is nice usually. People are respectful. But sometimes it's invasive, offensive, scary even."

"Oh, you mean like stalkers? Or people who don't like the, uh, group you grew up in?" From everything she understood it was a cult. But it wasn't relevant what she thought on that point. Not right then.

"Both." He shrugged. "The people who were either part of my former church or who were wronged or hate groups like Road to Glory pop up less than they used to. New outrages I guess. New self-appointed prophets all too eager to drain people dry and ruin lives."

"I'm sorry," she said simply.

"I got away. Mostly. As far as being a celebrity and getting recognized, that's complicated. It's nice that people care. That's why they watch my shows and buy my books. I like that. But some people have messed-up filters. Or they forget I'm a real person." He turned to face her. "And sometimes it encroaches on my personal time. I want to be all about you right now, so I would be aggravated. Which is why I generally avoid eye contact if I get that buzz that they might think of intruding."

Damn. "You make my stomach all floaty."

He smirked. "Is that good?"

Cora nodded.

"All right then. What's next?" He indicated the area all around them.

Cora considered following up but he clearly wanted to change the subject so she let him. She went to her toes, kissed him quickly and pointed. "Let's head that way. I see some fat ones. I need fat ones." Cora danced away, taking in deep gulps of the fresh air, happy with her life and the sight of one pumpkin with super deep grooves on it that she decided she had to have.

Each time she would pause to really examine a pumpkin, and then later the gourds, he patiently waited for her to do whatever she pleased. He never glanced at his phone. Never looked bored. In fact, he began to point out his own pumpkins, even grabbing a few he said he wanted to put in the windows of the apartment he was staying at.

He never complained about the weather, even after a light rain began to fall, or how heavy the wagon got once it was laden down with pumpkins. He didn't bat an eye at how many she ended up buying and unloaded them all at her side, making her smile the whole time.

"So, what did you think of going to the pumpkin patch?" she asked as they headed back toward Seattle. She held a big bag of kettle corn out for him to grab a handful.

"I liked it. Food, a pretty girl and a huge bag of fresh vegetables to go with a thousand pumpkins make for a pretty enjoyable outing. Thanks for bringing me along."

"Probably less than a thousand. I'm all about new

experiences," she teased, undeniably pleased that he'd apparently enjoyed their day. "Next up is decoration. I pulled the Halloween boxes out of my crawl space and I've got a general idea and some notes."

"Notes? Crawl space? I feel like such a newbie to the Halloween decoration game."

"Remember I just told you about how I was all about new experiences? Anyway, you'll be there making me food, which is like, way more important than stringing lights and helping me create the super spider lair."

"Super spider lair, huh? Okay, I'm game. I'll make tacos while you get to super lair creating."

"Tacos? This day keeps getting better."

They listened to music all the way back up north to her place, where he then helped her carry all those pumpkins to her porch.

"I'm on call for you if you need anything heavy moved or whatever. Just yell, okay?" he told her.

"Thanks," she said before he gave her a kiss and allowed her to watch him walk back into her house looking all hot and tasty.

Once he'd gone, she began to set her porch to dark, spooky fun with spiders tucked all around. Some with glowing red eyes. A few with realistic-looking bristles on all eight legs. And at the end, she installed the ones on motion-detected triggers that would have them dropping from the ceiling or jumping across a trick-or-treater's path.

After that she strung all the lights and draped the fake spiderweb, giggling to herself as she thought about all the scary fun she was creating.

All while she peeked through her front window and watched him in her kitchen. He moved like magic. All to his own rhythm. He cooked like he was totally, utterly sure of himself.

Sexy as fuck.

And he wanted to spend time with her.

If he'd been smooth about it, or calculated, she could have just let it be a fun fling. But he wanted to go to a gallery event. Not to buy art. Not to meet artists. He didn't need her for that. No, it was about her.

No one could have ever described to her just what it would feel like to have someone focus on her like that. Put all their attention, attraction and ability into her. It was by turns flattering, confusing and thrilling.

He looked up from where he'd been sautéing something at the stove and met her gaze. A startled smile broke over his mouth and holy shit he was just stupid gorgeous.

All points south of her eyes stood at attention.

She smirked at him, letting him see that she was done with the spider lair and was coming inside.

"Damn, you make me sassy," she said once she'd put away her tools and the boxes were back in the crawl space.

He leaned back, resting his butt on the counter behind him, crossing those fine legs as he looked her up and down. "That so? And how do *I* make you sassy? Seems to me, you were sassy when I got here."

Laughing, she swaggered over, pausing just a foot away. "That's a fair point. You make me sass*ier*. The way you look at me sometimes just revs me up. Makes me feel all sexy and goddess-like and stuff."

"You *are* sexy." He all but growled it.

She let out a shuddering breath.

"Food and then." He lifted one shoulder and sent her a smoldering leer.

If he weren't a chef who'd just spent all that time and effort cooking for her, she'd have jumped on him right then.

"Oh, you mean after we carve the pumpkins?" she teased.

He grabbed her, yanking her to him. "The idea of you with a knife is alarmingly arousing."

Cora would have laughed, but he bent to kiss her before she could, stealing her breath for a moment.

By the time she managed to gather her wits, he'd broken away, again wearing that sexy smile of his.

"Lunch is ready, my spider queen."

"I'll set the table," she told him after clearing her throat.

CHAPTER SEVEN

In my kingdom I will rule
as the ocean foams at my feet
and the birds do my bidding.

"OH MY GOD. How did you manage to make this taste so good?"

Cora hoped she didn't sound like she was having an orgasm while eating a shrimp taco, but she sort of was. "At first I thought it was the crema. Because the lime and avocado are so perfect together. But now I'm leaning toward the cabbage slaw type thing on top. The sweet hot tang of it is my favorite thing right at this moment."

"You're irresistible when you love my food. And you haven't even had the pork yet."

The pork had mangos and red onions and had her seriously considering licking the plate at the end. The most unexpectedly delicious was the veggie taco with roasted eggplant and mushrooms with a tomatillo salsa.

She pushed back from the table with a happy sigh. "It's not even one in the afternoon and I've had a great day."

"When do you need to be at the gallery?" he murmured, taking her plate so he could get closer.

"Are you going to make my day even better?" Cora asked, turning so they were nose to nose.

"Oh yes. Yes I am. I just need a timeline so I can plan accordingly."

"I really like the sound of that. I need to get down there by three. It's a ten-minute walk from here so we've got some time. We can always carve pumpkins another day."

"I like your priorities," he told her, pulling her to her feet.

Three steps toward her room and she found herself pressed against the wall, the full length and hardness of him weighted, holding her in place.

Desire had been simmering in her belly but now, as he licked over her earlobe, and then nibbled down her neck, it burned inferno hot.

She hung on as he continued to feast on her throat, as his hands rucked up her sweater, spreading more heat against her belly where he brushed his fingertips.

Why was she wearing pants? From now on, she needed to wear skirts when she was going to be alone with him. For easy access.

She nearly laughed but that was before he pulled the sweater up and off, leaving her there in her bra, the cool surface of the wall a counter to the heat of him.

All she wanted was him. On her. In her. All around her. That sort of focus was something she only usually had for art. But this? He filled her with so much naked greed it surprised her.

She struggled momentarily with his button and zipper, but then, with a groan, she grabbed his cock. In both hands.

He snarled, spinning them a few times until they burst through the half-open door of her bedroom, nearly taking them both to the floor as she tripped over several pairs of shoes she'd left out.

Laughing, he heaved her up and then onto her bed. She managed to pull her jeans and panties off as he got his jeans and shirt off.

She paused, hands at the hooks of her bra as she took him in. His eyes were glazed slightly, drunk on hormones and sex. His upper body was *so much* better than any of the pictures she'd seen in magazines or on television.

She hadn't been able to get a good look when they'd been together a few days prior; it had been rushed and they'd still been totally clothed. But he stood in her room, stealing the oxygen, pumping out fuck-me heat like a furnace.

And that was before she'd really gotten a look at the line-and-dot elephant head across his upper chest. Later… Later she'd ask about all his ink, including the numbers and letters on his left side and the jellyfish on his thigh.

After.

For that moment, however, she tossed her bra to the side after surging to her knees. He didn't need her to hold a hand out, instead, he looked her up and down with a light in his gaze and then moved, taking her to the mattress, his body against hers, skin to skin, hot.

She hissed, writhing against him as sensation rushed through her system.

So FUCKING BEAUTIFUL.

Beau looked at her on her knees, tits still jiggling just a little from her movement.

Curves for miles.

Not wanting to wait another second, he joined her on the bed, pulling her underneath him. Before he could kiss her again, she wrapped her legs around him, opening herself up to him so his cock brushed against the scalding heat of her pussy.

"You're so wet," he mumbled, sliding his hands over all the skin he could reach.

"Thank *you* for that," she replied.

He wanted to laugh and groan and snarl for more.

So he bent to kiss her and let himself fall.

Nothing tasted the way she did. Sweet and tart and totally Cora.

She dug her nails into his shoulders, trying to hold him in place, but there was more of her he wanted to kiss. More of her he wanted to explore.

Always more and never enough it seemed.

He tasted the salt of her skin as he licked over the blade of her collarbone. Drew in the sweetness of her sigh and the shiver that followed.

Kissed her over and over all the way down her body, over her ink, including a lovely bit of lace and gems just underneath her very fine breasts.

After looking his fill, he licked over a nipple until she made a sound—breathy and needy—and then he blew until it stood hard and dark.

He hummed his delight. Wandered over to her other

nipple, repeating the lick and blow, and was rewarded with her nails digging into his biceps and a snarled *yes*.

At the hollow of her hip, he inspected the firefly in full color inked there. She yelped into a fit of giggles when he nipped it.

She was ticklish as he rained kisses over the inside of her thighs.

The laughter stopped as he spread her open and looked his fill.

Yes. Utterly beautiful.

She arched her back on a gasp when he took his first lick. And let himself drown in her. In giving her pleasure and taking his own.

In his hands, she was fire. Lush and sensual. But at the same time there was an edge to her. A vibrant— and in places, dark—energy.

There, between satiny thighs she was slick and totally open to him. There she was more addictive than he'd imagined she could be.

Bone-deep craving seemed to slice through his senses, shredding his control.

The muscles of her thighs trembled as her breath caught. Close. He knew she was close and though he wanted to feast on her for a lot longer, he had to satisfy himself with knowing he'd have another chance, hopefully more than one, to get back to where he was exactly at that moment.

Making Cora Silvera come so hard she pounded the bed at her sides as she brokenly whispered his name.

He had to rest his cheek against her belly, gasping for air the same way she was doing. Not because he was physically tired, though he liked to think his oral skills took some energy. She seemed to yank his emotions free with the way she not only touched his skin, but reached inside him with her reactions. With nothing more than being who she was.

He'd been through a lot of traumatic crap in his life. A lot of highs too. He was generally easygoing with it all by that point. But the way he felt with her, around her, was just shy of overwhelming.

So seductively good he just didn't have the energy— or the will—to make up reasons to resist.

Cora was an adventure he wanted to experience.

Her smirk when he lifted his head enough to look up her body sent an arc of lust straight to his cock, so he jumped up to dig through his pants to grab a condom before returning to her.

She grabbed the packet from between his teeth before he could bite down and tear it open. "That's bad for your teeth," she told him, ripping it by hand and giving it back.

He could flat-out guarantee that he'd never had a lover tell him to be careful of ruining his teeth. Perversely, that only made him harder. So hard that he had to zone out a bit as he got the condom rolled on his dick or else come all over his hand and end this—at least for twenty minutes—before it got started.

Still on her knees from when she'd grabbed the condom, she waited for him, lips slightly parted, pupils large. Her hair was tousled all around her face in a way that screamed, *I just had an orgasm.*

"On your belly," he told her.

She rolled over and gave him a look. Inviting more as she thrust herself back toward him.

He swore under his breath as he took in the antique chandelier taking up the entirety of her back. An old-school design. Strong and feminine. Sexy as hell.

"I love this ink," he said, leaning down to kiss her between her shoulder blades. Settling between her thighs, he pushed one leg up, keeping it bent at the knee.

The sight of his cock disappearing into her body as he slowly entered her short-circuited his brain. His hand at her hip, fingers digging into the muscle there slightly to set the pace he wanted.

Slow. Because he wanted to draw it out.

But that was difficult when she was so snug and hot around him. Still soft and slick from her orgasm, her inner walls stretched, and then tightened around him.

Deep. Even deeper once he'd tipped her hips just a bit. Knew he'd gotten it right when her moan got raspy at the end.

He fucked her with hard, deep digs. Concentrated on how it felt, on how her skin tasted, on the wall holding back his climax.

"Harder," she said over her shoulder. "More. Please."

Beau bent himself over her. "I want your hand on your pussy. On your clit."

He knew she liked it by the way her inner muscles seemed to flutter around his cock. And the surprised moan as she slid her hand between her body and the mattress.

Knew she'd begun when she got even hotter and

wetter. Even through the latex it was enough to bring the orgasm he'd been holding back roaring toward him as he stayed where he was, his body caging hers, thrusting deep and hard.

She whimpered into the blankets as she started to explode around him and that was it. He continued to fuck her as it sucked him in and held him under. He came so hard his thigh muscles burned and jumped.

"SWEET BABY JESUS eating jerky," she mumbled, rolling over so she could watch him get out of bed to dispose of the condom. She just had some of the hottest sex of her life with a dude who *looked* like sex on legs.

"Wait. Did you just say *sweet baby Jesus eating jerky*?" he asked, a wary expression on his face.

"I did. I was just thinking about how you're just so damned gorgeous and hot and it occurred to me what a delight that was."

He snorted as he joined her in getting dressed, and then pulled her into a hug, taking a long, leisurely trip around her mouth and throat before letting her go at last.

Leaving her needing to lean against the wall a moment because she was weak in the knees.

"Glad to be of service," he said. "I like the way you objectify me."

"That's a big relief because I gotta tell you, looking at you gets me all warm and tingly. And then you add the cooking and the sense of humor and the way you fuck and it's just downright impossible not to objectify you."

Smiling, he walked two steps back to where she leaned against the wall and caged her in with his body. Yum.

"I'm not the irresistible one here," he murmured before bending his knees to kiss her slow. "I have dreams about your taste," he said, stepping away from her.

How did one even process a man like Beau saying such things? It made her light-headed in the best way. Made her feel like a gorgeous queen and damn it was really fucking wonderful.

The start of something really fucking wonderful. She hoped, even as she knew it could be a quick thing, she had a very strong feeling it wouldn't be. There was something compelling about not only Beau, but the energy they had as Beau and Cora.

She shouldn't think on it overmuch at that point though. Let it be magic. Magic was lovely.

CHAPTER EIGHT

GALLERY SILVERA SAT on a corner, next to a wine bar and across from a café. It was the perfect sort of place to wander after enjoying a glass of wine or a cup of tea. There were several other galleries within a four-block radius, all having a different perspective and emphasis. It created a lovely, artsy atmosphere.

Cora's town house was close enough that she usually walked during the warmest months. But more, she herself was part of the neighborhood she worked in. When she chose what went on the walls in the gallery, what could be seen through the big windows facing the street, Cora expanded her gallery outside. Connected with those other places, and through Seattle Center, they were part of something vibrant, pulsing with music and art and dance.

It'd been in the current location in the shadow of the Space Needle for thirty years. Most of them had been as a moderate success. Her father had originally bought it as a gift for his wife—and as Cora believed, a way to give Walda roots. To give her a sense of place to build a life and a family. Which she'd done, but in her own way because no one told her mother how to live.

Like any kid who grew up in a family that ran a

business, she and her siblings had spent a lot of afternoons and weekends at the gallery. It had brought color and creativity into her life at a very early age. She'd learned her multiplication tables while tucked into a back corner. A young painter who now had an established, successful career had helped her with a book report. Their dining table had always been surrounded by artists, art lovers and all manner of exciting, interesting folk.

The gallery and the people who came through it were what she always thought of as another room of her childhood home.

She would get dressed and in makeup in her office once all the last touches were in place. For the time being she was in jeans and a long-sleeved shirt and wore sneakers as she rearranged some of the bouquets and floral baskets while making sure all the descriptions and associated materials with each piece were free of errors.

The caterers and bar staff had arrived and were beginning to get set up when she finished up all she could do for the event.

Maybe knocked on the door of Cora's office not thirty seconds after she'd gotten her clothes and accessories for the night laid out. "I brought you a coffee," Maybe told her, kissing her cheek as she handed the travel mug over.

Her friend was not only a fantastic hairdresser and barber, she also did makeup for her friends on special occasions. Maybe had shown up with her case, ready to work.

"You're my favorite," Cora said as she got into the chair.

"Naturally. You can tell me about the pumpkin patch and the sex you had afterward while I'm doing your hair."

"How the hell do you know we had sex?" Cora looked at herself in the mirror, carefully making sure she hadn't missed a love bite or something embarrassing.

"You have the glow. Your hair is looking fantastic. It's got sex volume. And you didn't deny it immediately. Also, you seemed pretty hot for one another and so it was a natural assumption."

Maybe began to do her magic on Cora's hair while she sipped her coffee and sighed happily.

"He was cute at the pumpkin patch. He pulled the wagon without complaint. Then he made me three different kinds of tacos while I decorated. Then we had terrific sex. Like stick your finger in a light socket electric sex. And in the afterglow what do you think we did?"

"Ate more tacos?"

Cora sighed. "I hadn't even thought of that. Hell, eating more tacos totally would have been a wise choice. But no, after he fucked me silly, he helped me with some of my pumpkins. We even carved some before I had to leave to get here. Oh, and he's coming tonight."

Cora kept her eyes closed as Maybe worked. Pinning, curling and spraying her hair before moving on to makeup. At some point, Rachel arrived and Cora recounted the same story, catching her up.

"He'll be more comfortable because he knows everyone already except for Beto and Finley." It was less pressure that way. If, for whatever reason, he hit his limit on Cora time, or their chemistry cooled or soured, there'd be other people around to make it easier to avoid one another.

"Finley is curious about him. She's done some internet sleuthing so be ready for all her questions about his, um, more colorful days," Rachel said of Cora's sister.

"She runs a tattoo shop. She's around colorful people all day long. Hell, she *is* one."

"Don't get defensive. She loves you and you're the baby," Rachel reminded her.

She didn't want that feeling lodged in her gut just then. Resentment and maybe a little bitterness. She adored Finley, who'd always been there for her. But if she was so concerned, why not help with their mom?

"I'm sure it'll be fine. He's charming. And it's not like I'm harvesting his organs for dinner or anything. We're just having fun," Cora said.

"Hold your breath I'm getting ready to set your hair with spray," Maybe told Cora.

They helped her get into the dress without smearing makeup, mussing hair or getting deodorant on anything. A bonus was the way the high neck and illusion panel on the front accentuated her boobs without having them in danger of falling out of anything.

It was a grown-up, sexy dress and she couldn't deny she chose it with Beau in mind.

"Dayum, baby. You lookin' good," Maybe said as she circled Cora slowly.

The three friends laughed as they headed out to the main gallery floor where the candles were lit, the wine had been decanted and music played in the background.

It smelled like cinnamon and oranges so she knew her brother was around somewhere, a mug of Market Spice tea in his hand. She followed her nose and found him setting that cup of tea down so he could open the doors for their parents as they approached the gallery.

Before she could head to them, Finley stepped into her path. Her sister wore an amazing jumpsuit that would have looked awful on most other people. Her forearms and chest were mainly bare, all her ink on display. Her dark brown hair was pulled away from her face into a loose knot at the base of her neck.

Finley was unique. She had an edge, but she put makeup on it, winged its eyeliner and used her tattoos like jewelry. Her sister was a badass. Gorgeous. Fierce and deeply thoughtful. Her artistic nature was the closest to control freak of the sisters.

She loved hard, including her family. They weren't perfect. The Silveras could be total assholes to one another. But their connection was bone deep. Their commitment and loyalty to the family was something Cora never doubted.

"So. Where's the dude?" Finley looked around before settling back on Cora. "Oh, and you look particularly dishy tonight."

"I clean up okay," Cora told her. "Digging that jumpsuit. We need to go shopping soon. As for Beau, I told him not to show up until after eight. I think he's going to check in with Gregori and Wren since they'll be here tonight too."

When Cora took a look around the space, she noticed immediately that her mother had begun to move things around, and at first, Cora stood, furiously stock-still. Walda had nothing to do with the gallery events by that point and hadn't for several years. She knew nothing about what hung on the walls. But that didn't stop her from coming in and fucking shit up because why not? Her mom always wanted her way.

Clearly, it was obvious to her friends because Rachel sighed, getting Cora's attention back. "You're going to pop a vein," Rachel said, pushing her toward Walda. "This is your gallery. Your event. You'd never let *anyone* else do this. I'm not saying you should punch her in the face," she snorted. "Just be in charge. You got this."

Finley sighed before linking her arm through Cora's. "She's right. If you don't stop Mom now, she'll only get worse. You know how she is."

Maybe cocked her head, saying nothing but lending her support with a smile.

"You stay here," Cora told her sister. For a long time Finley had worked really hard to get their mother's attention and affection. She'd been the bridge between the older two kids and Cora and Beto. Their oldest sister's lieutenant when their mom was focused elsewhere. Cora had watched over and over as their mother took things for granted or her attention wandered. She did say thank you from time to time, but that need for approval had never been filled completely.

The energy between Finley and their mother was often tense because their mom either just didn't get it, or overreacted to something, launching a passive-aggressive period that blew up into an argument.

And then Cora would have to fix it.

She took a gulp of coffee before handing it off to Maybe, straightened her spine and headed over.

"Hey, you two," she said as she approached her parents.

Her father kissed her cheek. *"Ta bom?"* he asked in Portuguese. *Are you okay? Are you well? Is everything all right?*

The words, his tone, always centered Cora. It was his way of checking in. Something he'd done their whole life.

She smiled in response to his question and began to undo all the stuff her mother had done when Walda was paying attention to something else.

Until she noticed Cora and turned, pointing an accusing finger her youngest daughter's way. "What are you doing? I just did that."

"I'm putting it back the way I had it. Better flow, if anyone is wearing long sleeves they won't drag through the candles and start a fire. The breeze from the doors opening and closing will also be far enough away that they won't constantly blow out."

"You don't need candles." Walda turned back to undo what Cora had done.

She very nearly gave in and just let her mom have that moment. It wasn't that big a deal in the larger scheme of things. But she remembered it wasn't just about a candle right at that moment, but about how she wanted her future to look. She needed to stand up for herself.

"I like them there. So I don't *need* them, I want them." Cora attempted to sound matter-of-fact as she got between Walda and the candles, putting them back to rights.

Her mother narrowed her eyes at her, not very used to being told no. Cora just smiled and gave her mother a hug, leading her, along with her father, toward where the others still waited, pretending they hadn't watched the whole thing.

"You look nice tonight," Cora told her. "I didn't know you were coming. It's a happy surprise."

And it would give a bit more attention to the artists whose work was being sold, which was a very positive thing.

Walda meant well. Usually. Cora just had to remember that while she continued to work on ways to find her own place in the next phase of her life.

Even so, Cora's heart still beat fast in the wake of pushing back against her mother's interference. It was ridiculous for her to be so anxious about it. She wasn't weak in other areas of her life.

For a long time, people thought they could tell Walda no and she'd hear it. But her mother wasn't there for hearing things she didn't like.

Cora could steer her mother, which is what she did to manage her. To keep her out of trouble. But now, she had to tell her mother no, not as an employee, but as a daughter. A younger woman. And one, Cora saw in Walda's gaze, who was a potential rival.

Cora now had to step away from her role as Walda-keeper and, as she'd been reminded by several people in the last week alone, into the gallery full-time. She knew more about this gallery from an artistic perspective than anyone other than her father. The time had come. She felt it to her toes.

Both women, mother and daughter, were undergoing a huge change. Cora *wanted* to deepen her roots professionally and socially.

Beto approached with his suave-ass smile that charmed oh so many men. He handed Cora a glass. "Vodka and soda with extra lime. Drink up, sweetheart." He squeezed her shoulder. "You did well with her," he murmured.

That made Cora feel better. "I'm trying. Thanks for the drink." Cora held it up in salute before she took a healthy gulp.

"The place looks fantastic. You did a great job with everything. Even though most of it was over the phone or internet when you were gone, you still handled it. I do notice. So does *Pai*."

One of her goals was to be sure her father had faith in her leadership of the gallery. She'd needed to hear it.

Beto tipped his chin to where their parents stood with Maybe and Rachel, who'd been keeping Walda busy so she couldn't get back to messing with things. "Those Dolan girls are good friends."

"They really are. Okay. I need to get circulating. Be nice to Beau when he arrives."

Her brother's eyes widened slightly. "Can't wait. Not going to lie, Finley and I looked him up on the internet and saw all his modeling shots. He's not hard to look at."

Cora nodded. "Not at all. Naked, he's like one of those magical things you're not supposed to look at directly or you get ensorcelled."

Beto laughed, leaning in to kiss her cheek. "We haven't had much time to check in since you've been back. I can see you have a lot to say."

"I've been mulling. I think I might be ready to share. Let's all have brunch soon. I want to talk to Finley about it too."

He nodded and she headed off to do her thing, mask firmly in place.

THOUGH HE'D PLANNED to play it far more cool and make his way to wherever Cora was in a casual, nonchalant cruise, Beau saw her the moment they walked into the gallery and there was nothing but his desire to get to her.

A dress of midnight blue skimmed from midthigh up over her body in a caress that displayed the curves beneath. The neck was high and it had no sleeves. The combination worked, hinting and showing off equally well.

With her hair pulled back he saw the lines of her face better, noted even in the lower lights the darker lip and the dramatic eyes. He liked it when she was in jeans and T-shirts, but this dressed-up version was hot.

When he drew close, he listened to her speak about

the artist of a series of pen-and-ink drawings she stood in front of.

This wasn't just the boss's daughter. Cora clearly loved what she was doing, but also had a sound foundation on which to speak about art. She was intelligent and quick-witted. Intuitive.

She was far more complicated than he'd given her credit for at first glance. Every time he saw her, he learned something new. Something more.

After the people she'd been speaking to moved on, she looked up and their gazes locked with a sensual punch.

He cupped her elbow as he leaned down to kiss her. He'd been intending on a cheek kiss but ended up with a brush of his mouth against hers.

"Good evening," he said, stepping back but not very far. "You look fantastic."

Her smile seemed to light her from within. "Thank you. So do you."

"Do you have time to give me a tour?" Beau indicated the gallery's contents with a wave of his hand.

"Of course."

She led him through the gallery, pausing here and there to show him something or answer his questions.

All the while, her friends and her mother all watched them with undisguised curiosity.

"You're aware your friends and I assume more of your family are clearly waiting for you to introduce me to them," he asked her when she paused in front of a hyperrealistic painting of a scarlet leaf swirling toward a drain.

"Finley's been playing internet sleuth. She and my brother have been looking at your modeling shots online. They've all seen your butt and tasteful shots of your dick."

He nearly choked on his spit at that but she was amused so he could relax a little. His life had included a period of time when people took pictures of him to sell their products. Clothes, shoes, fragrance, lifestyle based products, he'd done them all. And there were pictures to prove it.

"If it helps, they both think you looked hot in the pictures," she told him, a smile on her face. Damn. He wanted to kiss her again and then once more.

"I'd be lying if I said it didn't."

"You remember that my mother is a kook, right? I mean, look—" Cora lowered her voice "—she might bring up the, uh, way you grew up. I mean, I'm sure my father coached her not to, but, she does what she wants. So. I apologize in advance."

Adorable. Good god. This woman was beyond adorable.

"I'll be fine. Whenever you're ready." But it looked as if one of them was going to bolt and come over to them if they didn't get a move on.

She stood taller and gave him a look. "All right then. You were warned."

He leaned down to whisper in her ear. "You made up for any potential issues with your family earlier this afternoon if I recall."

Her blush charmed him.

"We'll see what you think after you meet them."

"I've met your mother," he said.

She snorted. "Dude. You met W. Silvera. Another famous person who lived in the same complex. That woman over there? That's Walda, my mom and also the queen of this space." Her tone held a bit of bitterness and it tugged at him. "She's the gatekeeper, or so she thinks. It's different."

Cora smiled at some people who passed by before turning back to him. He could see that bitterness had been swept aside.

She was also correct that this time, coming into contact with her parents and siblings was different. Which he'd been in denial about until that moment and now a little anxiety churned in his belly.

Regardless, he understood Cora enough to know her family was important, and if he meant to be around her, he'd have to accept it. And have them accept him.

"Ready?"

"As I'll ever be," he said.

With a smile, she took his hand and they walked over to where the Silveras stood, not even pretending they hadn't been watching him with Cora the whole time he'd been there.

"Everyone, this is Beau Petty. Beau, you already know my mom and some of the others, but this is my father, John."

Her dad gave Beau a once-over before giving him a firm handshake. Walda gave him a far more imperious look before she held her hand out.

"It's nice to see you again. You've aged well. Why

are you in Seattle?" Walda continued her regal look like that was how everyone met new people.

"I'm Finley." A tall, dark-haired woman who shared the same eyes as her little sister stepped forward, interrupting her mother's question.

"Nice to meet you. And you're Alberto?" Beau asked, turning to her brother.

"Yes." His handshake was firm, his look assessing but not hostile. "Call me Beto—everyone else does."

"You were going to tell us why you were in Seattle," Walda repeated.

"I'm in Seattle for work. I'm writing a cookbook, creating my new show around it. And for personal reasons. I have several close friends in Seattle. I find it easy to relax here. There's a great food culture." Beau gave Cora a look. "And now I've got even more reasons to stick around."

"Are you in the market for some art?" Walda asked him.

She wasn't his mother so it didn't poke at him the way it did Cora. He'd been around more than his share of strong, manipulative personalities. His father was a master of the mind fuck. So Beau knew not to engage like that. Better to let the other person either run out of steam, or if they continued, he had other ways of dealing. Changing the subject, moving away, pretending to be totally ignorant of the intent because once you gave in and responded in kind, the other person would only think it was all right to act that way in the future.

No one pulled his strings.

He *chose* to be laid-back and easygoing. Chose to

be amused, so he said, "I'm told by a very good source that I should always be in the market for some art."

"He means me," Cora said with a smile, relief clear at the edges. "Speaking of being in the market, I see a collector I know over there in front of the watercolors. She *definitely* needs some new art. I also see Gregori and Wren," she told him. "Let's go say hello on the way."

Beau tipped his chin at his friends, who headed over. "Not necessary. They're coming to us. Go and sell the hell out of some art. I'll be here when you're done."

Cora turned to her mother. "Behave," she urged before sailing off to do her job.

She had a way about her, an air of competence and authority. She knew her shit and was confident without being overbearing. Warm and charming. It was sexy just how well she worked the room.

"Why don't you model anymore?" Walda asked, breaking into his thoughts. She wasn't done with her questioning, and while her manner bordered on rude, it was a fair enough question.

And he wanted her family to like him. He'd enjoyed Walda well enough in the brief interactions he'd had with her. Beau needed to reach a little deeper now that he'd pushed back and established his boundaries with her.

"It's a hard life and as my friend Ian likes to remind me, beauty fades. I wanted to have something else to do to diversify my career. Because of the opportunities I was presented with, I found that I really liked to cook. It turned out to be a good pivot. My manager knew someone who was looking for a new face for a cooking show. That's how I got the first television job. It's been seven years now and my second iteration ended six months ago so I'm working on version three. I do still model from time to time. Good to keep a toe in and it pays the bills." It also enabled him to support the different organizations he wanted to.

She made a sound. If it was good or bad he didn't know, but then she nodded as if he'd passed some sort of quiz. Not that Beau fooled himself. This was her nature. To be the queen in every room.

He turned his attention back to where Cora stood, across the gallery, selling the hell out of some rather striking pen-and-ink drawings.

"You should come by the shop sometime. Have lunch with us all," Finley said.

"If you scare him off, Cora is going to peel the skin off your body and rub you in salt," Rachel replied easily.

Wren laughed. "I love you guys. No one is going to scare anyone off. Beau is made of sterner stuff."

Appreciating the backup, Beau sent a smile Wren's way before turning his attention back to Finley. "I'd love to come by the shop. I'm thinking on some new ink so that kind of works out. Cora says you're both really good."

"See? Sterner stuff. Charm and good looks." Wren shrugged with a smirk.

"We'll see. There's no shortage of handsome, charming men around," Finley said with a lift of one shoulder.

"I know. Life is pretty damned awesome, right?" Wren said with a wink, setting everyone to laughing.

CHAPTER NINE

The shape of your mouth
A lush, pillowed haven
Giver of pleasure
Curved with secrets

A FEW WEEKS LATER, Beau knocked on her door, knowing he could have easily texted her.

She opened up, looking sleep rumpled, and he should have felt guilty but all he felt was pleasure at the sight of her. The intensity hadn't worn off as they slow danced through the first weeks of their relationship.

"I just…" He paused and then ran a hand through his hair. "I have to fly to LA. My house sold and I need to sign stuff and handle some last details."

She held a hand his way. "Do you have time to share a cup of coffee or are you on the way out now?"

He took it, going into her little town house at her side. "I have time. I'm not flying out until tonight. I woke you up. I'm sorry."

"I was still in bed, but awake. Just writing a little, listening to public radio. Sit. I was about to make coffee. Honestly. And even if I wasn't, it's not a big deal to make it."

Beau watched her, her hips swaying slightly as she measured out coffee and got everything started.

It had been two days since he'd seen her last. She'd been busy, as had he. And yet, she'd never been far from his thoughts and he found himself making the time, pushing her to the top of his priority list, even if it was to just have a quick lunch or share a cup of coffee. He wanted to spend some time while he was gone to think on that. About how he wanted to be around her on a regular basis.

But the impact of just how different this attraction to Cora was than anything he'd experienced before still had him a little unsteady.

"I'll be back Friday night," he said. But instead of sitting, he moved to her fridge. "What's in here?"

"Look for yourself. I went to the produce market yesterday with Rachel and Vic so there's all sorts of goodness."

Her face was bare of any makeup, she wore flannel pajama bottoms and a long-sleeved shirt, and yet he couldn't take his attention away from her.

"What? I brushed my teeth already, I promise."

He didn't resist the urge to cross her kitchen and kiss her silly. Her taste seeped down into him, spreading through his system in a slow, warm tide.

Recognition. She tasted like she knew him and wanted him anyway.

"Just wanted to kiss you, that's all," he murmured before breaking away to continue poking around to see what he could make them for breakfast.

"If you like smoked salmon there's some in the

cheese drawer thingy," she told him. "Vic's mom makes it fresh, and then sets some aside for me. And there's some black bread over near the toaster. There were these Danish things called *vatrushka*, but I ate those."

He laughed. "Why'd you tell me then?"

She shrugged. "Gloating, I suppose."

Holy shit did he adore her. "Can we get together when I return?" he asked her as he began to assemble a quick scramble. Step one in his being-with-Cora-more plan was to simply speak his intentions.

"Yes, of course. I guess...well, I figure we're in a thing of some sort, right? So yeah, I'd like that. Was the house on the market long?" The coffee maker began to gurgle merrily as she pulled out plates and silverware.

Relief hit that she seemed as off balance as he when it came to how well they connected. "Luckily for me, the house was in a neighborhood in high demand with really low availability. My broker hadn't even officially listed it when we got the first offer."

"Are you a real estate genius or was that a stroke of luck or what?"

"Can you toast the bread? The eggs are nearly finished," he said, and once she agreed, he answered her question. "I bought the house years ago when the market was crap and my accountant suggested it as a good way to diversify my portfolio. The cool factor of the area is the final reason I decided to get out. Constantly surrounded by young, rich fucks who have no jobs, party constantly and race through the streets in Lambos they don't deserve. I liked it when it was mainly old people. They make less noise."

The toast popped up to put a period at the end of that statement.

"Is the next sentence, get off my lawn?" The giggle at the end let him know she was teasing and it was good-natured. "Want butter?"

He snorted. "I've never had a lawn really. Even at my house, it was more drought conscious so it was rocks and succulents and fire-resistant stuff. I think I might yell at people who walked on my emerald green lawn if I had one."

Her delighted chuckle pleased him nearly as much as the way she went to her toes as she yanked him her way by his shirt. The kiss she followed up with was rousing and comforting at the same time.

"You're pretty charming. You know that, right?"

Beau banded her waist with his forearm, holding her to him. He knew. He'd be a liar to deny it. Usually it was sort of automatic. He'd been trained early on to charm people. Make them like him as a way to get people to come to church.

With Cora, it was more a desire to please and delight. He wanted to be the one to make her laugh, to bring kisses and her attention. It was one of the reasons he was there instead of texting that he was going out of town.

"I would very much appreciate butter on my toast, thank you," he said after kissing her one last time.

Once they settled at the table, she poured them both a cup of coffee and they dug in, eating in companionable silence.

"Your life is so quiet here. Even with the super spider lair on your porch and a dozen pumpkins it's quiet. Peaceful." It called to him nearly as powerfully as she herself did.

"The rest of my life isn't always so quiet. I wanted a place that I could retreat to. There are only six units here. And all of us facing an internal courtyard seems to really cut noise from the street. It's nice and shady in the heat of the summer and cozy warm in the winter. It's a good place to be. There's just one drawback. Or two. Dave and Lani. I call him The Hugger and she's Nip Slip. They have a hot tub they're always inviting people to. He's a close talker, all up in your space. Loves to grab you into hugs while telling you he's a hugger. Like it's not obvious. Anyway, their place is two down. Be warned."

"Making a note not to walk down that way." He paused. "I had a good time at the gallery event. I think I forgot to say so that night or the days after."

"Yeah? Good. I did too."

He hadn't stayed over after the gallery event, though he'd come home with her and they'd ended up having sex twice more before he shuffled out after two.

As he'd lain in the borrowed bed, in a borrowed luxury condo, he'd realized he wasn't as adrift as he'd been before she'd come back into his life. Cora, always at the center of his thoughts it seemed.

It had been so rare in his life to feel this *connected* to another person. Nearly every other time though it had been lightning fast, as well. So he paid attention because it felt like he was supposed to be there with her eating breakfast at her little table.

Not that he was entirely comfortable with the intensity between them. He was drawn to her and lacked the will to do anything but obey that call.

It should have felt lowering. He couldn't recall the last time he'd been this way with a romantic interest. He was used to being pursued so the flip of perspectives, being the pursuer, wasn't entirely steady. But while he was uncertain, he had no plans to do anything but keep on with her to see where he ended up.

"Once I buy my own place, I'll be coming to you for all my art and art-related needs. It's nice to have connections who show me their boobs."

She laughed, nearly choking on her coffee.

"I should amend that to singular." He was suddenly embarrassed he'd said it out loud but he wanted to make it clear. Wanted her to make the same declaration. "I just thought you should know. That it was just the one. You I mean."

"Okay. Even if I had the time, which I don't, I wouldn't be looking for anyone else just now," she teased, and it made the knot of anxiety in his chest loosen.

"Good. Yeah." That was smooth. "What are you up to this week then?"

"I'll be at the gallery. I'm seeing my brother and sister for brunch on Wednesday. I always have lunch with Maybe and Rachel on Friday afternoon. It's our ritual. Probably dinner out a few times. Especially as this hot guy I know who cooks like a dream will be out of town."

That pleased him a lot.

"I'll make you lots of food when I get back," he promised. "So, to be nosy, what's up with the gallery? It's clear you run it now, but your mom seemed…"

PLEASED WITH HIS PRESENCE, with the way he looked at her, like he couldn't get enough, she leaned back in her chair to look at him.

He came to her before he left town. He even told her he wanted to be exclusive. He made her breakfast and now was wanting to know about her life. Right then and there with this man, Cora knew, just knew, she was meant to open herself up to the magic of what might be.

"My father bought the gallery for my mom thirty years ago. But two years later she won the Oscar for Best Original Score and her career exploded. He stayed here in Seattle, running not only the gallery but his business. He's a landscape architect—I think I told you that? Javier, that's our oldest brother, he and Beatriz pretty much helped him raise me, Beto and Finley. I grew up at the gallery. It's my second home in a lot of ways."

"Javier and Beatriz aren't local, right?"

"Javi is a choreographer. He lives in Toronto. Bee lives in Virginia. She's a psychiatrist." That they'd moved to the other side of the continent hadn't been lost on Cora. "Bee took me to school more than both my parents combined. Even when she was an undergrad at the UW, she lived at home to help."

"Are you close with them still?"

It was more complicated than that. "There are a lot of ups and downs in life, you know? Lots of low times when you're not sure how you'll get through. But no matter what, no matter how chaotic things are, my family is always a united front. I'd give my kidney to my siblings." Cora paused.

"But?" He got up to grab the apples he'd sliced and peeled to bring them to her table for them to share.

"They escaped. Both of them would deny that. But of course they did and it was absolutely what they should have done. They had the weirdest childhood of all the kids." Cora winced and looked up at him. Speaking of weird childhoods…

He burst into laughter as he reached across to squeeze her hand briefly, and then left their fingers tangled together. "Well, look, your childhood is another universe of weird. Which sounds insulting—I'm sorry."

"That's not insulting. It *was* weird. No doubt about it. Back to Javier and Beatriz though. We can talk about my stuff later on.

"I'm closest to Beto. We're only a year apart so we had each other as playmates and confidants when everyone else was doing their busy thing. I'd say Javi is more an uncle to me than a brother. He's fifteen years older than I am. But we're connected. He's a lot like Walda in that he's all about his art. He was a dancer until he aged out, sped a little by a series of injuries and surgeries. Dancers are hard on their bodies." She shook her head. "Anyway, that's his focus. He works and when he's not working he's watching other people work. He comes back home at Christmas but stays with Finley or here with me. He and Walda are very complicated."

"Part of the reason he's in Toronto?"

She laughed. "It's not really a coincidence that he and Bee got as far away from Seattle as they could."

"And Beatriz?"

"Bee is Bee." Cora shrugged. "Rachel knows more about her personal life than I do. She's easier with friends than she is with family." Which was most likely connected to their mother too. "She loves us and we love her. It works for everyone that she's where she wants to be."

"Makes sense. And you're the fixer. I can see that already."

"It's a family joke that I'm the only adult of the whole lot." Not so much a joke at that point, it was the truth. "Anyway, I'm in a transitional phase. I want to run the gallery. Beto has been taking most of the load while I travel with Walda, but his artistic love is development. He's actually quite good at it. Probably helps that he's handsome and good with people."

"And what does your mother think about that? You replacing her?"

Cora snorted. "She's never really run the gallery anyway. She's the face because she's already well-known in the art world. She likes a place to show her own work when she decides to, but mainly, she's disinterested in the work of running a gallery and really just wants to make art." And take credit for other people's work. "It's going to be a matter of presenting it to her in the right way because it's really not a case of me taking her job."

She was about to jiggle her boobs at him to get his

attention pointed in the direction of her bedroom when her phone started to buzz. She looked at the screen and sighed. "I have to take this. I'm sorry."

Beau waved her apology away. "I'll clean up while you deal with that."

It was her mother. "I need you to get me those aloe juice drinks."

"Okay. I'll order you some. In the future though, you can let Kay know so she can pick you up some when she goes marketing."

"She never gets the right ones. You do."

Kay was the house manager for her parents and she took a lot of the day-to-day load from Cora's shoulders. Still, there were always these little things Walda insisted no one knew how to do right but her youngest daughter.

"I'll let her know which Trader Joe's has them." Cora was fairly sure Kay already knew exactly that, but it never hurt to just underline for her mother that she had a full-time person to run her errands.

"I don't know why you need to do that when you know where they are."

"Because it's Kay's job and she does the marketing so why wouldn't she want to be sure to get your favorite aloe juice?"

"You do it best," her mother told her.

"There's no doing it *best*. It's grocery shopping. It's a matter of getting the things people want and need."

"But then you make sure I have everything else I need." Walda's voice had a tiny bit of petulance at the end.

"*Mai,* I love you. But I promise you this isn't a matter of skill, just a matter of knowing what to get you. There are things only I can do, but this isn't one of them. Be sure you get all your prescriptions filled this week."

"You can do that when you get the aloe," her mother said as if she hadn't planned that from the first. "Anyway, I'm not sure I even need that blood pressure medication. It makes me tired."

This was officially an old argument. Her mom's *I do what I want* gene was one thing when she was younger and when she focused it on her work, but the older she got, the more it began to creep into her health and other things.

And became another issue Cora had become responsible for. "We've talked about this. You can't just stop taking your pills so if you really do want to go off them, you need to do it with your doctor's supervision." Cora massaged the space between her eyebrows where her headache had begun.

"So bring my aloe juice with the pills later today. We'll have lunch after."

Just like her mother to just change the subject.

"I can't. I've got appointments all afternoon. You know how to call in your pills. The number is on the bottle. I'll touch base with Kay on the juice. 'Bye." Cora disconnected with a heavy sigh.

"Every time I try to leave they pull me back in," she muttered, looking up to discover Beau standing very close.

"Everything all right?" he asked.

"She and I are experiencing some growing pains. I have to be firm and she has to listen and respect. And then I have to be forgiving because her strong suit is not listening."

"I'm sorry."

Cora shrugged. "It's the way of things. We'll both survive and thrive in our new roles. Hopefully. I'm not under any misapprehension that it'll be smooth or always easy, but it's what needs to happen."

"I have to get moving. I still haven't finished packing. If you need me to, I can probably put this on hold. Go sign things later in the week," he told her, taking her hands and pulling her closer.

"Aw thank you." She reached up to kiss him, missing his lips but getting just beneath, against his beard. Yum. "I'm good. I'll see you when you get back. Travel safe."

She kept it light, though she knew that since he'd come back into her life she'd miss his presence in it. He'd return to Seattle and to her. She felt it in her gut.

Then he picked her up, taking them to the couch, resting her butt against the back of it. Cora wrapped herself around him as he bent to kiss her long and slow. He tasted of coffee and strawberry jam and felt like nothing else she'd ever experienced.

"I'll talk with you soon. Have a good week," he said, stepping back at last.

It was a good thing the couch was there to support her because he'd gone and made her knees all rubbery again.

"'Bye, Beau." She walked him to the door, and then watched as he loped with long, ground-eating strides, out of her sight.

CHAPTER TEN

It's no coincidence
my lips cannot forget
the way you taste

"Thing is, Cora, Dad needs to be doing this stuff, not you. Not me. Not Finley or Bee or Javi," Beto told her after they'd ordered their food.

She'd just finished relating the phone call with their mother the day before.

"I think she scares him," Cora said. "He *wants* to take care of her. She's cool with it but not when it's anything that might make her look or feel weak. So he can drive her around and take her to all her favorite restaurants and that, but medicine pickup or doctor's appointments might be difficult."

"*You* need to tell her no. She calls you because you do what she wants you to." Finley shrugged. "You don't want to work for her anymore. Quit your job. People do it every day."

"Mom isn't just *people*. She's a force of nature. You can't tell her no. You can't quit her. That's not how it works," Beto said.

"What is it *you* want?" Finley asked her. "You're part of the problem here. You let her get away with it."

Cora rolled her eyes at her sister. "I *let* her? You've met your mother, right?" She chose sarcasm instead of giving in to the hurt that her sister's casual comment brought.

And it wasn't altogether inaccurate.

"Stop being an asshole, Fin. What do you want to do, Cora?" Beto asked.

"I want to run the gallery. I've thrown myself into it since I got back from London, wanting to see if it was something I was really suited to or if I'd built it up into more than it really was." Cora paused. "I love my job. I want to curate. I want to build something that is uniquely mine and that can be passed to our kids. I want a dog. I want to be in a relationship that could develop into something long-term. I want to travel for pleasure."

"Fair enough. All of it. But you said yourself you're already working at the gallery. So what's the real issue?" Finley asked.

"I do it, but I have to deal with Mom's stuff too. That's what I need to change." It was making her bitter and resentful and Cora didn't want that.

"I vote we get her a new personal assistant," Finley told them, pouring syrup on her freshly arrived waffles.

"Whatever we present to her, we need to show a united front. If she senses any weakness she'll seize on it. Cora has been the person who makes her life effortless. She won't let go of that easily," Beto said.

"We all need a Cora, that's all I'm saying," Finley told them both.

"You don't feel like I'm trying to push you out?" Cora asked Beto after winking at her sister.

"I like art and I love the gallery, but I don't want to curate. And I don't want to be the director. *You're* good at it. I'm tolerable when you give me very specific instructions. I'd really like to dig in more with Dad, you know?"

Their father had a landscape architecture business. It was his art and he was marvelous at it. And Cora had no doubt her brother would be good at it in concert with their dad.

"Okay. I support that and whatever we need to do so we can make it happen. I guess we have some discussion points for the next family dinner, huh?" Cora said. "Now let's talk about your lives a bit. I missed you both."

BEAU LOOKED AT the black SUV he could have sworn he'd seen drive past the café where he sat with his agent—and friend—Jeremy more than once. Probably looking for a parking spot. He hoped it wasn't the paparazzi.

"Now that I'm moving to Seattle, you can add me to your list of people to see when you come to visit. I know you have other clients up that way," Beau told him.

"I'm up there a lot, actually. I've got friends and clients in Hood River, Oregon, as well as on Bainbridge Island and in Seattle proper. I'll be up in the early summer for sure for a graduation. I've considered relocating a time or two. But…"

Jeremy's ex-wife was a certified rock star. They'd suffered the horrible loss of a child and it had broken their relationship. Remarried and a mother with someone else, she lived in Seattle *and was still one of his clients*, which made for a big reason not to relocate, Beau supposed.

"I get it," Beau assured him.

"Ian tells me you're seeing someone and it's serious," Jeremy said, changing the subject.

"I actually met her seventeen years ago. She wasn't even an adult yet and I was only barely one. She's friends with Gregori and Wren so that's how we reconnected. It's, I don't know, super intense."

"So, she's in your circle of friends. That's new."

"I can't stay away."

Jeremy snorted and raised his glass. "Then don't. You don't mind being a hedonist in every other aspect of your life—why not let yourself like this woman as deeply as you want to?"

"I'm trying to give in to my urges less. Before I think about them a little at least. I've been doing little else but think about her."

"Ah. You're not in control and you don't know how to handle it," Jeremy said with a shrug.

"I've done plenty of out of control things in my life. Part of her appeal is that there's an edge to it. Something that challenges me subtly and yet completely. It's alluring and terrifying. She writes poetry and loves my cooking and the sex… It's astounding sex."

"You're vulnerable with her. That's necessary. If you don't have that, you don't have what it takes to get through the rough spots."

"It's been just less than a month. I find myself aiming my schedule to align with hers. I make up reasons to drop over because I really love her place." Beau shrugged, a little embarrassed but lighter for the admission. "I've been trying to fight it and we've both been so busy it's been easier to tell myself to go slow. But… I don't want to anymore."

"Something I've always admired about you is the way you're open to the truth of things. You ask questions. You seek learning. You're the kind of person who wants to *know* but once you do, you're not going to play games to pretend the truth away."

"Which is a long way to say I should trust how I'm feeling?" Beau asked.

Jeremy nodded. "More or less, yep. This person was thrown into your path for a reason. You can trust yourself when it comes to cooking and your on-camera work, you can trust your gut when it comes to other things too."

It had been hard to trust his gut after he'd left Road to Glory. Everything he'd thought was true had been a lie. And not just a lie, but a devastating series of lies told over decades. Lies he still had to deal with to that day.

"Christ." Beau ran his fingers through his hair.

Jeremy said, "I know what happened to you fucked you up. It was terrible and it would have fucked anyone up. You're strong, but you're not superhuman. Of course you doubt yourself. You always have when it comes to people instead of business decisions. But look at your close circle of friends. You've done right by yourself and by the rest of us. And if I can be totally honest, it's sort of gratifying to see you all uncertain over someone. All these years and you dicked around and moved on when it was over with no feelings hurt on either side. This is raw and scary. That's why it's so hot."

Beau laughed. "Perhaps. It *is* really fucking hot. And raw. It's intense and all, but I don't feel rushed. It's making this move a lot easier. Most of my shit is in storage until I get a place. But I'm going to call a real estate agent when I return so I can start looking."

And he wanted Cora to come along with him when he looked at houses. If for no other reason than she'd be amusing as hell and make him think about each property in a way he never would have alone.

Jeremy examined Beau's face a moment before speaking. "Keep me updated and I'll make things connect on this end when you're ready. My assistant will be in contact with some appearance possibilities. It's good to keep a hand in during this break between projects. Stay busy so you don't end up making questionable lifestyle choices. Your liver and your bank account prefer you engaged and productive."

Jeremy was totally right. Boredom *wasn't* his friend. Beau too often delved deep into his head, and then tried to drown out all that noise with substances and a great deal of empty physical encounters.

"So. Let's get to it. You said you had some new information from the investigators?" Beau asked, changing the subject to the seventeen-yearlong search for his kids. Nearly all the time the answer was no new information. Even when there was something new, it hadn't ever led to anything important.

"Obadiah Petty has been sighted in the United States."

Obadiah was Beau's dad's youngest brother. He'd left the group on and off as Beau had been growing up, but he'd always come back, usually with some new skill. Computers and other technology—though never for anyone but his father and those closest to him. Sometimes weapons. In fact, Obie had mined the land all around their original homestead and was most likely the reason the remaining church members hadn't been arrested and put on trial. He had the skills necessary to keep them under the radar, usually in Central and South America, where a group of American missionaries wasn't so unusual it caught a lot of attention.

However, before his father had run totally off the rails, he and Obie were thick as thieves. Obie was a calming influence on his big brother. One who kept his father's worst ideas at bay. For a while anyway. At times Obie helped Beau's father, at others, well, at others Beau wondered where his uncle's true loyalties lay.

"He may not be with them anymore, but chances are, he knows where your father is. And if we can finally find him, maybe we'll find your sons," Jeremy said.

It'd been multiple years since anyone in the group had direct contact with Beau. The last had been the final in a series of demands for money in exchange for information or access to his sons. Another fruitless payoff.

Beau ruthlessly tamped down any hope he'd allowed himself. His uncle could be the link they'd been waiting for. Or it could be another dead end. There'd been so many disappointments that it had become a defense mechanism. It was that or let it eat him alive.

"Where?"

"South Florida. He didn't enter the country under his own passport. We know that since his has been revoked. The team is down there now. I'll update you when and if I hear anything else. I debated telling you at all. I hate reopening old wounds."

"I want to know. Always," Beau told Jeremy.

Jeremy nodded. "I know. It's why I told you. And it's why I'm going to ask you if you want me to have a background check run on Cora and her family. Just to be safe."

Beau was paranoid sometimes when it came to what people might want from him. It made no real difference that it was due to how he was raised. The result was the same. He doubted people's motives and was slow to trust. Usually. Cora was an exception it seemed.

"Look," Jeremy began, "wanting to be sure she's not a criminal and that she doesn't have ties to anyone at Road to Glory doesn't make you a villain. It makes you careful. Maybe even tell her you do it with everyone? I don't know. But I do know you're going to wonder until it's done so let me have the standard run handled."

"It feels wrong. With her it feels wrong."

Jeremy appeared to follow up on his point but then

just sighed, sitting back in his chair. "Fine. Tell me what you decide." Beau got the feeling Jeremy would do one anyway and if it was bad, he'd say so. Otherwise he'd stay quiet.

CORA LOOKED DOWN at her phone to read a text from Beau telling her his plane was delayed. Again.

Poor dude. That had been the third time and it was already after nine and it looked like he wasn't getting in until the following day.

Disappointment tinged her concern for how tiring it was to deal with that sort of flight delay after delay. Thankfully it was a relatively short flight and she'd see him soon enough.

She texted back.

Check into a nice hotel room and get a good night's sleep. I'll see you when you get back.

"What? You have a face. A sad face. What did he say?" Maybe demanded, underlining her words with a stab at the air with her pizza crust.

"Ease up there, sport," Rachel mumbled.

"I just want to be sure he's being nice," Maybe said.

"You're being very aggressive there, ma'am. How much caffeine have you had today?" Cora asked Maybe, who snorted. "He's actually quite nice to me. I promise. His plane was delayed again so they booked him for a morning flight instead," Cora told them with a shrug. "It happens."

"But you have sadface." Maybe hugged her. "You

didn't even have sadface when Dr. Cheaterpants broke up with you."

"Oh him. Whatever." Cora waved a hand. Nearly three years before she'd caught her ex with another woman's underpants in his bed. "He's a cliché. Then again so am I because I haven't had a serious relationship since then." And not even because she'd been in love and had her heart broken. Just because she'd sacrificed parts of her life so she could straddle the world between her mother and the gallery.

Rachel said, "You're not a cliché at all. You've been busy. Your focus was elsewhere and that was what you wanted. You chose your priorities. Don't apologize for that. Now your direction is shifting at the very same time Beau Petty shows back up in your life. It's not a coincidence."

Cora dropped her gaze down to her phone when it buzzed with an incoming video call from Beau. "How do I look?" she asked her friends quickly.

Maybe tousled her hair and Rachel brushed pizza crust crumbs off her boobs so by the time she answered, Cora looked pretty damned cute.

Beau didn't look cute. He looked tired and sexy as hell. So far away.

"Hi. I'm sorry about all your flight stuff," she told him.

"Corny as it sounds, seeing your face makes things a little better. I'm on my way to the hotel now but I just wanted to call. To check in. You look pretty."

Every once in a while, his smooth demeanor would slip just a little and he'd be very sweet. Even slightly hesitant. It got to her, made her want to bring a smile to his lips.

She knew she sighed and had heart eyes at him, but she wanted him to know he made her gooey in more ways than one.

Maybe and Rachel found things to do in the kitchen but Cora knew they were listening.

"You look handsome as usual. But tired. Drink some hot tea when you get checked into the hotel," she urged. The light from the city and traffic outside the car he rode in cast shadows over his face in all the right ways. "And I need to add that you look like the hero in a gothic romance novel."

His puzzled smile shot straight to her swelling heart. "Is that a good thing?" he asked.

"Oh yes. I love gothic romance. Love, love, love. You're broody and mysterious. A scandalous past." Broken and not a little torn at the edges. Unattainable almost certainly. But she wanted him anyway.

"Well okay then. Remind me to follow up on this sexy little side story when I finally get back," he said with a look that made her go hot all over.

"You betcha," she managed to say. "Hot shower. Cup of tea. Bed. I'll see you tomorrow."

"Are you working?"

"Tomorrow? From three until ten or so."

He frowned. "Can I see you after that? Would you like to eat a late dinner with a bunch of chefs? You can meet Ian. And afterward…"

She smiled. "Okay. Yes to all that."

"Good night, Cora."

"Night, Beau. See you tomorrow."

Cora tucked her phone, screen down, onto a nearby table, cheeks heated with her blush.

"You're dumb over him," Rachel declared with a happy sigh. "This is the best."

"I'm enjoying myself and the sex, as I've said but will share again, is incredible. That much sex appeal is enough to render certain parts of myself dumber than others," Cora said.

"Ignorance is bliss I guess," Rachel deadpanned.

After the giggles subsided, Cora settled back and sipped her soda.

"Finley said you'd had brunch and were finally going to tell your mother you wanted to take over the gallery," Rachel said.

"That clearly falls in the Cora's news to tell folder," Cora grumbled. Having her best friend work with her sister meant sometimes news would get shared by other people and not always on her schedule.

Finley couldn't keep a secret to save her life so it was frustrating to expect anything else, even if it was annoying sometimes.

"You could have told us first," Maybe reminded her.

"This is the first time I've seen you both where we've had some privacy since that brunch. Anyway. We're having dinner with my parents to talk about it."

"Good. I know it might come off like Finley isn't taking you seriously. She is. She's just got her own business with Walda and it gets in her way sometimes." One of Rachel's gifts was her insight into other people's hearts and minds. And what seemed to be a bottomless well of empathy.

"I can't take anyone else's shit on right now, Rachel. She's a big girl. Older than I am. I've done the heavy lifting and I'm not going to keep it up because Finley can't be a big girl and confront her mother. If I can, she can."

Maybe's clapping and cheering made Cora feel better about standing up for herself.

"Neither of you has just yet," Rachel reminded her. "But you shouldn't take Fin's shit on. Other people shielding her is why she and your mom have this messed-up dynamic even now. I'm *always* on your team. Always. I'm just providing some context, that's all."

"Have you talked with Javi or Bee yet? To get their support?" Maybe asked.

Cora shook her head. "Neither of them is involved. To try to drag them into it would only complicate everything. You know how my mother is when it comes to Javier." The oldest child and the overbearing mother. It was like textbook family drama. "It's best for everyone that an entire continent separates them. I've already shifted my hours. Traded off the load with Beto—who really wants to work more with my dad and he can now. It's a good time for this to happen. Walda is close to home for a while so the possible upheaval at this point is mainly emotional. We've all lived with my mother enough to weather one of her tantrums." She hoped.

"I'm super proud of you," Rachel told her with a

quick hug. "You're a pleaser. You like making people happy and taking care of them. You're doing this for yourself. Which I know is really hard. For whatever it's worth, I think you're doing the right thing for your mom too. I mean, I do feel pretty sorry for whoever you hire to replace you."

"Even if it means I'll be at Ink Sisters less?" Cora wasn't just leaving her mom's full-time service, she was giving up doing the books for her sister's shop.

"It was time for that too. Not that I won't miss you but it's not like we don't see each other pretty much every day outside the shop anyway. And let's be honest, she needs to depend on herself more too," Rachel said. "So much amazing change about to happen for us all." She looked back and forth between Maybe and Cora. "I'm pregnant."

Cora smiled so hard her cheeks hurt. "Shut the front door!"

"Get out of here! How did you not tell me until right now? How long have you known?" Maybe demanded. "All that talk about uteruses a few weeks ago! Did you know then?"

Cora couldn't stop laughing, even as tears started rolling down her cheeks.

Rachel shook her head. "I didn't know for sure until two hours ago. I promised Vic I'd cut tonight short so we can go over to his mom and dad's place to tell them. I was late when we had that conversation about kids but I honestly just didn't think about it too much. But the throwing up started and Vic started to nag me about taking a pregnancy test and finally just brought some home tonight. Five of them."

"This is good news, right? I mean, we're all laughing and crying and schmoopy over this but how are you?" Maybe asked after the hugging stopped.

"It is. I wasn't even sure if it was possible…after all the physical damage." Rachel had been kidnapped, tortured and held captive by a serial killer several years before. It had left her in a coma, and then facing multiple surgeries and physical therapy. The emotional therapy had taken longer, but it was there. She'd done the work, and then had fallen for Vic at just the right time.

Cora dug out a box of tissues and handed them out to everyone.

Rachel mopped her face before she grinned at them. "It's good. Let's just hope the baby isn't as huge as Vic. At least not until after the birth. I'm going to be a mom. Holy shit." Rachel thumbed away her tears.

"Thank god you finally told them," Vic burst out as he came into the room. "I've been lurking like a creeper, just waiting. You all talk a lot." He frowned but once he caught sight of Rachel he smiled so big Cora started to cry again.

"You two will be aunties and that's a big deal," Rachel said. "You have to help me not be a terrible mother."

"You don't need help to be a good mom. You're going to be a *fantastic* mom." Maybe hugged her sister once more before settling next to Cora so Vic could sit with Rachel.

"It's totally a big deal and I take it so seriously. I'm

ride or die for that baby," Cora said, making an X over her heart. "Maybe is right though, you're going to be good at this mom gig." She looked to Maybe. "We have so much baby stuff to make and buy and design and shop for."

"Yay!" Maybe hugged Cora and then they all hugged Vic and Rachel and it was a weepy, sweet, happy mess.

"Now will you please marry me already?" Vic asked, still in the midst of a hug pile.

He'd asked her once a year since they'd started seeing one another, and she'd said she wasn't ready. Even when Maybe had married Alexsei, Rachel had said she wasn't ready.

Cora and Maybe sat back, unsure as to whether or not they needed to leave. But hoping they didn't have to.

"You don't have to marry me just because you knocked me up," Rachel told Vic. "No matter what your mother says."

Vic rolled his eyes heavenward and muttered in Russian. "Have I not been asking you to marry me for years? Long before you got pregnant with what will surely be the most beautiful baby ever born."

"It's nice that he's keeping his expectations manageable," Maybe said to Cora with a snicker.

"Oh. Well, that's true." Rachel's mouth quirked up into a smile. "Okay. I guess I need to make an honest man out of you or people might think you were easy. But we get the final say with the wedding stuff. I don't want some gigantic affair at the church with eight thousand people. I want it to be small and full of the people

we love and your mother needs to be kept in check."
She sized him up. "And I don't mean by me. I mean *you*
have to tell her no if and when it comes up."

Cora tried not to snicker but it was impossible.

"And I will never ever want to eat beets so let's es-
tablish that," Rachel added.

Vic made an admirable attempt not to look confused. "Duly noted and witnessed by Cora and Maybe."

"You must really love me to want my crazy mixing
up with your crazy. You do realize we might have just
bred the Kwisatz Haderach, right?"

"Did you just make a science fiction reference from
Dune as a way to accept a marriage proposal?" Vic
asked her.

"Yeah. I'm totally weird. Are you new here?" Rachel asked.

"So much happiness!" Maybe said as she threw her
arms around her sister again.

Cora headed home not too much later, wanting to
snuggle down in her bed and sleep a solid nine hours.

Beau would be back the following day and her dear-
est friend was going to have a baby and get married.
Things were really freaking good.

CHAPTER ELEVEN

Unexpected. A storm of tears washed over me, leaving my insides clean and peaceful.

BEAU ROLLED INTO his borrowed apartment just before noon. The temptation to drop by the gallery or even her house since she said she wasn't working until three was strong.

But he had a dinner to plan. Friends to corral and lecture and/or threaten into good behavior in Cora's presence. He wanted to clean up a little around the place, change the sheets and all that just in case she wanted to stay over.

"So, this is new," Ian said, tone very dry. "You've never asked any of your romantic interests into my kitchen before." They stood just outside the open kitchen at Luna, the smallest and most intimate of Ian's restaurants. And where they often ended up after closing, taking turns making meals for the crew of local chefs and other restaurant people who made up his knot of friends.

"I want her to meet you. Or you to meet her. Both. I want to cook for her when she's surrounded by my friends."

Ian smirked. "You want to show her off. Show off for her too."

"Fuck yes I do. She's not only pretty and funny and weirdly fascinating, she's smart. Charming. I want her to know I have a community. I'm not some aimless pretty boy."

"Even when you *were* an aimless pretty boy you weren't really that bad," Ian said. "She's someone you want me to meet and that alone would be enough. I've got to admit I'm seriously curious about this woman."

"You're going to like her. It's impossible not to." Beau had watched in serious awe as she'd worked that gallery and the patrons and artists who'd come in.

"You want to do leftover roulette?" Ian asked of the game they made of creating an after-work menu with whatever each particular chef brought with them, or had remained after dinner service had ended.

Because Cora would like the game and he was pretty sure he could make something delicious out of most ingredients his friends would present him with, he agreed.

AT THE END of a very long day Cora usually just wanted to go home, take a long hot shower and go to bed. But that day had started with a text asking her to be a maid of honor in a Christmas Eve wedding and was going to be ending with a guy she hadn't seen all week and had missed more than she'd really thought she would.

She'd sent Beto home an hour before but she needn't have worried about being alone when she closed up because Cora looked up to catch sight of Beau coming in from the street. He wore a navy blue peacoat with a pale gray sweater beneath. Dark trousers showcased just how tall he was.

She watched him as he searched the room, looking for her. And when he found her and his gaze locked onto hers, she felt it ping-pong through her, that zing of chemistry they shared.

Beau looked like he'd walked straight off the photo shoot for a menswear line, or a line of luxury cars. All predatory and masculine but smooth as fuck at the same time.

As they were the only people left, she allowed herself to go to him and let him hug her before brushing a quick kiss over her mouth.

"Hi. You didn't have to come in. I told you I'd meet you at Luna when I got changed," she said, pleased he'd come anyway.

"I wanted to see you."

Which was nice to hear, because she wanted to see him too. And now that he was right there she could admit to herself that she'd missed him a lot. More than she'd wanted to. More than she'd expected to.

"I just need to lock up, then we can head out. Tell me about your trip while I'm doing that," she told him.

He gave her an update on his house in Los Angeles, talked about seeing some friends, including his manager, who apparently wanted to meet her when he came up to Seattle to visit next.

It meant he'd talked about her to these people in his life.

Giddiness flitted through her belly as she turned

out the lights, hit the security system and then they headed to his car.

He held her hand, opened her door and was present in a way that comforted her but didn't crowd. That wasn't something you could plan; it simply was the way you fit with someone else. Or not.

It had been *or not* for most of her life. Not that she'd experienced it in a negative sense, but now that she had it with Beau it was hard to imagine a future without it.

The energy between them built from the moment he'd walked into the gallery and by the time they'd reached her apartment, and she'd closed and locked her front door and looked to him, a fire raged through her.

He stared at her so intently it was like a caress. All she could do was breathe a yes before he took the last three steps, pulling her into his arms as his mouth found hers.

The sound of all her belongings clattering to the floor as she dropped her purse and tote bag was the only thing she heard other than the pounding in her ears and the rustle of clothing.

He slid his hands down her sides and to her ass, grabbing two handfuls and holding her in place as he ground his cock into her belly.

A moan wrenched from deep in her gut, one he echoed as they bumped into the wall at her back.

Nearly frantic to have him, she struggled against his body to push back and grab at his button and zipper.

The heat of his bare skin—velvet stretched over his cock as she grabbed and gave him a few slow pumps of her fist—nearly stole her breath.

He cursed, a snarl of sound against her neck, where he'd been licking over her collarbone. "Condom," she urged in a broken whisper.

"Back pocket," he said, half turning to get his wallet out before he grabbed a condom and tossed it on top of the mess from her bag.

She threw her leg up, hitching her calf around him and holding him in place just in case he thought she needed him to go slow or some such nonsense.

"Now," she said, underlining that.

"Impatient."

She tried to laugh but wasn't entirely successful as he rucked up the hem of her skirt over her hips. The cool air brushed against the backs of her thighs and the sound of her tights being ripped only made her wetter.

His fingertips brushed between her panties and her pussy, sending bursts of sensation through her, rebounding straight to her clit. Enough that when he swirled over it, slowly but surely, it seemed to ripple from there out.

"You're like liquid heat," he said, lips against her neck. "It's all I think about. The way you feel. So soft and hot and wet all for me."

He shoved aside the material of her underpants and in one thrust seated himself to the root within her.

She writhed, moving what little she could against him as he began to fuck her in earnest. Cora buried her face in his neck, breathing in the scent of his skin, sweat and sex. It made her feel *alive*.

Each thrust and the pictures hanging on the wall at her back rattled. And it didn't matter. She wanted him so much it was all she could think about. He had her pinned, angled how he wanted, the fingers of the hand at her hip dug into her flesh.

The other hand though... He'd been cupping her breast, pinching the nipple through her blouse and bra before reaching between their bodies to find her clit again.

He grunted as she tightened up around him, rocketing to climax after just a few touches. She bit down into the muscle and tendons at his shoulder and he tipped his head back, exposing the throat she wasn't tall enough to get to, even if she had the energy.

He came on a snarled whisper of her name as the echoes of her own climax still rang through her.

Beau pulled out carefully, making sure she was steady on her feet before he headed to take care of the condom.

"Should I be apologizing?" he asked as he joined her in her bedroom, where she'd gone to change her clothes.

"What? Hell no. What makes you ask that?" She pulled off the ruin of her tights, balling them up and tossing them in the trash.

"Because I just showed up after being gone almost a week and fucked you three steps into your house. And because I ripped your tights."

She danced his way, throwing her arms around him a moment. "See, those are *positives* from where I'm standing. I can replace torn tights gladly if they get that way because you're about to make me come."

He was quiet a few long moments as he watched her

change into jeans, boots and a soft gray sweater with tiny unicorns eating doughnuts on it.

"Maybe gave this to me for Christmas a few years ago. It's seriously one of the best things about winter."

"Trying not to get whiplash from the way you were classic and elegant at the gallery to this version with goofy sweaters." His smile was all sexy and even though she'd just come a few minutes before, things were still awake down there. "As homecomings go, that one ranks at the top." He bent to kiss her.

"When I get back from a trip, I'm coming to your place so I can fuck *you* against a wall. It can be our thing."

"As far as those things go, I'm cool with wall fucking as a welcome home being our thing. Like a song, only with orgasms."

"I really like this idea," she said.

He grinned, hugging her again before heading toward the door.

It hadn't occurred to her to be nervous about meeting his friends until the moment he reached out to open up a rear door to the restaurant. Suddenly the unicorns and other whimsy made her wonder what they'd think.

It was too late to do anything about it, so she let him take her hand and guide her through a kitchen she'd expected to be empty because the restaurant had closed an hour before. But it wasn't empty.

There were several people appearing to finish up and one of them had to be Ian Brewster because he looked even better than he did on a magazine spread or in some local news piece on the very successful gorgeous restaurant entrepreneur.

He caught sight of Beau and Cora, leaning to speak to one of his employees briefly before coming over to them.

"Cora Silvera, this is Ian Brewster," Beau said.

Instead of a handshake, Ian's smile shot into a grin and he caught her up in a hug.

"It's a pleasure to meet you, Cora. Welcome to Luna."

Ian then explained the leftover rules and that Beau was going to make a meal out of all the wonderful tidbits the others had brought.

Beau took her hand and tugged a little, bringing her closer as they approached the twelve-person-sized chef's table in a corner of the kitchen. Three people lounged there either nursing bottles of beer or a tall glass of something else.

They all looked up, openly curious about her.

Beau slung an arm around Cora's shoulders, holding her at his side in a way that was comforting while also being a clear signal that she was with him.

"Everyone, this is Cora. She's nice and smells good and has manners. Behave yourselves so she'll stay."

Cora snorted.

"Len is the one with the septum piercing. On his right is Wyatt, who tells me your sister has done some of his tattoos. On the end there is Jayden."

She raised a hand in greeting.

"Len, move so Cora can sit there. I want to look at her face when I'm cooking," Beau said.

The lanky guy with the piercing and a very complicated neck tattoo vacated his chair for Beau to help her into it.

"I hope you're all hungry," Beau said after he kissed the top of her head and wandered over to the nearby countertop, where all the different contributions for the evening's meal sat.

They all stared at her.

"You're making me feel like a bug," she said to them.

Beau chuckled, his attention on whatever was going on as he began to unwrap things, Ian acting as his assistant.

"A bug?" Jayden asked.

"Yeah. You know how when you're a kid you bent down to stare at bugs? Like they were so crazy and wild looking it was hard to believe they were real much less so regular and everyday they lived in large numbers in the grass or the trees," Cora explained.

Jayden appeared shocked a moment, and then he threw his head back and laughed. "That's totally how bugs seemed when I was a kid. We're just nosy. Tell us about yourself."

"Are you saying you're crazy and wild looking?" Wyatt asked her in a sexy drawl. "Or that we are?"

"In this group?" Cora gestured to them all, indicating ink and piercings. "Um…" she teased.

"You're wearing a sweater with unicorns eating doughnuts on it," Wyatt offered.

Cora shrugged. "Cool, right?"

The laughter that came after that was easier. Genuine.

"STOP STARING AT HER. You're working with an open flame and my insurance will go up if you burn yourself," Ian murmured.

Beau just had the most ridiculously hot quickie he'd ever been involved in, only made all the more hot because she'd been as mad to have him as he'd been to have her. More than that, she'd soaked into his system like he'd been parched.

And he'd known it was right to seek her out. Right to want more and tell her so.

"What are you making?" she asked, catching his gaze and smiling that smile she had only for him.

"We've got ourselves some shredded beef, roasted sweet potatoes and red pepper, various cheeses, pesto." He paused to sniff. "From Len I believe as I can smell the cilantro olive oil. Which will go with this pasta. Fresh eggs, some olives and pickled onions. We're going to eat well." He winked at Cora.

"I was half expecting something like those wacky baskets on that show with ingredients that shouldn't go together or that I've never heard of but are preserved goat pancreas or whatever," Cora said, bringing laughter as the group warmed to her.

"Have you ever eaten goat pancreas?" Ian teased.

"I don't even know if goats have pancreases. I learned from all my travel—I generally don't ask if I'd be freaked out by the answer. Things taste better that way."

"That's a very good rule," Ian agreed.

Cora absolutely adored this group of friends. They had such a wonderful back-and-forth with lots of humor and patience for each individual's way of communicating. They asked her questions and listened to her responses.

They seemed to want to know her because Beau had brought her around. They were foulmouthed and fascinating and gave her insight into Beau she'd not expected. There was caring between them. A shared history.

Her memories of him as a young model featured more of an entourage instead of a circle of friends. This was something else entirely.

And their reaction to her also told her something important. This very close-knit group didn't have a whole lot of guests of the significant other persuasion. It wasn't the kind of thing one had a casual date for.

An ember of satisfaction banked in her belly that wasn't entirely about the food she was planning to shove into her face.

And holy shit did her man look *good* in a kitchen. Making food. For her.

She'd been amped up since the moment he walked into the gallery. Tall and gorgeous and sexy as fuck.

She'd missed him. More than she'd realized until his hands were all over her as he thrust deep and hard into her body. The fire of their energy sizzling between them.

He was back. He'd come to her and now he was bringing her into his friend circle and yet again making her food.

Ian had an inner light. One she thought complemented Beau's. They had a rhythm in the kitchen, clearly used to working with one another.

Food began to be ferried to the table as whoever was left seated lined up shots of excellent tequila.

Cora didn't talk nearly as much as she listened, learning each one of the people around the table.

Beau finally joined them, resting his arm along the back of her chair.

They told restaurant stories and kitchen stories and laughed and gossiped and cursed. Beau updated them on his house sale and surprised her when he said he was going to start looking in Seattle and that he thought she'd be a great person to have along.

It was a good surprise.

He wanted her opinion.

He was laying the foundation for a long stint in the city.

He was including her in that step.

It was delightful and a little magical.

LATER, AS HE led her on a tour through the condo he was staying in, she thought to ask him why he hadn't opened his own restaurant.

"I like to cook. I like having a television show. Having a restaurant is a whole different level of responsibility. I like being my own boss. Ian is good at it. He likes restaurants as a business. Having employees and insurance and all that. To me? It's suffocating. I don't want that relationship to my food."

Cora nodded, understanding his point. "Fair enough.

It's no skin off my nose to watch you on television. You look good on camera. Like really, *really* good."

Quick and smooth, he reached out to grab her around her waist and haul her close. "You watched me? Before we got together I mean."

"Well, of course I did. Food porn is always better when it's served up by an attractive guy. Oh man, when you went through that Mohawk stage? Yum. That was super sexy. Two thumbs up." She ran her fingers through his hair. "I do like this look too though. Makes me want to grab a handful and yank you down to my mouth for a kiss."

"That's exactly the thing I'm going for." He smirked before she did indeed yank him down to her for a quick smooch. "I'm flattered. You smell really good. Like your perfume and sex all bound up. Irresistible." He nuzzled the spot below her ear and rendered her a little dizzy.

She didn't have the words to reply so she hummed instead.

After a kiss that left her lips tingly, he continued the tour. The condo was elegant and modern and didn't feel lived-in at all. Like a gorgeous hotel.

"This is beautiful. What sort of place do you think you want here? A high-rise condo like this? A house?"

He thought awhile. "I like the ability to walk to wherever I'm working. But with the right house and the right kitchen, I could film there."

"Or maybe if you had an *ohana* flat you could have the kitchen and filming done there? Have your office or a production space out there too? Makes things easier.

Perhaps a house with land so you can put a tiny house out there to make it your workspace and customize it?"

He cocked his head. "Yeah, that would be good. I had a pool house in LA and if I didn't have guests in it all the time, I could have used it for filming."

"People don't come to visit here as much as they do LA, where there's sunshine, fantastic Mexican food and theme parks. It's a good exchange I think. But I have hermit tendencies so I may not be a good example."

"I grew up in a place with communal living. It's great when kids are really small because more hands make for light work. But then it's...not so great. I like my space and my privacy. If I had to have a crew in to film, it'd be far easier to have it in a back house or what have you than in my main house."

She filed that away to keep in mind.

"Yeah, I imagine."

He brushed a curl back from her face, cupped her cheek briefly. And then neatly changed the subject. "I never did formally ask for your assistance. I really appreciate the help."

"I'm glad you assumed I'd help. Because I will and I'd do it for any friend." She took his face in her hands, an echo to his previous gesture. "And for whatever you are to me now."

"I really missed you this week," he admitted.

"It's good to miss someone. Makes it better when you come back together." She smiled at the snatch of words caught in her mind. The beginning of a poem that'd be about him. Something that was becoming far more common as a theme in her work.

"Except I fucked you against a wall. Not very romantic." He appeared sheepish, which only made it hotter.

She let herself lean in, drew her mouth up his throat. "Unless the person *getting* fucked against a wall very much *wanted* you to fuck them against a wall. In which case, it was very romantic. Some women like roses— I like getting fucked against a wall. But to be fair, I like roses too."

"I'll keep both in mind." In a dizzying move, he switched positions so it was he who kissed her. First her nose, and then he took her mouth. Sank in slow, stayed awhile as he tasted and teased until he released her, leaving her a little breathless.

"Wow," she managed to say.

With a smirk and one last quick kiss, he said, "My friends like you."

"I like your friends," she replied. "And now I have half a dozen new restaurants to try."

"Will you stay here tonight?"

There was a little vulnerability at the edges of his words.

"Will you make me something yummy for breakfast?" she asked.

"Waffles?"

"Deal."

CHAPTER TWELVE

JUST A FEW days later, Beau awoke to sunlight breaking over Cora's still-sleeping form. In the time they'd been together he found himself at her place or she with him most nights. And still he wanted her. Burned for her.

She was goofy as hell and there was nothing like it in his world. It filled him up in ways he hadn't expected.

He eased from bed, wanting her to get all the rest she could. Especially as he'd kept her awake the night before. Twice.

In her kitchen, he'd noticed she now kept things he liked and used, like the coffee he scooped into the filter to get a fresh pot started. He didn't have any plans until that evening when Cora got off work and would go with him to look at some houses.

Since she'd have to be up within the hour to get her day started he figured he'd send her off with coffee and a full belly. Waffles seemed to be a favorite and they were easy to whip up and add fruit to to change things up.

Before he quite got over the flutter in his chest at the way his life had gone from lonely to this connection he shared with Cora, he remembered it was her recycle day and hustled back to the bedroom, where she'd just finished pulling on jeans, sleep still on her features.

"Recycling," she said, her voice momentarily muffled by the sweater yanked over her head.

"On it." He shoved his feet into shoes, laughing as she danced out of his reach on her way out the door.

Clutching the little bins for glass and paper, they ran through the rain out to the main collection containers on the street just as the big blue truck turned the corner onto her block.

"Score," she said, grinning and rain-soaked.

He grabbed her hand and they headed back to her place, pausing on the porch to toe off their shoes.

"Thank god I turned the fireplace on before I started to make coffee," he told her.

Cora tossed a towel at him. "Get dried off before all the women in the area start banging on my door demanding more hot, wet model in their day. And who can blame them?"

"Not that I'm complaining. But I prefer when one person in particular demands hot, wet model in her day." He peeled off his shirt. The pants were in pretty good shape though so he left those on.

"Lucky me," she murmured, yanking her shirt off and standing in her living room just out of his reach. Bare skin over perfectly sized tits. The swoops and swirls of all her ink added an edge.

"You have time to get luckier before you have to go to work. I mean, I might have to rush a little, but I do get the job done."

Her laughter warmed his belly, and right as he

reached to grab the waistband of her pants to pull her nearer there was a sharp knock at her front door.

"Ignore it," he said.

Shrugging, she wrapped her arms around him, sliding warm skin against his warm skin. She climbed up his body like a monkey, wrapping her legs around his waist as he carried her into the bedroom. "Make me late for work."

Half an hour later they emerged a little mussed up, but smiling as they headed into the kitchen for some breakfast.

On the way out though, as she opened her front door, an envelope that must have been tucked into the space between the jamb and door flitted to the porch.

Cora picked it up and made a sound of surprise so Beau looked over her shoulder and recognized his name on the front. "Weird. It's for you."

No one knew he was there but Ian and Jeremy. He had some superfans who tended toward bad filters rather than instability, but the idea that anyone would come at him through Cora rendered him a little nauseated.

She handed it over her shoulder to him. "This is weird," he said. "Stay back when I open it just in case." Confusion washed over her features and he gentled his tone. "We don't know what it could be. I just want you to be safe."

"If you think this will blow up why the hell are you thinking of opening it? Why not call the authorities?" Cora demanded.

Damn it, why was she so fucking cute all the time?

Even when she was disobeying him and demanding answers, she was cute. He kissed her, picked her up, set her back inside the house and closed the door at his back.

"Oh no, you did not just pick me up and put me in my house like a puppy!" she yelled through the door.

He opened the envelope and pulled out the paper inside. No powder, nothing sticky or strange on the contents.

As he finished reading it the second time, Cora came around the side of her house and up to the porch, where she pinched his side. "Don't do that again."

"Listen, let me get this out so we can be clear," he said. "I will do it again. Or anything else that I think is necessary to protect you."

Her outrage was also cute but he decided not to share that thought. He liked his balls unkicked.

"I'm not a kid. Or a thing. You can't just move me around how you want," she said. "Well. Except for sex. But that's not what we're discussing right now."

He turned her way and paused, giving her a slow up and down.

She had on high-waisted red trousers and a white blouse. She'd done something to her hair, a twisted bun thing that gave her a vintage air. Of course it was the killer heels she wore that made the outfit. That and the bright red lipstick. She looked like a noir villain. The annoyance on her features, god help him, made the entirety of her more than he could resist.

"You look fantastic," Beau told her, bending to kiss her. "Beautiful Cora, I know you're not a thing.

I know you're independent and intelligent and capable of making your own choices. But I'm not going to take chances with your safety. If that annoys you, I am sorry. But not sorry enough to stop putting you first."

Her sigh had a snarl in it, but she stopped looking like she was going to punch his junk any second. "Tell me what the hell is happening. What is it that's gotten you so freaked out?"

"I need to make some calls and handle a few things. Let me take you to the gallery. I'll be back later to pick you up and I'll tell you more then."

"Are you in danger? Is someone threatening you?"

That she'd be concerned about him when the damned note showed up on her doorstep was another disarming thing about her. It also made him worry a little more.

"No one is threatening my safety," he said carefully. Beau wanted her safe at work so he could get in touch with Jeremy about the note. "This is related to Road to Glory." He tucked the envelope into a pocket. "I promise," he repeated, "to explain more when I see you tonight. Everything is fine. There's no danger. I'd never lie to you about that."

She allowed him to check to be sure she'd locked the door, and then led her through the center courtyard and out to the street where he'd parked.

If there'd been more than three minutes to the gallery he might have given her some background. Still, when he pulled up out front he paused, a hand on her forearm. "I need to move on this information immediately. Please understand."

Cora nodded, leaning over to kiss him quickly. "Be careful. I'll see you later when I will expect a full explanation. And smooching."

He was still smiling when he pulled away from the curb and headed back to the condo so he could get in touch with his investigators to tell them what had happened.

CORA BURIED HERSELF in work as much as she could to avoid obsessing about whatever it was that had Beau going so pale and then very stoic when he'd read whatever it was in that envelope. Expression closed off and more severe than she'd seen him. If he hadn't been all bossy to protect her she might have been more unsure as to what was going on between them. But he'd looked at her, asking for her patience and that's what she'd give.

She sold a few paintings and a sculpture and considered it a day well spent when she finally locked up. She was ready to go home, change into leggings and thick socks and look at her hot former model boyfriend as he told her whatever was going on.

He'd cook for her. At the very least make her a cup of tea and pull out something sweet to go with it. He liked to take care of her that way. It was simple and lovely and quieted the noise inside her chest to be treated like that.

Even all his picking her up and moving her around earlier that day had been annoying but borne of a real desire to be sure she was all right. She'd never experienced the like.

A more than brisk wind kicked up and she was glad she remembered her gloves. But before she even got three steps from the gallery doors, he beeped the horn of his car as he pulled into the loading spot in front of the gallery.

"Hi," she said when she got in and leaned over for a kiss.

"Hi yourself, beautiful."

He took her hand and didn't let go until he found a parking place.

"Your porch looks naked without all the spiders," he said as they approached her place. "I'm bummed I missed Halloween while I was in Los Angeles."

"Me too. It was pretty epic. Everyone came over here and hung out, taking turns handing out candy and scaring the trick-or-treaters."

Her only excuse was that she was paying so much attention to Beau that she hadn't seen The Hugger fast walking over to them until it was too late to avert their collision course.

Damn it.

"Cora! It's been too long since I've run into you." The Hugger moved in but she stepped around to Beau's other side and he kept between them to help her evade.

"Hi, Dave. It's nice to see you. We were just on our way home so…" Cora smiled, tugging on Beau to keep them moving.

"Is this your boyfriend?" The Hugger looked up and up some more into Beau's face. "I'm Dave!" He stepped in for a hug but Beau just held a hand out to hold him off.

"No hug, please. I'm not a hugger."

Beau managed to make it sound charming and apologetic instead of insulting. And Cora liked him more for it. Dave wasn't malicious; he just had weird boundary issues and an attachment to attempting to live every day like it was 1977.

Dave put his hands up and smiled. "No problemo. Lani and I are firing up the hot tub and cracking open some wine. You two should come over. Get to know you better since you're dating Cora. I even have a spare suit for you if you like."

Cora withheld—barely—a shudder at the idea.

"Thanks for the invitation and say hello to Lani for me. Beau and I have plans though. You have a good night and enjoy the hot tub." Cora smiled and tugged on Beau to get him moving again.

"Nice to meet you, mate," Beau said as they walked away.

"You too!" Dave called out and kept on his merry way.

Once inside the house, she made sure everything was locked up. "Just in case they want to come back for another crack at you. When Lani sees you, well, she's going to want to take a bite. Not that I blame her or anything. But if she were to try I can't say I'd take it well."

Beau cocked his head, smirking. "Well now. I've never seen this side of you. Makes my dick hard."

Cora snorted a laugh.

"Go get changed out of your work clothes and I'll start dinner. Then we'll talk." He bent to kiss her.

After she scrubbed off her makeup, she pulled her

hair into a ponytail and dressed in those long-awaited leggings, a long, soft sweater and thick socks before heading back out to the kitchen.

She'd texted Maybe and Rachel before she'd left the gallery, just saying she and Beau had a thing they needed to work out that night and she'd talk to them tomorrow. Hopefully that would be enough to keep Maybe out of her business until the following day, when they had a lunch date.

He was pouring her a rather large glass of wine when she approached the counter. "Um. This doesn't bode well. You think I need that much booze to handle whatever you're going to say?"

"Before you walked into Gregori's kitchen that night I really had no idea how sexy I'd find it to be spoken to so plainly."

"Stop being so hot and charming. Oh! What's that?" Wariness forgotten for a moment, she leaned in to see what he was making for dinner until he started to unload the sacks he'd brought in with them.

"I've been working on pasta today so we're having ricotta cavatelli with eggplant and sausage," he told her as he rolled up his sleeves and pulled his hair up and back into a bun.

"Whoa," she whispered. He was just so damned beautiful with all those delightful lines and shadows on his face. His forearms exposed, along with the ink and the muscles as he washed his hands gave her a little thrill. She knew his strength. Knew the way his muscles felt as they flexed and bunched.

And he was bringing her handmade carbs. "You're a unicorn, Beau," she told him.

"I am?" He appeared amused as he cleaned off her countertops even though he had already done the same that morning. Another hot as fuck thing about him was that he seemed totally content to clean her kitchen with a depth and zeal she never even wanted to approach. But she was happy to watch him at it.

"You're gorgeous and sexy and you're making me pasta, which is like my all-time favorite thing to eat. You're smart and I love your sense of humor." Cora tried for a nonchalant shrug but really it was more embarrassed. "You're a lot of really good things rolled up into one person. I like you."

He glanced up, surprised pleasure on his face. "I like you too. I think you're the gorgeous and sexy one who appreciates my food and lets me take over her kitchen even though I'm a little compulsive about cleaning it."

"Feel free to compulsively clean my bathroom anytime you like too."

"I think showering together might qualify. For future reference."

She clinked her wineglass to his. "We're on the same page. Now. While you're cooking you can tell me what's going on."

She hopped up on a stool on the other side of the island from where he worked. Normally he didn't need her to be his assistant and the way he moved around, using all the space, told her he needed to be alone in there.

"How much do you know about Road to Glory and

my history there?" he asked her as he began to clean and peel the eggplant.

"I know you grew up inside a religious group your dad ran. Still runs I guess. You're the oldest son so they were grooming you to take over. Some stuff happened and you needed to escape. They left the country and haven't been found."

He barked a laugh before sobering. "You *must* like me to be so politic about it. Be blunt. I want to tell you, but there's no need to have to repeat everything you already know."

"Okay. So your dad decided to hook up with underage girls and you helped the FBI. There was a gunfight situation but your father escaped, along with your mom and some of his other followers. A lot of people got hurt. Some went to jail. A bunch of children were taken without permission from the other parent if I remember right."

"When I was fifteen my dad decided it was time for me to marry and start the process to first replace my uncle and then take over for my dad. It was time for me to have children and show the rest how healthy and fertile the church could be. Our marriage wasn't legal by state law, but at that time, the only law that mattered was my father's law. The law of the Road."

He kept moving. Putting a pot of water to boil for the pasta.

"Okay, let me back up a little from my wedding. Things started to change when I was about thirteen. We moved from suburban Nashville to the middle of nowhere Arizona. On a compound. All the kids were homeschooled but once we moved we weren't allowed to go out into the world unaccompanied. No outside media. No internet back then like it is now. There were cell phones but no smartphones. It was a creeping slow sort of snuffing out of all outside influence. Any influence but that of The Anointed, which was what my father had started to call himself by the time I was sixteen.

"Then one day, after I'd been married, I woke up to an envelope that'd been slid under my door and inside was a letter from a mother in the group. Her thirteen-year-old daughter was being *courted* by my father and she was terrified. The daughter and the mother. She begged for my help."

Cora's breath caught in her chest as she had to hold back any appearance of pity or horror. Though she felt both in the pit of her stomach. She knew somehow that he needed to get it all out before she said anything so she didn't.

She did, however, finish her wine and got herself and Beau another glass, pausing to kiss him before she hopped back up onto her stool.

He leaned over the island to tap his glass to hers.

"I believed her. Cora, I read that note and there was never even a struggle to believe it. It was a moment I was confronted with the truth I'd been hiding from, and I would either stand up and call it out, or go along with it and damn myself.

"So I looked into her claim to get all the facts so I could go to my mother and uncle for help. I asked around, and when I was allowed to go to the private mailbox the church rented about two hours away from the compound, I was approached by an FBI agent who had more information for me. Some of our members who'd left had gone to the authorities about punishments. There were parents trying to gain access to children still living on the compound. Weapons charges. Wire fraud."

He dumped the sausage along with the eggplant into a pan and the scent of garlic lifted into the air on the steam.

"I have some bread. Would you like me to make a quick batch of garlic bread? Nothing fancy, but it should be really good with dinner," she said, needing to move or she'd do something stupid like cry or try to comfort him with dumb words.

"Perfect. Yes, that's good."

She slid down and began to assemble her ingredients to put together the bread. He kept cooking and began speaking again. "I came back shaken up. I knew there were problems but what I'd learned that day meant everything I'd grown up believing was a lie. My dad was a monster. And by association, through the proof I'd seen, my mother had known, as had most of my father's closest associates. I told my wife that I was having doubts. I admit it. I hedged a little and didn't tell her about the FBI. And thank god I didn't because once I fell asleep she went to my father, who sent his goons in to kidnap me and toss me in one of his punishment houses.

"I was out there in the heat for three weeks. In and out of consciousness. Compared to the others I was soft. My father's favorite. And I'd been tossed out of the circle of his affection and it sucked. My cousin Patience is a nurse—she managed to see me out there as often as she could. I was dehydrated and in declining health. I don't know who exactly helped me get out, but I suspect it was Patience and my other cousin Macie. The cops found me left by a road mile marker after it had been called in. I was in the hospital overnight but I was panicked about my kids. My babies. Four-month-old twin boys. At that time I was worried about my wife too, even though she'd been the one who turned me in."

Cora turned on the broiler to heat up and imagined myriad ways to punch these people who hurt him so much in their stupid faces.

"But the standoff happened just a few hours later. Many escaped. Some died. My wife had our marriage annulled in the eyes of the church and has, as rumor goes, married another one of my cousins who has taken my children as his own. I helped the authorities as much as I could, not only because it was the right thing to do, but because it was a way to keep them working on finding the church members. I wanted my damned kids back and the government had more tools than I did.

"I started modeling as a fluke but it was a way to make the money I needed to hire investigators on my own. It's been two decades I've been searching and aside from sightings of some of my father's cronies I have had no real leads on my sons. They were four months old then. Even if I'd had a lot of photographs they're both men now. Adults who certainly don't look like babies anymore. They're not in trouble or on any watch lists the way my father is, which makes it more difficult."

The emotions in his voice at the end were too much and she walked into his arms. Burrowing herself into him, she hugged tightly and told him without words that she was so terribly sorry he'd gone through all that pain.

Finally she pulled away and he tipped her chin up with the tip of his finger and kissed her before he got back to dinner and his story.

"Most of this is common enough knowledge that I've had a few people try to extort me for information about the group over the years. I paid because I had the money and I'd rather spend it and find them than not spend it and risk the info being real."

Someone was trying to extort him? On her own doorstep? Oh. No fucking way was that allowed.

"However, four times in the last twenty years I have been contacted by someone in the group still. They say they have information on my sons and want to set up a meeting. Twice in those four times there were other pieces of information that I forwarded to the authorities and they turned out to be real solid clues on the whereabouts of the Road. Once they even caught up to my dad's most recent location and managed to take in one of the members who'd stayed behind to handle any loose ends that needed tying up for their move. That member refused to say anything in his own defense and pleaded guilty. I'll count myself lucky if he does three years of his eight-year sentence.

"But I've never been able to meet this contact in person. He or she, each time, has either gotten spooked or simply not shown up. Though, like I said, twice the source left information that actually helped. That's what the note on your doorstep today was. That's why I had to contact my agent and the investigators right away."

Cora waited for him to tip the pasta into the boiling water before she put the bread into the oven.

"That sounds like a nightmare. I hope you find your children so they get a chance to know you," she said. "What all did it say?"

"My uncle is back here in the US. Which I did know because my investigators reported that to me. But the note says he's here because one of the group is really ill."

She took his hands. "Your sons?"

"The note didn't say and all I can do is hope not."

"Does the church, or your dad, whatever, believe in getting medical care or is it not okay?"

"When I was younger there were no problems with going to the doctor. But over time and especially after we moved to Arizona, the rules for daily life got much more strict. Fortunately there were two nurses who were part of the church and most things could be dealt with by them. Something serious though? Diabetes or anything more than basic surgery or setting of bones, cancer? George, my father, was into laying on of hands when people were at their most ill and desperate. They died and he said it was that they didn't work hard enough or that God called them home. I have no doubt that it's something similar even today."

She moved to take the bread out and he tossed the pasta with the other ingredients and took the pan to the table while she transferred the bread to a plate.

"This is nowhere near as flashy as the food you make but it's pretty hard to mess up good bread slathered in butter, garlic and cheese," she told him.

They settled in and she was beyond words until she'd shoveled food into her face for a few minutes.

He finally spoke again right around the time she realized she must have looked like a hungry teenager as she gobbled her dinner.

"So what's your verdict? Should I include this on my short list for the cookbook?"

When she blushed and hid her face behind her napkin, he laughed. She said, "As if the way I just inhaled my plate wasn't enough? It's amazing. I might even let this get to second base I dug it so much."

"I love it when you enjoy the food I make. It's a huge compliment to see you eat with such relish. Sexy too."

"I'm so glad you find my virtual inhalation of everything but the fork as a positive instead of a slovenly bad habit."

"Maybe if it was someone else's food," he teased.

She snickered but sobered quickly, returning to the subject of the letter. "I mean, they told you someone was ill but not who specifically. Are they asking for money or medical assistance or what?"

"You're not even going to mention the fact that the

letter came *here* to your home? I honestly can't believe you even let me stay after I told you all that."

"That's not your fault though. So how could I be angry at you about that? I'm a bitch sometimes but I'm not an asshole," she said.

"It *is* my fault. It's not like that letter would have shown up here if I weren't here so often. Which means they're watching me as much as I watch them only they're doing it better because I still don't fucking know where *they* are."

"Because you're not hiding! You're not on the run from the FBI and Interpol or whatever. I don't blame you for this. I'm glad they found you and I hope you don't end up disappointed."

"The letter just had the info in it. No ask. But it will come. That's how this person has worked in the past. A contact note that shows up via courier. Like this one. My investigators will call the place to get any info they can, but there won't be any. They'll have paid in cash. Usually to a middleman in need of some quick money to take the letter in on their behalf. Next will be the ask. Sometimes it comes via phone or email. It's a waiting game now."

"I don't even know what to say. Nothing wise or helpful I'm sure. Your dad sounds like a dreadful asshole. I'm sorry your ex stole your kids. What can I do? Tell me what I can do to help."

"At this point I'm doing it all. Just listening to me helps, so thank you. I'm sorry this involved you. I don't normally…" He shoved a hand through his hair. "I usually see people outside my circle. So they don't get involved in any of my personal business other than my dick. It sounds shallow, I know. But now that you've been dragged into this it makes me nervous for you."

"How I'll feel or that I'm somehow in danger?"

He honestly didn't think she was in danger. But he could admit—to himself anyway—that he was worried she'd get turned off by all his drama and want to break things off.

"I just don't want you to think all I bring to your life is this sort of crap."

Cora burst out laughing. "Earlier today I was feeling a little guilty because honestly you're the most deliciously gorgeous creature on this earth and I can't stop thinking about how fucking hot you are. And then I thought *oh no, I'm objectifying him and he's so much more than that*. Like the way you always make me food. And you're tall so you can reach stuff and you're great at getting us through a crowd. A note on my door isn't a deal breaker as long as I can keep wanting to eat you up with a spoon."

He had no idea how she managed to do it, but she just had a way of cutting through bullshit and taking things down to what truly mattered. It wasn't like he was unaware of his looks. That *she* found him so delicious meant something altogether different to him than it had with anyone else.

"Always feel welcome to nibble or lick or suck any part of me."

She fanned herself at his leer and he relaxed a little more.

He'd come a long way from that uneducated and woefully unprepared for the world teenager who'd escaped Road to Glory with nothing more than the clothes on his back. He understood that he'd been a child raised to believe in everything his father said. Sometimes that alleviated some of the guilt he felt.

His father had stolen his childhood, but Beau had taken his adulthood and all that potential and made something of himself. But he also had two children he'd only held a handful of times before his wife had taken them and run off with the rest of the group.

He wanted Cora to know that about him. Wanted her to understand he'd never give up looking for them, and given her reaction and the way she looked at him, she did understand.

What experiences and opportunities had his sons lost a chance at because of George Petty?

"So. You still cool dating me?" he asked her. He was aiming for teasing and flirty, but there was a whole lot of truth wound through the words.

Cora frowned and got up to circle the table and straddle his lap, facing him. "Thanks for sharing all that with me. I'm obviously still cool dating you because you have a meaty penis and you cook me food. Plus you look damned good naked." She patted his chest over his heart. "And you have a big, good heart. I want you to find your sons. I want you to be able to hug them."

Emotion swamped him as he swallowed against the

lump in his throat and pulled her to him, wrapping his arms around her tight.

He took a deep breath and let it out slowly. He wanted to be able to hug them too.

CHAPTER THIRTEEN

I can hear
the music of the universe in the way
you say my name

CORA ROLLED INTO Whiskey Sharp the next evening,
pleased at the sight of her two best friends standing
near the bar.

Vic was in deep conversation with Alexsei and Gregori on the other side of the room. The family resem-
blance was striking at some moments and that was
one of them.

"Christ. What the fuck kind of genetic lottery pro-
duced humans who look that good?" she asked after
she gave Maybe and Rachel a hug.

"Right?" Maybe said. "Imagine the baby cooking
in Rachel's uterus right now. Adorable to the power
of a million."

"Where's Beau?" Rachel asked.

"He'll be by in a few. He had a sauce breakthrough
apparently," Cora said.

"Ha! Really? My dude has yeast emergencies and
yours has sauce emergencies," Rachel said. "Life's
weird."

"It is. But now that mine has really great sex and food in it I've got to say yay for weird life." Cora ordered a whiskey sour. "How's things in gestation today?"

"I want to nap a lot. Vic makes me go to bed at like eight with him. Which works because he's up at four anyway to get to the bakery and I end up sleeping another few hours after he leaves. I'm nauseated followed by periods of intense hunger. I mean, it's not that far into the process but damn, I hope I want to be awake in the hours where I don't want to vomit and soon."

Cora frowned and gave Rachel a gentle hug. "Sorry, punkin."

Wren bounced in and after a snuggle and a kiss from her husband, she headed over to Cora.

"It's the coolest thing ever that you and Beau are together. I mean, it's nice not to have to vet an outsider. Plus he cooks. And if the modeling pictures from his younger days are accurate, he's got a very prodigious rod of justice."

Cora and Rachel both burst into laughter. "Rod of justice?" Cora asked once she could speak.

"It's weird to me to call someone else's man's equipment a cock. Gregori has a cock. Dick is fine. But sometimes you just need to bust out the purple prose and make it extra creative. The more I can fluster Gregori and make him blush or laugh, the better. Thunder stick, meat staff, mighty spear of pleasure."

By that point Cora was laughing so hard she got the damned hiccups just imagining the look on Gregori's face at any of those descriptors. "I love you guys so hard," she sputtered.

"It's going to be a while before I can look at Gregori straight on without snickering," Maybe told Wren.

Vic looked over at them, narrowing his eyes. The others followed suit.

That's when Beau came in, lighting up Cora's heart. She watched as he scanned the room and felt that *click* of connection when their gazes locked.

"Be back in a sec," she told her friends over her shoulder before meeting him halfway.

She wasn't expecting the hug or the lingering kiss he laid on her, but she wouldn't be complaining anytime soon.

He kept her close and in his arms for long moments. "Good evening."

God, he made her smile.

"Hey there. I just ordered a whiskey sour. They're on special for another hour or so. You want one?" she asked.

He spun her neatly but kept her hand in his as they walked toward the bar. "Yes, and then we'll eat. I'm getting pretty hungry."

"I can make us dinner from time to time too, you know," she said.

"I'm sure you can. Tonight, though, Ian has asked us to Luna to sit at the chef's table. Along with Gregori and Wren."

"A double date with your besties? Awww."

"More than that. The table seats twelve so Maybe,

Rachel, Vic and Alexsei are invited too if they can break away."

"Pardon me for overhearing but yes to dinner," Maybe said as she leaned around Cora to speak to Beau.

"Pardon your nosy ass, you mean?" Cora teased.

In the years she'd been coming to Whiskey Sharp or gone out with her friends, it had been as a single person around people slowly coupling up. And now here she was, part of a couple. Falling for this dude who'd come into her life when she wasn't planning on anything like love. It was not overrated.

ONCE THEY'D GOTTEN everyone rounded up to go to dinner they headed out. It was cold but not rainy so, buttoned into coats, they all began to walk over to Luna.

"Are you okay to walk that far?" Vic asked Rachel in an undertone.

"It's four blocks. On First so I don't even have to walk up a hill." Rachel tugged on his beard, and then kissed him. "But thank you."

Cora kept her smile to herself, leaning against Beau awhile as they walked.

Maybe snorted as she bumped her hip to Vic's. "It's very sweet, but she's got like seven plus months to go. So ease up there or she's going to push you out of the air lock before the middle of her second trimester."

"Go bother *your* husband," Vic told his sister-in-law with a grin.

Laughing, Maybe skipped up to Alexsei, who took

her hand and planted a kiss on top of her head as they walked.

"Are you cooking tonight?" Cora asked Beau.

"Nope. I'm there to enjoy the food with you at my side and our friends all around. Ian's team is fucking amazing. Better chefs than me by far."

She scoffed and he hugged her to his side.

"There are no chefs better than you, duh." There might be better cooks or whatever, but none of them were him.

"I'm a decent, inventive cook who had the luck to land a television gig. I have good business sense and excellent management so all my money goes where it should be and everyone does well."

"Didn't you slay sauce today? Hello. Exhibit A. I said it. It's true. There. Glad we got that settled."

"I really have nothing in response to that so I'll accept the compliment and move on," Beau said.

He took them in through the restaurant and through the kitchen, where the large chef's table was set and waiting for them all.

Ian came out and, after greeting Gregori and Beau, he turned to the rest of the group. "Welcome, everyone. I hope y'all are ready to eat."

Beau and Gregori took turns introducing Ian, who'd been the one who introduced Beau to Gregori, who'd been a scrappy up-and-coming artist at the time. Not in the United States for very long, he'd become part of a group that included several other young men also out of place or far from everything they'd known. And from what Cora could see from the way they interacted, it had given them all a foundation of safety and brotherhood.

They'd learned about how to be better people, better men, through one another's trials and tribulations, and Beau was totally sure he would not be there without their support and example.

He wanted to show it off to Cora. Wanted her to see who'd been such an integral part of making him the man he was that day.

Cora leaned against her fist, a smile on her face as she listened to Len describe their first course.

Beau realized he hadn't ever in his life been so lighthearted. She made him laugh. Made him think. Respected him but didn't take him too seriously. Good to his friends and appreciative of their work and what made them tick.

He took the hand she wasn't propped against, threading his fingers through hers before leaning over to kiss her knuckles. Her smile deepened and she shifted slightly to be closer to him.

Ian came and went as he occasionally got up to take a cruise through the restaurant to make sure everything was going smoothly, but when the main course arrived, he settled at the table across from them, Beau knew, to get to know Cora better.

"How did you come to end up running an art gallery?" Ian asked.

"I grew up in the gallery. Surrounded by art and artists. Then as I started to travel and work all over the world with my mother, I took classes, got my degree in art history. Because my mom had connections

I was able to intern in some of the best museums with all manner of curators and directors. Taught me a lot about how I would and definitely would not run a gallery. Reinforced how much I love the gallery and the chance to run it."

"I know Gregori and I can't wait to see what you do with the gallery now that you're running it full-time," Wren said.

She talked about her plans for an upcoming series of shows and ended up recommending a few artists to Ian.

"Speaking of artistry, I've eaten at Northstar a few times and really loved it. Creative, solid menu. Well worth the drive up to Bellingham," Cora said of Ian's restaurant and bed-and-breakfast on several acres of a working farm about two hours north of Seattle.

It was Ian's pet project and a compliment of it probably raised her up quite a bit in Ian's estimation.

His eyes lit. "In the spring we're going to do a wine festival weekend. You and Beau should come up and stay."

"Awesome. I'd love to. You're Rian Brewster's son, right?"

Ian nodded, a little wariness back in his gaze.

"My father designed the garden at his house. I was just at Dad's office last week and he had photos of it. Gorgeous. Did you grow up there?"

The wariness washed away. Ian was second generation famous. His father had been a model and then an actor. He'd met Ian's mother when she'd been his orthopedic surgeon. Two utterly gorgeous and super successful and charismatic people united to form a marriage Beau held as a goal to achieve one day.

"Yes, I grew up there. Went to school in Bellingham. I got scouted at the mall, which is such a cliché," Ian said.

"The grounds look so lush and quiet. My dad said it was blissful and smelled perfect. That's a big compliment, in case that wasn't clear."

They talked a while longer as Cora revealed her brother was going to start working more with their father's business since she'd be taking on more over at the gallery. A happy set of choices and opportunities for both siblings.

After a really amazing dinner, they walked out to the front, where Ian had a car waiting to take them all back the few blocks to Whiskey Sharp.

"You want to sleep over at my place tonight?" Beau asked her. He had gotten used to her at his side as he slept, to the point that when they weren't together it felt off.

"I have an early meeting at the gallery, and then I'm going over to my parents' for a family lunch. I need to be close to work so it's better if I sleep in my own bed tonight."

He took her hand. "Say good-night to your friends and I'll drive you home."

She looked up at him, a smile playing at the corners of her mouth. "Will you stay at my house instead? I'll make coffee on my way out so you can have some when you wake up."

He nodded but it wasn't until they were nearly all

the way back to her house that he said, "I'm glad you asked me to stay over."

She made a happy sound. "I should confess it's easier to sleep with you there. And it gives me a reason to have really good cheese and butter because you make that little sneer if there are ingredients you find substandard."

He nearly guffawed. "I do not! I ate blocks of processed cheese on bread that was more corn syrup than baked good when I was growing up."

"There are things you have to do because your options are limited and things you don't have to do when you have the choice. Funny how when I look in your fridge at the condo I never find processed cheese or crappy bread."

"Busted. Life's too short to eat crappy cheese or awful bread when you have an alternative."

"I might embroider that on a pillow for your bed," Cora said. "Oh, and I had the opportunity to grab an extra parking place when someone else gave it up. So you can park there instead of having to hunt for street parking."

That gave him pause. Filled him up with a sense of belonging. Of home and safety.

CHAPTER FOURTEEN

I want you to know what I feel
as translated through my lips and fingertips

INSIDE, SHE DIDN'T bother with the lights, instead leading them both to her bedroom.

"No. Let me," she said, sliding her hands down the front of his shirt to his waist, drawing the material up.

There were no other words as she unbuttoned her way from the tail of his shirt to his throat and slid the fabric away from his torso. Sighing, she wrapped her arms around him, holding him close, her head pressed to his chest over his heart.

Usually there was so much heat between them that it was all teeth and snarls, fast and hard. But this time it was about slow. Taking the time to kiss the space between two of his ribs before licking, enjoying his taste.

He made a soft sound. Surrender. Assent. And because it was Beau, a demand.

It made her smile against his skin before she dragged her teeth over his left nipple. He dug his fingertips into her hips, holding her against him.

Heat and sex rose from him, blanketed her senses until she was drunk with him. Cora circled his body to press herself against his back. So broad and strong, muscles rippling as she swept her palms across it, down his sides and up his spine again.

From behind, she unbuckled his belt and pants, sliding them, along with his boxers, over an absolutely spectacular ass, complete with some freckles up near his tailbone, and then down his legs.

She knelt before him, placing his hand on her shoulder, letting him know to lean against her as she helped him step free.

So many people simply got one look at Beau and that was it. The stunning looks were all they were able to see. All he was.

But Beau was so much more. The way his hands rested on her, touched her without violence though he easily could have. He used his hands to cook for her. To nurture the people he cared about.

Every layer of him she was lucky enough to peel back revealed a person she desired to know even more.

Cora pressed a kiss to his knee and then up his thigh. The wiry hair there tickled against her lips and cheek. Content and happy to her toes, she breathed him in, brushing her cheek against his cock and hugging around his waist.

She had to close her eyes as he slid his fingers through her hair, freeing it from the pins holding it up.

"Your hair is so fucking soft. And when I take it out of whatever complicated thing you're wearing it doesn't just come loose, it tumbles down around your shoulders," he murmured. "Sweet smelling and a little spicy, like a wave of sex."

What could she even say to that? How could she express just how it made her feel to know he saw her the way he did.

She breathed him in, the subtle scent of his skin, the tang of him on the flat of her tongue as she laved from root to tip. His moan shifted into a snarl and the hands that had only moments before been caressing, tightened in her hair.

She went hot and cold all over at the feeling. Overwhelmed to the point where she had to let go and trust him. He paused; she knew he was listening to her cues, giving her the space to take a step back or indicate she was uncomfortable.

The way he checked in with her, always making sure her pleasure was central and definitely willing, was deeply sensual.

He was so patient.

Respectful.

Sexy as hell. Oh my god, he turned her to jelly.

Cora wanted him to know she found him beautiful, yes, but that she saw to the bone and wanted him. Knew him—and that was what attracted her the most.

She kissed down the length of him and back up as his impatience practically vibrated from the muscles in her thighs.

Taking him into her mouth, she made herself go slow. Teasing. Tasting. Wanting him to know through every touch just how she saw him.

It turned her upside down, shoved her out a window and into free fall to be so connected with him.

He groaned and she gave in to the delight of having that sort of power over him, sliding her hands up his calves and thighs and over the planes of that seriously fantastic belly. She dug her nails in before dragging them down, one to grip the root of him and the other to cup his sac.

Let herself wallow in the salt of his skin.

SOMETHING DEEPER AND sharper edged than mere desire swelled through Beau as he watched her. On her knees. It wasn't just that it felt good. It was that she took her time. Her attention was totally on him, the weight of it a comforting thing.

And it was blisteringly hot. Because it was Beau and Cora. The combination wasn't just physical but emotional and it made everything more raw and intense.

In his life, given his past, he'd learned and exhibited control when it came to the people in his life. Letting her in, letting her this close had been out of his control because there was nothing *but* letting her in. She was meant to be there.

But it meant being more exposed with her than he had been with anyone else. Knowing what he knew as an adult, understanding what it truly meant to tell secrets to someone—and to have that trust violated—what it was to be that vulnerable.

It terrified him, just how much he craved that with her.

A rush of pleasure swelled from his balls straight to his scalp as she took him into her mouth, swirling her tongue over the head of his cock, stunning him into a grunt as his orgasm began to dig itself into his gut.

She wasn't just erotic; she managed to make him

feel comforted after all the strangeness of the last several days.

Cora drew him deeper and deeper into her mouth, hot and wet, tempting him with glimpses of her face. Flashes of disappearing between those lips over and over, as her hair moved, rendering it in bits and pieces like an old-school flip book.

When she added her fist just below her mouth it was too much. More than his control could manage and he came hard and fast. In such a rush it felt as if every last bit of sensation was being wrung from his cells.

Still, he stumbled to pick her up and plop her on the bed so he could be the one on his knees.

He made short work of getting her naked, exposed to his hands and mouth. She drove him to pet, to cosset and delight. He ached to wrench every sigh and gasp of pleasure he could from her.

When he parted her and breathed softly against her pussy she sucked in a slow, shaky breath. Made him feel like a superhero.

Once he took a taste with a long, slow lick, he paid her every last bit of his attention. Kissing, nuzzling with lips, the gentle tug and suck until she writhed against him, rocking her hips, seeking more sensation.

She was velvet soft at the spot where her leg met her body. Super sensitive as he licked across it. Soon enough though he was drawn back to the heart of her. Drawn in by that slick, delicious, inferno-hot pussy.

A stuttered breath and then one of her hands tangled in his hair, tugging him to her as she came in a hot rush.

He got into bed on what he now thought of as his side of the bed, working up enough strength to pull her fully onto the mattress and into the curve of his body.

"Even better than the brown butter cake with plums we had tonight," he said into her neck as he kissed her there.

Her quiet laugh made him smile.

"That cake was pretty amazing. As was the whole dinner. Ian was awesome to have invited us all," she said.

It had been Ian's way of opening their group up to begin including Cora and her friends and that she seemed to get that pleased Beau a great deal.

"Telling him about how much you liked Northstar was a nice thing," he told her. "It's been something he wanted since back when we first met." Beau's friend wanted to prove himself to the world. On his own, not because he was the son of Rian Brewster.

Northstar had been Ian's flag. Planted to say he had a unique vision that included gardens and an inn along with a restaurant that would be something worth taking the time to visit. To savor fine food and wine. To roam through vast gardens that would supply the kitchen. Views of the land and water around.

"The whole place is part of the plate," Cora said sleepily.

"I really can't wait to look at properties with you." Beau hadn't meant to say it but it seemed impossible to keep himself from telling Cora things. "You see the world through such a unique perspective, I mean," he added.

She snickered. "Nice save."

"I mean it. You're going to notice how the light might reflect off the kitchen cabinets, or how the trees might sound in the spring."

She turned in his arms and snuggled into him, burying her face in the crook of his neck. "That's a really nice compliment."

"It's a really nice quality," he returned, kissing the top of her head. "How did you end up best friends with the Dolan sisters anyway?"

"I met Rachel through Ink Sisters. She came recommended by Bee but Finley saw the same spark in her too. Rachel was so determined to live. I don't know any other way to describe it better. She had a plan and she was so focused on it. It just… She needed a friend and I needed a friend so we ended up friends. Maybe and I ended up meeting at this little sandwich shop that eventually turned into our regular lunch spot. She liked orange soda and so do I. She had a great sense of style. We just clicked. And then as a group of three it worked too. Like I became one of their sisters and they became two of mine. The family of my heart, I suppose. What about you? Are you in contact with any of your family at all?"

"A few cousins from the branch of my mom's family. They gave me a place to live for the first six months after I left the group. I'm not real close to them, though they always remember my birthday and I do go to the special occasion events like graduations. The family of the heart thing though? I totally get that. Until I met Ian and his grandfather, the only older men who'd had any real influence on me had been my father's bishops. They were all under his control. He told them how to parent."

In his arms, Cora settled against him a little tighter. Giving comfort without words.

"Ian's parents were really busy working so when he had work outside Seattle and one of them couldn't be there, Pops would come. Whatever apartment or house they were in was where I wanted to be. Pops worked at The Northwest Grand in the kitchens there for forty years so there was always something good on the stove or in the oven. I was taught that cooking was women's work. Pops made sure I learned just how silly that was. He taught me how to cook. He's the reason I am where I am now. It was nice that Ian came along with the package since he turned out to be my closest friend. But Pops became the father figure I needed. He taught me what it was to be an adult. To be a good man."

"He did a very fine job of that. Is he still around?"

"He is. He lives on the grounds at Northstar now. Keeping an eye on things in Ian's stead." And it gave Ian a way to keep an eye on his grandfather, as well.

"He sounds pretty amazing. I'd love to meet him. Especially now that I know what a huge impression he made on you."

He'd never told anyone he'd dated about Pops. But he knew without a doubt how much one would like the other. Cora would adore Ian's grandfather and he'd flirt and charm her while tempting her with bits and sips of whatever deliciousness he was cooking up in the kitchen.

She'd listen to stories and ask all the right questions,

and yes, Beau needed to take her up to see Pops, present her to him.

"He is pretty amazing. I owe him a visit soon so next time I do, I'll bring you along. Make lunch for you in his kitchen."

"I'm never going to complain that you're making me food. Just so you know," she added.

"Do you want me to come with you tomorrow? Just to lend you some emotional support? I have it on good authority that I'm excellent with the ladies when I put my mind to it."

Cora snorted, laughing against him. "My mother would soak up all that flattery, and then eat you for lunch. She's a shark. But I do appreciate your offer. It's going to be all right. My siblings will be there. I've even started the search for my replacement."

Somehow Beau got the feeling that Walda was far more attached to having her youngest daughter be her keeper than Cora anticipated. Her mother was a big personality who drew energy from those around her. A master at reading others and getting them to do what she wanted them to.

His father had been a big personality like that. Beau knew more than a little about how hard it could be for that person to go anywhere they didn't want to.

He hoped her brother and sister backed her up.

CHAPTER FIFTEEN

"YOU SURE YOU don't want me to come along?" Beau asked Cora the next morning as she was about to head over to her parents' house.

He was so sweet. If he was going to be an asshole she could fend him off. But it felled her, ripped all her defenses down, when the tenderness he evoked rushed through her. He'd gotten up and made her coffee. Kept her company while she'd gotten ready to leave. Even walked her to her car. And now he was offering to be a human shield between her and her mother.

"Thank you but I think it's going to be okay. The last few times I've spoken to her on the phone she's been mellow and happy. I'll see you tonight."

They were headed out to some art opening with Gregori and Wren. Most of their friends would make an appearance, she figured. It was her chance to dress up a little. Look extra sexy. A coming-out party of sorts for their relationship and also for the next stage in her life.

"Fine. I'm at the condo working today so if you need me, text or call."

Then, he captured her heart by actually blowing her a kiss. His smirk at her pleased reaction only thrilled her more.

"Don't forget to save me some of everything tasty," she managed to say. She'd been going for sassy but mainly she managed to pull off slightly askew.

He rapped three times on the roof of her car and stepped back. "Drive carefully and text me when you get there."

She could have scoffed at such a thing, but instead she nodded, agreeing because she knew she'd like the same in reverse. He still stood watching her as she turned the corner and headed toward the freeway.

Her parents lived about twenty minutes east of Seattle, across the lake in old Bellevue. Their house, the one Cora had grown up in, was surrounded by three acres her father had slowly transformed into a series of garden spaces that she never failed to find magic in.

There was always something new like the bench carved from the prow of an old sailing ship he'd surrounded in a wash of some sort of purple-and-white flowers he said would appear in late spring.

Her mother rarely came out into the gardens, but for the one he'd designed for her just outside the sunroom. Elegant. Roses with marble benches and water features. In the winter he made sure the portable heaters were in place near where she liked to sit best and in the summer, he'd created a pergola of wild climbing roses and wisteria that had made the most wonderful shady spot to while away the day.

The rest of the acreage had been changed at least once over the years. Sometimes he'd come back with a ceramic pot or some wind chimes that turned out

Dear Reader,

IT'S A FACT: if you answer 4 quick
questions, we'll send you **4 FREE REWARDS!**

I'm not kidding you. As a leading
publisher of women's fiction, we value
your opinions... and your time. That's
why we are prepared to **reward** you
handsomely for completing our mini-
survey. In fact, we have 4 Free Rewards
for you, including 2 free books and
2 free gifts.

As you may have guessed, that's why our
mini-survey is called **"4 for 4".** Answer 4
questions and get 4 Free Rewards. It's
that simple!

Thank you for participating in
our survey,

Pam Powers

To get your 4 FREE REWARDS:
Complete the survey below and return the insert today to receive 2 FREE BOOKS and 2 FREE GIFTS guaranteed!

"4 for 4" MINI-SURVEY

1 Is reading one of your favorite hobbies?
☐ YES ☐ NO

2 Do you prefer to read instead of watch TV?
☐ YES ☐ NO

3 Do you read newspapers and magazines?
☐ YES ☐ NO

4 Do you enjoy trying new book series with FREE BOOKS?
☐ YES ☐ NO

YES! I have completed the above Mini-Survey. Please send me my 4 FREE REWARDS (worth over $20 retail). I understand that I am under no obligation to buy anything, as explained on the back of this card.

194/394 MDL GMYP

FIRST NAME	LAST NAME

ADDRESS

APT.#	CITY

STATE/PROV.	ZIP/POSTAL CODE

READER SERVICE—Here's how it works:

to be the seed of some new plan either at home or in someone else's.

It made her happy to make that left turn up the long, meandering drive, lined by maples and ornamental cherry trees. The house sat around a curve, positioned perfectly to catch views of the mountains and the grounds beyond.

Finley's car and Beto's motorcycle already waited out front and Cora wasn't ashamed to admit how relieved she was that they were already there.

She parked on the other side of Finley and headed inside through the big hand-carved door her mother had brought back from Italy twenty years before.

The house smelled really good, which meant her father had spent the morning making the fish stew that starred in many a family meal.

He came into the hall from the kitchen, smiling big when he caught sight of her. "Come give me a kiss then, Cora," he told her, opening his arms for a hug.

He embraced her, and then kissed her cheek before offering his arm and taking her into the dining room where her siblings waited, along with their mother.

There was a flurry of greetings, cheek kissing and exchanging of compliments as Cora managed to put her bag and coat down.

Big band music played throughout the house and her mother already had a glass of rosé in her hand.

"I just pulled the bread from the oven. Beto, bring the salad and the vegetables. Finley, the rice," her father called out. Cora brought over a pitcher of tea and one of juice. Even Walda helped, bringing over a platter of fruit.

Once they'd been eating awhile, her mother gave Cora a careful once-over. "So tell me already."

"Beto is going to join Dad's firm full-time," Cora said to start.

Her father smiled, happy about that choice as he sopped up soup with a piece of crusty French bread.

"Maybe now you can work less," Walda told her husband. "Who will take his place at the gallery?" she asked.

"It's the other way around," Beto said. "I've only been there as a stopgap when Cora is away. She's already running the gallery."

Their mother turned to Cora. "And you? You're going to do the job of two people? Who'll manage when you're gone? I suggest we hire someone to run the gallery. That way no one is impacted by Beto working with your father."

No one? No one but Cora, apparently.

"You make a good point about staffing. I think it's time for me to step away from being your assistant and to put all my focus on the gallery."

Walda didn't move any muscle in her body but the ones that brought her left eyebrow to slowly rise. Imperious.

"I see."

Cora didn't take the bait. "I've written up job descriptions for replacements. I've divided up what I do between a house manager and a personal assistant for your business affairs."

"Very tidy."

The air hung thick with tension. Normally Cora would be finding ways around it, but right then it just pissed her off.

"Not really tidy at all. I do a lot for you, so it's not easy to find a replacement. There are multiple steps." Cora waved a hand, a conscious echo of when her mother waved away things she didn't care to hear. "We'll muddle through. I've spoken with several people who are assistants to high-powered people and have received great advice and a few referrals. I've brought you over copies of the ad. I've spoken with Kay, who will continue to work here, along with whoever we hire for you."

"Strangers in my house? You know my feeling about that. I won't have it. I used to handle my career myself—I'll do it again," her mother snapped. "If you're going to abandon me, fine. But you won't spend my money to dump me on strangers while you run my gallery like an ungrateful brat."

"Hey!" Beto cried, his hands up in entreaty.

Cora pulled herself together. Her mom struck out when she was uncertain. If she responded in kind, the entire discussion would get derailed.

She shot a grateful look at her brother before she said to her mother, "You haven't handled your career yourself in nearly three decades. Before it was me, it was Dad and your manager. You still have a manager, of course, and I'm working with her on this process. In your contracts, you have the option of the label paying for staff. That enables us to cast a wider net and also, let's be honest, get someone willing to deal with you."

It was worth whatever fallout to get to watch her mom's eyes widen so comically at being spoken to that way.

Her father hid a smile behind his napkin and Finley gave a slow clap.

"I don't need you and I certainly don't need two people to replace one," her mother said after a glare Finley's way.

"Two people doing the work will save them both from getting burned-out. I want you to take the next few days to think about just exactly how many things I do for you on a daily basis. It'll be an excellent exercise so we can make sure to hire someone who knows how to do each job best." And perhaps it'd give her mother pause when she realized just how much Cora did for her. In any case, Cora had no plans to engage with her mom's claim that she didn't need to be taken care of.

"That's an excellent point," her father said. Ever the peacemaker.

"Stop trying to handle me. I detest being handled."

If Cora hadn't known her mother so well, she might have missed the hurt in her tone. Hidden behind the aggressive bitchiness.

She was scared. And getting older. And things were changing and that was hard on everyone no matter what the age. Cora reminded herself to be gentle with her mom when she could.

"Why am I only hearing about this now if you've been so miserable working with me?"

Beto muttered something under his breath but it was such classic Walda that all Cora could do was be amused by the drama.

"I've spoken to you about this a few times. About what I wanted for the gallery. This last trip was very hard on you and we discussed changing what your schedule looks like. I did consider talking to you privately, but to be frank, this is a family business. You're the family business just as the gallery is the family business. And *Pai's* firm. Beto's shift there and my move to the gallery full-time will change the dynamic at both places as well as here and with you. It seemed best that with all those moving parts that we handle it as a family."

That, and she deserved the backup from her siblings and father.

"But you *assume* you have the job running the gallery? Without even discussing this with me? You're very young to be a director. We should do a wider search," her mother said.

"I know that gallery better than anyone else. You included," Cora said. "You could fire me—because you have to know I'd leave if you hired anyone else. It would suck. I'd have to find another job and it would take some time. But I would. Because I'm good at what I do." And if they hired anyone else, she'd never speak to her parents again.

Her mother's back was ramrod straight. She was pissed off because she knew she was boxed in. She'd said something in the heat of the moment and it was fire Cora right then or admit she was wrong.

Her father smoothly entered the fray. "You're very good at what you do. Of course you are. I think this is a fine idea, Cora. Walda, wasn't I just saying that the next time you have to travel I wanted to be there? With Beto at the firm, I can do that. And the gallery has flourished with Cora at the helm, which I'm sure you already know," her father said to her mother.

"So you knew about this?" she asked him.

Her dad took her mother's hand, kissing her knuckles before putting it back. "I knew Beto was coming to work with me full-time. I had my suspicions about Cora's intentions but figured she'd tell us all when she was ready to."

"I had no idea I was a burden to be discussed in quiet tones behind my back." Her mother sniffed, all offense and spines.

Cora wanted so badly to lean over and grab her mom's glass and take a big gulp of wine.

"No one is saying you're a burden," Finley said, exasperation in her voice.

"She knows that," Cora replied. "I'm discussing you in a regular voice to your face. This isn't a negative thing. Your career has changed. You don't travel as much but when you do, it's for long stints. I don't want that anymore. I want to build a life here, with roots and a dog and a job that fulfills me. I'm not rejecting you, as you well know."

Finley gave her an approving look.

"You do have a life here! An overpriced town house in Queen Anne. Friends. Your family. It's not as if I forbade you from having a dog if you worked for me.

I'm eccentric after all. I'm allowed to bring a dog with me anytime I like. You can too."

Cora said to her mom, "I love you very much. And I had a wonderful time working for you. I'm grateful for all I was able to see and do. But I want something different. Which is not about you. It's about me. I'll help this transition be as smooth as possible. Things will work out and be just fine. I'm not falling off the planet. If there are questions, I'll still be around for your new assistants to contact. I can be here in minutes if necessary and my phone is always on."

Walda, backed into a corner, said nothing else, but the flat line of her lips hinted at future trouble for Cora.

And still Cora couldn't deny the invigoration pumping through her system. She'd taken a stand and held her own and hadn't allowed herself to be baited into saying something she'd regret.

She wasn't an angel or anything. She'd save all her shit talk for behind her mom's back, in private to her friends or Beau.

"This is a good time for us. For our family," her father said as he held up his teacup. "I love you all and I'm proud of what your mother and I built."

The stubborn line of her mother's mouth softened. For all her flaws, no one could say Walda didn't adore her husband. And when he was sweet and charming, like he was right then, absolutely impossible not to be sweetened up by.

As he'd planned.

Everyone raised their various cups and glasses in salute and drank.

"Did Finley tell you Ink Sisters was named one of Seattle's best tattoo shops?" Cora asked her parents, hoping she could keep things on a positive track.

Her sister blushed, ducking her head a moment to hide her pleased embarrassment.

As Finley filled their parents in on the upcoming magazine issue featuring her shop, Cora sat back, smiling. Fin worked her ass off to build her business. Slowly but surely creating a client base and a good reputation. Bringing on artists across the spectrum of styles and approaches until Ink Sisters had come into its own.

Cora thought it was totally badass and said so, only a little less curse word filled.

Her sister was still pink from her blush, grinning as she thanked Cora.

"Are you still seeing that boy?" her mother asked.

"Beau? Yes, I'm seeing him still." It made her warm inside that he'd offered to come with her that day, even if he really had *no* idea what he'd been volunteering for.

"You turn red every time you mention his name and I think that's adorable," Beto said with a wink.

"Hmm. This is uncharacteristic, much like this whole plan to abandon me and run the gallery. Is that related to him?" her mother asked.

Cora sucked in a breath and steeled herself. She hadn't expected her mother to go that way. Silly, of course, a blind spot when it came to Beau perhaps.

"Related to him how?"

"This rejection of your family!" her mother exclaimed.

"Oh for goodness' sake," Cora muttered. "I'd already decided to shift to the gallery full-time before we returned from London. Before I'd even reconnected with him. And I'm not so weak that I'd just let some dude tell me what to think or feel."

Her father patted his wife's arm before interjecting. "What I think your mother means is that we don't know him and he's clearly important to you. I think dinner together would be nice. If and when you get serious with him that is."

Of course that wasn't what her mother said, or even what she thought. But whatever. Cora didn't want to get bogged down in a beef over Beau when her mom was just striking out to see what landed. And if she got a reaction to it, Walda would use it again.

"Dinner would be great. Getting to know him would be great," Cora said with a smile at her dad.

"Then he can explain just what he's up to with you," her mother added.

"He likes my boobs, my friends and my life. It's not that hard to believe he'd want to be around me because I'm wonderful, is it?" Cora asked.

Beto interrupted, "Not at all. Of course he wants to be around you because you're wonderful. It'll be good to get to know this guy."

Thankful for the backup on multiple fronts, Cora moved the discussion along to something else, pleased they'd all made it through the argument. For the time being anyway.

CHAPTER SIXTEEN

"So YEAH, ALL that happened," Cora told Rachel and Maybe later that afternoon. She'd stopped by Whiskey Sharp after the gallery had closed up for the night so she, Rachel and Maybe had tucked up off in a corner with some tea to catch up.

"I think Fin finally gets it. Not that she didn't understand how much you did for your mom before. Because she does and she did. But I think she sees just how much of a toll it was taking on you. And on your relationship with your mom. And let's face it, your relationship with your siblings. How can you not resent the way you had to do it all?"

Rachel was one of those people who listened more than she spoke. She was insightful—though not always when it came to her own baggage—and had excellent advice. It meant she not only understood Cora, but saw right down through all Finley's layers to the battered heart of her.

Rachel continued, "I don't usually get between you and Bee. I love your sister and I know you do too. But whatever it is, whatever she took on as you and your siblings were growing up, it's burned some important bridges between them. I don't want to see that be you.

I like this Cora. Happy and all schmoopy over someone who deserves it. Excited about her career. This is *good* for you."

"Bee and Javi had to raise us. You know that." Whatever the present, Cora knew without a doubt that her two oldest siblings were the reason she was sitting there that day. They'd done the work her mom just couldn't or didn't want to.

"*You* were a teenager when you started working for your mom too. And don't even get me started on Javier." Rachel shook her head.

"I haven't spoken to him about this whole situation. But he'll be supportive."

"Do you know that for the first few years I knew you, Maybe and I thought Javi was the youngest and Beto was the oldest? Because your big brother is a baby. Don't defend him. I don't want to hear it. He did what he did when you needed it and I am grateful obviously as I adore you. But he ran off, like Bee did. Only he stayed gone. He reverted to some kind of perpetual state of acting like he's twenty-three."

Cora loved how fierce Rachel got in her defense. Especially when it was hard for Cora to do it herself.

"I hope he finds what he needs. Hell, I hope he figures out what he needs, and then goes out and grabs it for himself." Cora shrugged. "I can't do this for him. Or for Bee. Or anyone else but me. I love running the gallery. It's not like I'm doing more than I did before, it's that I'm doing it with the knowledge that I'll be doing it next year and beyond. I love that. And I'm selfish enough to know it's selfish. And to do it anyway."

"I don't agree that it's selfish for you to want your own damned life. Your mom has one. She's got to let you have one too. If your dad gets involved, it should be good too I think. Hey, what are you doing tonight anyway? Maybe and Alexsei are coming over to hang out. I was going to order pizza. Vic will bring home a bunch of sweet stuff. We can gossip more." Rachel reached out to take Cora's hand, squeezing it a moment.

"I'm meeting Beau in an hour. He's looking at some houses tonight and wants my opinion. Which is pretty sweet." She remembered to update them on the note on her door and then the whole story about his kids.

"It's got to be a big mind fuck to have grown up that way to start with. But he overcame it. Even so, he lost his children. That's just awful. I don't even know how you could get over something like that. He lost his whole family. Everything and everyone he'd ever known. I'm glad he's got his close group of friends who are so protective of him. Like say, *my* friends who checked into who he was when he came around me at first."

Rachel snickered. "Look, I have skills. I need to use them from time to time or they get rusty. And you're important. You're our family. We don't want anyone messing with you. So yes. Maybe and I talked and I looked around. Just to be sure he wasn't hiding anything big. I'm betting someone on his team looked into you. I would."

"Oh god, what if he finds out about my secret life fighting crime?"

Rachel nodded. "Your secret's safe with me."

Vic walked in and strolled their way but got snagged by Alexsei so they got to talk about him.

"How's pregnancy going?" Cora asked.

"Vic has decided to follow me around and ask if I need anything to eat or if perhaps I should nap. Pretty much constantly. He's like a giant version of his mother, who also comes to our house to follow me around and ask me if I'm hungry or if I need a nap. It's easy for her to do that because like a dumbass, I moved in with my boyfriend who lives in a house pretty much across the street from his parents. This is going to be a really long nine months."

Cora snorted. "I bet you won't have to make a meal for yourself until the kid is in middle school though." Irena Orlova was a force of nature. A nurturing, avenging badass who baked bread and managed a lot of big giant alpha males like it was easy. Cora adored Vic's mother but she knew Rachel was going to have to fend off all sorts of well-meaning intrusions. Especially now that she was pregnant and officially marrying Vic.

"Probably." Rachel's annoyance seemed far outweighed by the affection in her tone. "Keeps the Orlovas busy if they can make food and cluck over people. I have to keep all this in mind for when I'm further along in my pregnancy and slower to get away."

"Just one of the many reasons I think Vic is going to be an awesome dad. I mean, just think of all the photo opportunities with big giant dude holding sweet tiny baby," Cora said. "But when it gets too much, you have a key to my house. You're always welcome to hide there. Knock first because now I'm having sexual relations on a very regular basis and you never know if I'm doing it on my kitchen counter."

"Was that bragging?" Rachel asked.

"It totally was. Are you jealous? Did it work?" Cora teased.

"I'm knocked up because I was getting it on the regular. And you've seen my man. I have no jealousy in that department," Rachel said. "But I'm fucking thrilled for you. Because you deserve it. And Beau is pretty snacktastic as the kids say."

"He totally is. I've never in my life been with someone just so gorgeous. And capable. He cooks for me after he makes me come. Like, how did that even happen? Whatever the case, I am all in on this."

Cora stayed for a little while longer before heading home to change before Beau came by to pick her up.

BEAU STOOD IN the wide-open farmhouse-style kitchen of the third house of the night. "What do you think?" he asked Cora.

She walked through the space, opening drawers and peeking into cabinets. "You're the cook."

"Yes, but I know what I think of this kitchen as a cook. I want to hear what Cora thinks about it."

Her grin was quick and filled him with pleasure. "All right. All the windows will give you plenty of daylight, and though it's dark, I can tell you for sure that your view will be gorgeous. Skylights too." She tipped her chin upward. "I love the white cabinets. Very clean and bright. The granite countertops are fabulous. The floors—the real estate agent said they were specially done for you to stand on comfortably for long periods of time?"

He nodded, watching her as she rocked back and forth on her heels a few times, and then bounced. He especially liked the bouncing part.

"I'm no expert, but I wish I could have the gallery floors done like this. It really does seem to absorb the impact but it's still really nice. The dark wood is contemporary and classic at the same time. Sexy. It would probably look good on camera and you have the space for sure."

It was the largest kitchen of all the houses the agent was showing him, she'd mentioned. And it *felt* big. Open with a sizable island in the center that would indeed be perfect for filming him behind.

"The pendant lights are fantastic. I love the touch of copper. I can see you cooking here. For me, obviously," she added with a smirk that made him step to her for a quick kiss.

"Obviously my cooking is primarily for you, yes." He kissed her again. "However, one does make a living from being filmed while cooking so there is that."

She snorted. "Whatever. As long as your priorities are in order we'll be fine."

"I do make it my aim to keep you well fed."

"You do succeed on *multiple* levels," she said in an undertone. Speaking normally again—though the real estate agent was actually outside—Cora said, "The color scheme makes you look super sexy. Highlights all your gingery goodness."

"You're really good for my ego, gorgeous." And she

was. In so many ways. He took her hand and tugged her through the kitchen and attached dining room and into the large living room with soaring ceilings and a wall of windows that looked out over a sizable yard and Puget Sound beyond.

"What's this area like?" he asked her.

"This is Magnolia. Swanky digs. It's quiet and you have great views because you're on the bluff. Even better, this house is set back and the agent said they'd done some sort of work to put thingamabobs down into the foundation under the house, which made it extra safe or whatever."

Certainly Cora had her own way of delivering information but it was what he'd been interested to know and he got what she meant, remembering the things the agent had said after she'd given them a quick tour of the house, and then had left them to wander some more alone.

The place was stunning. One of a kind as it had been a custom build. The master suite took up half the second floor with foldaway glass doors that opened the entire room out to a balcony that spanned the entirety of the back of the house. The views would be part of the high price tag, he knew.

Heated floors in all the bathrooms and gas fireplaces in each of the six bedrooms. Two walk-in closets in the master and it pleased him. He'd offer one to her, entice her to spend time with him there.

The lot itself was barely shy of an acre and at the end of a street so if he had a crew in to film it wouldn't rile the neighbors. The way the house was designed meant unobstructed views and privacy from every room.

Still in the city but it felt removed from it. Quiet. Way closer to the gallery than the other houses he'd looked at too. He wanted her with him as much as possible so it made sense to make it easier for her. Not having to deal with the hell of the bridges trying to get into Seattle, even midmorning when the gallery opened, would be a very good thing.

They looked at one last house before he drove them back to her place.

Once she'd changed into pajamas and washed her makeup off—he fucking loved to watch her do lady stuff—they'd settled on the couch with a cup of tea.

Because he knew she'd wait until asked before giving him an opinion, he asked, "What do you think of the places we saw tonight?"

"That second one? In the middle of the woods. Totally quiet. Three acres. The house was on a river and the kitchen looked out over it so that was nice. I think you'd need to invest in another generator as the one it has only works on a few things and the house is so big. And your power will go out because you're in the middle of the woods. It'll be gorgeous in the winter when it snows. And if you don't have to drive anywhere it's even better."

He had a gut-wrenching hatred of rural or off-the-grid living. He would never go back to that place. Not willingly.

"I hadn't thought about that. See you're helping al-

ready. I don't like the idea of the power going out. Are
generators a common thing up here?"

"Well, not here where you and I are living now. But
certainly out where several of the places we looked at
tonight are will have power outages. Windstorms are
common enough. Rain most definitely and snow too.
So if you have a generator you can keep the fridge
going. The freezer. There were gas fireplaces, which
is nice so you don't have to worry about burn bans and
they're good to heat the house if the power goes out."

Hmm.

"What did you think of the Magnolia house?" he
asked.

"It and the last one we saw were the only ones not
on at least two acres. But it's the closest in to the city.
I loved the kitchen, most definitely, and though it was
dark outside, the yard and all the outside entertainment
spaces had really nice energy and the lighting is really lovely so it would be really easy to be out there a
lot, even in the fall and winter when it gets dark early.

"I can't really speak about camera or filming stuff
but it seemed bright and open enough that a big guy
could be comfortable. That last house we looked at,
and the first one too, the kitchens were big if they were
like, my kitchen. But you're a tall guy—you didn't have
to stoop or anything but it really did feel cramped."

He nodded because he agreed. "And how far is it to
the gallery from there?"

"Like ten, fifteen minutes most of the day. Com-
mute time you're going to face longer, but it's not like
it would be with the first four houses you looked at.

Add another five or ten to get to Ian's," she added before he could even ask.

"Okay, I like that. All of that. Which house do you like best?"

"Which house do you like best?" she countered.

"I know which house I like best. That's why I'm asking you what your favorite is."

She rolled her eyes. "The Magnolia house. Part of that is selfish because it's closest to my job and it's like ten minutes from Maybe's and Rachel's houses. And I already have art in mind for your bedroom. I mean, you probably already have art for your house. Can't stop won't stop when it comes to art. But I think you knew that."

He squeezed her calf. "I might have figured it out. Magnolia is my favorite too. By a lot. It's not just the fact that it's close in to everyone I like being around. The design, the way the lot was used, the light and all that stuff just blew me away. I really don't want to mess around with generators or any of that stuff that comes with more rural living. Plus the house there has a three-car garage so you'll always have a place to park."

She blushed. "Well. Thank you. Are you going to make an offer then?"

"I told her I'd call her tomorrow to let her know. I'll go in all cash just to be done. I hate dealing with all that paperwork otherwise."

Her snort had him giving her the eye. "What?"

"I just thought how far you'd come from that kid who'd lived in a house without electricity to a guy who can fork over millions of dollars for a house with radiant heated floors overlooking the Puget Sound."

"I do think about it. Every day when I turn on the water and it's hot. When I flip on the lights or get things from the fridge. When I'm warm in the winter and cool in the summer. It's a universe away and I prefer that." Clothes that fit. Doctor visits when he needed them. An education. Freedom.

Understanding softened Cora's features.

"I think about how my kids grew up without those comforts and it fills me with rage."

"I wish I could fix it. I hate seeing that look on your face. I hate that their mother stole them from you. I would very much like to punch her in the cooter."

Damn, he fucking loved her.

"I suppose I should say that's terrible and not to say such things. But she took my kids so I don't feel much charity toward her. But for tonight let's put all that to the side. I just decided to buy a house and to tell you the truth, I'm creatively energized by that kitchen. I have some new ideas to incorporate into the pitch now."

"I'm so pleased for you. I can't deny the appeal of you making a permanent home for yourself up here. And those heated floors in all your bathrooms."

"I can't believe we haven't had the time to discuss the lunch with your parents today. Other than your texts that it went fine, do you want to elaborate?"

She shrugged. "It did go okay. She balked a bit. Tried to talk around it. Went on about how I was abandoning her and how she was a burden. But I placed the ads when we left and I'll be moving this process right along now that I've told her."

"Big day for Beau and Cora, eh?" he said with a smile.

"Yeah, pretty much. Come to bed. I want you to sex me up. I'll sex you up back. It'll be lovely."

Laughing, he got up, tugging her to her feet and then to her room, where he closed the door behind them and made it just the two of them with nothing more to do than get naked and feel good.

A big day indeed. Ending with what was by far his favorite thing—and woman—to do.

CHAPTER SEVENTEEN

"BY THE WAY, my parents always have a big pre-Thanksgiving dinner for friends and family the week before the actual holiday. I've been instructed to invite you," Cora told Beau just a few days later.

Her mother had called earlier that day to tell Cora it was more than time for her to bring Beau around for inspection. Though they'd met him at the gallery and her mother sort of knew him from the old days, it cheered her that her parents were including Beau in what was one of their longest-standing family traditions.

They were furniture shopping for Beau as his offer on the house had been accepted and he'd be moving in two weeks.

"Really?" He smiled as he brought her close to his side. "When, and what should I bring?"

"Next Saturday and you don't need to bring anything but you and some wine. My dad loves a glass of port at the end of a meal. I can even tell you his favorite label," Cora told him as she wrapped her arm around his waist.

The salesperson was beside himself with joy. He kept stealing looks at Beau, and who was Cora to be offended? Beau was gorgeous. And rich and famous and was going to buy a bunch of stuff.

"I gave my couches away and my mattresses. No use moving them up here. I have a huge farmhouse table that will be perfect in the dining room, but I'd like to go with that same theme on the lower level where the common areas are," Beau murmured as he examined a light gray couch.

"Is it weird how anxious I am to see your art? Because I am. And that's not even a euphemism." She shook her head no when he pointed to a grotesque chair she'd set on fire if he actually bought.

"Your expression just now makes me think you'd be terrible at poker," he said with laughter in his voice.

Cora snickered. "I'm actually good at poker. But I'm terrible at hiding my disdain for ugly furniture apparently."

"Works for me if it saves me from wasting my cash."

"Somehow I doubt you doing anything you don't want to do, even if it was you wanting to buy a chair that looks like it's made of vomit."

The salesperson who'd been shadowing them to keep near Beau gasped and it made Cora laugh. It wasn't like she was insulting the guy's mother. Or even the store or the other furniture.

"Oh, and it's not weird. I think it's sexy that you're excited by what you might learn about me from the art I already own. I, to be honest, am far more excited to see what you decide to show me once I've moved in."

"I should tell you I'm rather aggressive about my opinions regarding what I like personally. But once I know what your artistic tastes are, I can tailor what to show you. It's one of my favorite things about my job." She *loved* her repeat clients. That relationship once she got to know what would fit them was fascinating. She learned new things about art every single day from how people received it. What they yearned for. What surprised them in good and bad ways. It gave challenge to all her preconceived notions and biases. That's what kept her mind open to far more than things that appealed to her personally.

An open mind and an open heart were things she felt were integral to being not only a better person, but better at all aspects of running the gallery.

Beau brushed a kiss against her forehead before moving on to a different couch. "What do you think about the stuff I've bought so far? Not the art, but the stuff for the house?" Beau asked her directly.

"I brought you here because I've found their work to be consistently good. The quality is always high. Lots of unique pieces as well, which I thought would appeal to you."

He straightened, examining her closely before smiling a little. "Yeah, you do see through right to the heart of me, huh?"

He was too compelling not to want to know him deeper. Beau wasn't taciturn like Alexsei could be, but Beau's silences were as complex as what he said aloud. There was, at times, a churning undercurrent of yearning that seemed to roll from him. It brought out the protectiveness in her.

"I think you have excellent taste." He did. Another

attractive thing about him. Everything he'd chosen thus far—except for the chair—had been what she thought was a perfect choice for the feel of the house and what he seemed to want.

"I understand that for the compliment it is," he said.

A few hours later, as they lay in bed catching some postorgasm breath Cora traced her fingers over his elephant tattoo.

"Why an elephant? Any significance, or did you just like the design?"

"Elephants are badass. They're smart and tough. They'll defend their family to the death. Did you know that?" he asked.

"I didn't."

"They're all about family and connection. And since I was sort of let down by that as a kid, I've decided that I won't let anyone else down that same way. The people you love should come first in your life."

She kissed his chest, over his heart. Touched that he'd share.

"I was on a shoot in Thailand and ended up at an elephant rescue sanctuary one morning. It changed me. These animals are massive but with their caretakers, the small humans who saved them from a life of cruelty, they were gentle and even a little protective. The old lady of the herd, the matriarch, is sort of the keeper of the memory. She'll watch over the babies. Anyway, I've been supporting that rescue for years along with a few others I've found since."

"That's awesome. Perhaps at some point we can visit the sanctuary or something. I loved Thailand." It occurred to her then that he'd probably be a fantastic travel partner. Open and curious. Interested in things. Easygoing. All things that made the frustrations that came with travel a lot easier to get through.

Plus he looked so good it would make her day every time she caught a glance and remembered he was with her.

He slid his fingers through hers, tangling hands. "Yes. I'd like that. I go surfing every other year down there and it gives me a chance to visit, as well."

"I won't be surfing. But I'm really good at sitting under an umbrella, drinking a beer and watching *other* people surf."

"Does that include having a cold one waiting when I finished up?" he teased.

"Heck yes. And sex. Though that would have to wait until after we left whatever public place we were in."

He laughed. "Why? I bet you could be very creative when it came to fitting in a round of rousing sexy times in some dimly lit corner."

"People take pictures of you. You're not just a pretty surfing tourist. You're Beau Petty. And so some video of you giving me the business would end up online and everyone would savage my thighs," Cora said.

Already a photo of the two of them standing outside Luna, Cora looking up into his face, a smitten smile on her lips, had made the rounds at the gossip sites. He hadn't been bothered by it really, but it was clear he'd been concerned about how she'd react.

It made her nervous, because she liked her life private. But she liked being with Beau and Beau was famous and getting attention on gossip sites came with the territory, even if it was uncomfortable at times.

"I'm sorry about that, you know. I wish I could protect you from it."

He'd been really upset on her behalf, worried over her safety. Cora didn't want him beating himself up over something that simply came with his job.

"You can only control how you react to what other people do. You're pretty. You cook in people's homes and so they want to know you and whoever you're with. It's weird, but it comes with you and I like you enough to deal with the rest."

"Lucky me," he murmured against her hair. He wasn't joking at all and warmth filled Cora's belly.

CHAPTER EIGHTEEN

"WHAT IF SHE acts like a bitch?" Cora asked Rachel, who despite being woken up from a nap was delivering the pep talk she so desperately needed.

They were set to leave for dinner at her parents' house shortly and nervousness edged along Cora's spine.

"She's going to act like a bitch, honey. It's what she does. Beau is a big boy and he seems to really like you a lot. He's going to figure out what she is soon enough if he hasn't already. She might even be calmer because there'll be a crowd there," Rachel said.

Cora sighed. "I'm dumb for calling. Of course she won't be held back by the setting. You've met my mother, right? Okay, okay." She took a deep breath. "I'm all right. He'll be fine and if it isn't good we'll leave."

She realized just how much she meant that right after saying it. One of their friends had been married for nearly a decade to a person who never defended her to the family. Never stepped in on her side. As a result, his parents had disrespected her so much there wasn't anything he could do to fix it as far as the marriage had been concerned.

Some damage could never be repaired.

Cora valued and respected Beau too much to allow her family to treat him poorly or make him feel uncomfortable.

And the bald truth was that she didn't want to lose him. Didn't want him scared off. If things ended between them, it wouldn't be because of some bullshit from her family.

"Things will be okay. She'll push. He's all charming and mannerly but not prone to letting himself be pushed. Stand your ground. Let her get used to it. She loves you and in the end, that's why everything will be fine. You can do this."

"You're my favorite," Cora told Rachel. "I'll talk to you when I get home so I can update you."

"You better. Remember that you're worth this effort. Okay? Not just the moving to a new job but this thing with Beau. And being treated the way you deserve. Don't get me all het up on your behalf or Vic will frown at me and probably call his mother," Rachel warned in a teasing tone.

"Did she help?" Beau asked as Cora came out into the kitchen.

"She did. Maybe would have tutted and worried and made me anxious for her. But Rachel is no-nonsense. I needed that today."

"Stop worrying. I promise I'm pretty good around parents. I just think of them how I'd think of a network executive."

That made Cora guffaw. "Network executives are probably easier to please. But my dad will be there and my siblings and some cousins too. I think it'll be so busy and full of people that she won't have the opportunity to be her normal self. But I have no doubt you're good with the ladies. I've seen it over and over."

Generally she found it more amusing than annoying, which was likely a good thing as she imagined it wasn't something that was going to go away anytime soon. Part of his image was that sexy charm. It worked on him and for him.

Rachel had been right. Beau was a grown-up and capable of handling himself. Cora would keep a close eye on the situation and, if necessary, extricate him from anything unpleasant.

"I know you're busy inside your head trying to figure out how to make this perfect," Beau said as they drove east. It amused him, yes. But mostly he was touched. Touched that she spent the energy worrying.

"I…can't deny that I want today to be a good day. Not perfect. Perfection is impossible unless we're talking about your shoulders. Because well, they're perfection. Otherwise, dealing with family is always far from perfect. My mom is a grab bag. You never quite know what you're going to get. She's not malicious, but she has her own way of seeing the world. A type of focus that makes her so successful at her work. But she's used to having her own way. Used to seeing herself as the center of all things."

He heard more self-consciousness in her tone when it came to her mother than anything else. He understood that down to his bones.

"As you can guess, my father had quite the personality. Magnetic. He's a leader in that very intense way only someone who leads a cult can be." He paused, realizing it was one of the first times he'd voluntarily used the term cult. "I'm used to being around people with very large and complicated personalities. Your mom is an artist. I'm an artist in a sense. And we both care about you. So. We'll muddle through."

She was quiet awhile as they drove, crossing the I-90 bridge and heading into Bellevue.

"Okay," she told him as they exited the freeway. "I'll do my best to keep her in line. But if she says or does something offensive and I'm not around, get my attention and I'll handle it."

He scoffed. "Nope. Look, you can't be my keeper too. I have to find my own way with them or they won't take me seriously. I want them to take me seriously."

"Why shouldn't they take you seriously? If they don't, they're assholes. You don't need to work so hard to receive basic respect when they've invited you into their home."

She was so outraged by the very idea that his own nervousness fled. He reached out to take her hand and bring it to his lips for a kiss.

"Let's not get ahead of ourselves. I'm handsome and charming and I make a good living. Most mothers love me," he teased.

Her reluctant smile made him glad.

"This is…your father's work, I suppose?" he asked as they pulled up a long road to the house. Gardens, greenery, all sorts of sweet spots with benches or water features, stretched as far as he could see.

"Yes. He likes to say this is his canvas. It changes from time to time. He putters and updates. Sometimes he does a sweeping redesign when the mood strikes. It's nice to come home to," Cora told him as she parked the car beside several others already there. "At the holidays I mean."

"I grew up living in a series of trailers and barely standing rental houses. This is pretty swank."

She paused as they headed up to the wide, inviting front porch. "It is. I'm sorry. Sometimes I do take it for granted. I appreciate what I have, and I work hard. But yeah, it's pretty swank and it was where I grew up so it seems normal to me."

Beau put an arm around her shoulders, pulling her to his side so he could kiss the top of her head. "I wasn't chiding you. Just admiring the property."

"Okay. I just want to be sure. You ready?" she asked before opening the front door.

"Let's do this."

Beau wasn't sure what he'd expected, but it wasn't the warm and nonfussy interior of the house. It smelled good, like a family dinner should smell. Bread and simmering meat, something rich and spicy seemed to embrace them as they entered a large family room.

A chorus of calls sounded as people began to notice their arrival. Beau recognized her brother and sister in a knot of what was most likely cousins. A pang hit, longing for those cousins who'd been close as siblings until he'd left and was excommunicated.

Cora brightened at his side but instead of moving

away on her own, she took his hand and tugged gently. "Come meet my family."

It was a maelstrom of noise. Of names and hands to shake. A few hugs and no small amount of curious looks. Her father came out from the kitchen, shaking his hand and clapping his upper arm.

"Welcome. Would you like something to drink?" he asked Beau with a smile and Beau understood why he and Walda clicked. John Silvera was charming. And the source of that same crinkly-eyed smile his youngest daughter wore on a regular basis.

"Yes, thanks." Together with Cora, they went into the kitchen. She grabbed him a soda, even pouring it over ice for him. He thanked her before taking a sip. "I don't know if Cora has told you or not, but I just bought a house in Magnolia. It's on just shy an acre and I'd love it if you could come out and give me an estimate on some landscape upgrades."

Her dad's face brightened, and then he began to pepper Beau with questions. Cora leaned against Beau's side as they spoke, chiming in here and there with ideas or suggestions.

He sensed her mother approaching and knew Cora and her father did too by the way their body language changed. But the smile John sent his wife was so full of love and recognition Beau couldn't help but like them both better.

"Hello, Mom." Cora turned to hug her mother and kiss one of her cheeks. "*Pai* and Beau are talking about gardens and I'm trying to figure out a way to steal some of that ham over there while he's engaged elsewhere."

Walda's expression was full of affection. "I'll get his attention so you can commit your theft." She winked at Cora, who grinned.

Walda gave Beau a once-over, and then smiled. Granting him some sort of acceptance, though it wasn't all the way through. She still had doubts and Beau could see it at the edges. He wasn't offended. Cora was special and he understood they wanted to protect her. He might have some colorful moments in his past, but he hadn't hid anything, most certainly not his feelings about Cora.

Her uncle came in to grab a beer, and then got into a very passionate discussion with Beau about dry rubs versus brines. Children came through, grabbing things to drink or snacks and before long, they were carrying bowls, plates and trays of food out to the massive table where everyone but the kids—who had their own table—got seated.

Her father said grace over the meal and like a switch had been flipped, the food began to make a slow circuit around as people began to pile their plates high.

"Will you be doing another series, Beau?" Beto asked.

"I hope so. I'm heading to New York early next month to meet with the network people so I can pitch my new idea," Beau told them.

"I find it interesting that when Cora decides to stop traveling with me, you come into her life and travel all the time," Walda said. "My daughter should wait around for you while you fly all over, surrounded by beautiful women who will tell you whatever you want to hear?"

"Mom, what the heck? That's out of line," Cora said, and Beau heard the disappointment there.

"It's all right," Beau told her before turning his attention to Walda. "The filming will be done here, in the house I just bought, so I'm fortunate I won't have to travel for work that often. I'm also fortunate Cora loves to travel for pleasure as much as I do, so we're hoping to get out there in the world within the next year."

He wanted to keep underlining to her that he wasn't going to get drawn into her games.

"That *is* fortunate," John said. "Tell us about what sort of theme, if you can."

BEAU DESCRIBED HIS show idea to her family, who, other than her mother, were interested and engaged, talking about their own lives and projects. Getting to know Beau because they could see he was different.

Walda was working Cora's last nerve though. Picking and sighing, giving looks down her nose and just being a dick.

Cora had to admit Beau was really good at handling her mother by redirecting her. Not letting her needle him. But it needled Cora. Big-time.

Which her mother doubtless knew.

Still, her father and siblings were being very sweet and helping keep Walda in line even as they nosily collected data about Beau. And he remained adorable and sexy as he dealt with it. Perhaps he was imagining her mother to be one of his crazed fans.

She snickered and Beau turned to her, a questioning look on his face. "I amused myself. Sorry," she told him.

"There's a story I'm very sure."

"There are millions of stories, Beau," she said in a mock serious tone.

"Damn, I am hurtling toward falling into all kinds of love with you," he murmured before brushing a kiss against her temple.

Touched and thrilled, she leaned into his touch, wanting him to know she was right there with him.

After dinner, Cora and her generation of cousins cleaned the kitchen and after portioning out leftovers, they put everything away and headed down into the basement, where her family had gathered.

A knot around the big television was in the process of getting a video game started. The card table was already full. Her father and uncle already teased one another and attempted trash talk. Her father was so silly, he failed terribly but all his taunts were wonderfully entertaining.

"I should have warned you to DVR any games you wanted to watch today," Cora told him.

"I can watch sports twenty-four hours a day. I'm here with you and your family. I'm slightly drowsy and wishing I'd worn sweats because I shouldn't have had that second helping of mashed potatoes and gravy."

He was trying. Not uncomfortably so. Slightly awkward on both his side and her family's. But it was the normal sort of awkward when someone brings a serious romantic interest to a family dinner.

"Let's avoid video games then. The little kids like the games where you have to jump around. Last year I had to tap out or lose my meal," Cora told him, aiming at the table where Finley sat with Beto. "What are we doing?" she asked as they sat.

"Beto won't let me play Monopoly anymore," her sister said with a glare at their brother.

"You bet your right to play it again away last year. I told you not to bet anything else and you would *not* stop. So we had to gang up on you so you had no choice but to forfeit your right to play it. You have a problem. You can't play that game and be calm," Beto told her with a shrug.

Beau snorted a laugh.

"Just because I'm passionate about it," Finley started in.

"Passionate? You throw things," Cora reminded her. "You get mean."

"Mean?" Beau murmured.

"You'd never guess this, but our sweet-natured, mellow Finley has no self-control when it comes to certain games. Just two or three. A few years ago she told our mom the scarf she was wearing made her look old."

"She lost her edge," Finley said with a shoulder raise. "Our mother is really intense and competitive so I knew I had to shake her up. It worked and I won."

They all laughed at that, Beau shaking his head at them.

Cora scanned the shelf of board games and reached out to grab Uno. "How about this? Fun. Fast paced. Not rage inducing."

"I've only played this a few times. No card games in Road to Glory households. But a friend's grandfather taught me a few. I'm always up for board games but only if you don't throw things at me or insult my scarf," Beau said.

Finley's startled laugh brought their mother's attention squarely to them once again.

Beau and her mother had done some complicated dance at dinner. She'd come in for an attack and he just flowed around her, deliberately not taking the bait. Walda had retreated but Cora knew it was only so she could watch her prey more closely to figure out her next steps.

"You look like you're thinking uncharitable things about Mom," Finley said in an undertone once she'd noted where Cora's attention had been.

"She's watching Beau so closely it's making me nervous. She's got that look about her." Cora kept an eye on her mother. She wasn't yet alarmed, but it paid to stay alert as Walda could go from zero to international incident in under fifteen minutes.

"Stop whispering. It's rude. If you're saying mean things you really need to share," Beto told them.

"Deal the cards and stop trying to start trouble," Cora told her brother.

After a few games of Uno, they moved on to Scrabble, which got *very* competitive so they created a game of insults where they had to use the words they played.

Beau soaked it all up in a way that told Cora board games weren't any more a part of his childhood than cards had been. But that kid in him seemed to shine right through him each time he rolled dice or played his turn.

Soaked it up in a way that meant she'd be setting up regular game nights once he got settled in his new house. Have friends over, or visit round-robin style to eat, catch up and play. They could all get to know Beau better that way too. See his sweeter side.

Cora wanted everyone to understand just what a sentimental, soft underbelly Beau had.

When they finally got out of there six hours later, she appreciated him more than she ever had before. He showed perfect manners. Gave her father the bottle of port on the way out the door and as far as Cora could judge such things, she felt he'd gone a long way at showing her family just what a very nice guy he was.

CHAPTER NINETEEN

BEAU PUTTERED AROUND the kitchen—his kitchen—
as be began the preparations for a post-Thanksgiving
Thanksgiving dinner with Cora. As the actual holiday
had been so busy for everyone and he'd been dealing
with his move, Beau had proposed they postpone a
big holiday meal until he had his furniture and was
all moved in.

So there he was, getting things prepped and watching her slide in her socks across the wood floors in his
dining room, giggling like a child as she did.

It was quite honestly a moment he figured would
be burned into his memory. How happy she was! She
filled his life with silliness and laughter as well as fantastic sex and a lot of great art.

"I'm glad the floors meet your very high standards,"
he told her as she slid past on her way to the coffee
maker where she topped up his mug and got one for
herself before making some toast.

"These are great for sliding, no lie." She moved to
the island, putting her mug down. "Hey, what's that?"

He turned to follow her out toward the front door,
which she flung open and headed out into the snow
that had started to fall.

"Cora, wait a second," he called to her, not knowing what might have caught her attention enough to have her run out in her socks and no coat.

When he skidded around a low bank of bushes, he saw her sitting back on her haunches, a hand stretched out to a shivering mound of dirty fur he realized was a dog.

"Hi there," she crooned. "I know he's super tall but I'll tell you a secret, he's a big old softie who'd never in a million years hurt a dog." Without turning to him she said, "Do you have any towels or old blankets? You had some from the move I put in your garage. Can you bring some so I can wrap her or him up? Maybe some cheese to give our friend some calories."

Within a few minutes, he'd gathered everything and returned to her side. If he thought she'd have a hard time getting the little stray into her arms he'd have been wrong. Nope, the little fuzz ball knew a good thing when he saw it and came right to her and into the blanket.

Beau held his arms out to take the dog while she changed into the dry socks he'd brought for her.

"No tags but she doesn't look like she's been out on the street a long time. She was someone's not too very long ago. I'll get her cleaned up and fed, and then check the shelters around here," Cora said as she handed a piece of cheese over.

"I'm home during the days so she can hang with me. No use taking her to the shelter unless she has an owner looking for her," Beau said before he'd in-tended to. He'd had cats before but a dog was a different kind of pet ownership. He hadn't thought himself ready for that.

But Cora? Beau watched her with the scrappy little terrier mix and knew he was not only ready for it, he *wanted* it. With her. Cora had brought up wanting a dog a few times over the last few months, and while he hated the idea of this little dog being abandoned, Cora was already invested in the little pup. And he couldn't help but hope the fur ball could be hers. Theirs.

She gave the dog a bath in the sink in his laundry room as Beau got the turkey into the oven. By the time she came back out, he barely recognized their new friend. "I cut her hair too because there were some snarls, and then it looked off balance so I kept adjusting. But she's very chill. Just hung out in the sink. Didn't try to jump out or anything. I promise I'll wash everything up. I know you just bought this very nice home without dog hair on the furniture."

Beau liked the little dog already, but seeing her squirm happily in Cora's arms, licking Cora's face only made him love the damned thing. He could give this to her. If not their furry guest, there were other dogs that needed a home. Other dogs that could make his Cora giggle and dance around singing.

And he was deep enough in love with Cora to be mercenary in the sense that he'd use a dog to lure her around as often as possible. In fact, he bet the dog would be just as happy as he was to have Cora around.

"I'm going to run out to get some doggie supplies," Cora said, setting the dog down. "A bed. Some food.

Keep an eye on that turkey and I'll be back as soon as possible."

After she kissed Beau, she smooched the dog's head and ran out the door.

The dog looked to the door and then back to Beau, deciding to settle just out of the way but still close enough to see if food might be involved.

"Okay, dog, so here's the thing, she just kissed you. I think she likes you. And I like her. She smells good and she's a great snuggler. So we're going to look for your owners because I'm not a fucking monster and maybe there's some sweet little kid crying because they miss you. If so, we'll have to hand you over and I'll spend my time trying to find a really cute little mutt with a lot of terrier in her genes."

He got a bark in reply that he took for an acceptance of the facts.

"But if I can be totally honest, dog, I'm sort of hoping we can keep you. You make my human very happy and making her happy is sort of my job. I think we might be able to come to an accommodation."

CORA CAME BACK to find Beau on the couch with the dog in his lap, hand-feeding her what looked like some egg. He'd been talking to her as he did it and she looked up with her pretty, big doggie eyes full of adoration. Cora was pretty sure she had that expression with him sometimes too and not only when he fed her cheese or eggs.

It was sweet enough that her ovaries pulsed a time or two, and when they both noticed her, the dog gave a version of the smile the human did.

Cora held up the things she'd procured. "I got more than I needed, I'm sure. But whatever."

The *clickity-clack* of nails sounded as the dog jumped down and scampered over to where Cora busily unpacked and set up the things she'd bought.

"I talked to your closest neighbors on the way home just now. They both said our gal got left behind when some people moved and she's been sticking around the area for the last few months. They've all tried to catch her but she won't get close enough. They had been feeding her. Even tried to contact the people who left but they won't reply. Assholes." She bent to look the dog in the eyes and got a lick. "You don't seem like a skulky type to me. I'm guessing none of those people appealed to you but you saw how handsome and sweet the new guy on the street was and you decided you wanted to live here."

Beau snorted in the background but Cora wasn't fooled. "You're the one who volunteered up front for her to hang out with you during the day, remember? I'll obviously share in the doggie parenting duties and I'm going to want to get her chipped and licensed and make sure her shots are up-to-date and all that stuff."

He tried to keep a straight face, hold the nonchalant dude mask in place. But it didn't work because their furry dog child farted and ruined the moment by making her nearly gag.

"No more deviled eggs for you," Beau told the dog, making Cora guffaw.

Cora fanned a hand in front of her nose but the

dog kept getting in her face to give kisses and get some love.

"You've been lonely haven't you, baby?" she asked as the dog settled into her lap. "You can live in our pack, okay? We need a name because I can't keep thinking of you as the dog. No one knew your name and we don't need to name you after the garbage family who abandoned you."

"So we're all in?" Beau asked her, a smile on his face that told her he certainly was. In more ways than one.

"We know she was left and that people tried to contact her previous owners. We know she's been out on her own for at least four months. I don't want to take her to a shelter. I like her face and she has a sweet disposition. I want her to be in our family."

Beau leaned over to kiss her quickly. "I like you saying that. Our family. Yeah. So. A name." He looked at the dog closely. "What do you think? Sally? Molly?"

The dog remained unimpressed.

"Sandy? Curly?" Cora asked. "No. None of those. Peaches? Cookie?"

They went back and forth with names as Cora set up one of the—three—beds in the little nook next to the kitchen. She'd be out of the way but also be part of the action when the humans were cooking.

"We'll eat in about three hours so I made some little bites to tide us over," Beau said as he pulled several containers from the fridge and she tried to pretend her mouth wasn't watering just looking at the stuff he'd prepared.

"Yum." Cora popped a meatball into her mouth and tried not to get sucked in by puppy dog eyes. "The guy at the pet supply store recommended a certain kind of food so that's what I got. I also bought food bowls but they're temporary because I don't like them all that much and I think they'll make your beautiful sleek house look janky."

When Beau bit into an empanada, the dog flopped onto her back and gave him a come-hither look.

Which is how Jezebel, Jezzy for short, came about.

"I should tell you not to get attached until we get Jez into the vet and all that. But I can see I'd be wasting my breath," Beau said.

"Like I didn't just walk in to find her on your chest while you hand-fed her deviled eggs?"

He blushed. "She was hungry. Eggs have protein!"

"And since you made them, they also had some shaved ahi tuna and a little scallion."

"No need to act as if we have no civilized manners, Cora."

That made her laugh and hug him while Jezzy shoved herself between them, wriggling for love and attention.

"If that means all the deviled eggs you make are fancy gourmet ones I'm all in with your idea of civilization."

She set the table as he began to assemble what she thought to be an excessive amount of sides, but again, she wasn't complaining because everything he made was fantastic and all she had to do was watch him cook for her.

Cora realized her life was pretty freaking perfect. And now she had a dog. One she suspected she'd have to share with her boyfriend, but that was all right too.

Her phone had buzzed twice that afternoon. Once it had been Maybe, checking in and letting Cora know her dress for Rachel's wedding had arrived and there was a fitting the following morning. The other had been her mother, asking a question she knew the answer to.

"What's up?" Beau asked her when she made a face as she listened to her voice mail.

"Walda gotta Walda."

He snorted a laugh and raised his glass of wine. "And Cora gotta Cora. Go on and return the call."

She'd been considering not doing it. Just ignoring her until she got the damned message that Cora wasn't her keeper anymore. But Walda was getting older and what if there was a problem of some sort?

"I'll take Jezzy outside to do her business while I do it."

He tossed her one of his hoodies, which hit her at the knees but it smelled like him and it was warm so she headed out, Jezzy excitedly scampering around, sniffing things, peeing and moving on to the next thing to sniff.

"Hi there," she said when her mom answered.

"Why do you have your phone if you don't even answer it when you get a call? Did you screen me out like I was a salesperson?"

So she was getting that version of her mother apparently. Cora couldn't win with that one and she was having a really good day so she had zero plans to let that get ruined. "I imagine you called for a reason other than yelling at me. If not, I'm actually in the middle of something so I'll be going."

"My new assistant doesn't know I don't like the childproof caps on my medicine. Your father had to open my blood pressure medication yesterday."

"Fair enough. Let's make sure Lilah checks in with you about this. She's the person who should be picking up your pills, not Gina." Gina was the new assistant they'd hired and Lilah was the house manager. Naturally her mother must have insisted on something and it got done wrong and so now she was able to complain. Really, her mom should give Gina a bonus for allowing her something to bitch about.

"You never mixed that up," her mother said.

"Years of learning. I'm sure Lilah will be fine once she knows your rules. And it's a good reminder to you to make your preferences known in advance so everyone can do what you expect. It's easier when we know what those expectations are."

"It's easier when you do it. You know how it all works. No one does things wrong when you're in charge," her mother told her.

"It's easier for you, yes. But not for me. Mom. I can't just be your keeper. I have more in my life to do. To see and experience. My life can't be about making your life better. It just can't. It doesn't mean I don't love you. You know I do. But you need to give Lilah and Gina a chance to learn you."

Because Cora wasn't going back. No matter how much her mother sabotaged her new staff.

Being at the gallery these last few months had strengthened her resolve. She knew it had been the right choice and even though Walda was unhappy at that point, she could get the hell over it and enjoy having two people running her life for her.

"Maybe if I give them a nice car," her mother said.

"Perhaps they'd tell you what I did—don't buy it if you plan to lord it over them for the rest of time. That's not how gifts work."

Her mom remained silent, understanding the rebuke in Cora's words.

"Okay, I'm going to hang up now. Be sure to let Lilah know to contact the pharmacy to have them add to your record to not use childproof caps. I love you. Say hi to Dad."

Cora waited for her mother to say she loved her too before disconnecting.

Jezzy dropped a stick twice her size at Cora's feet. "Look at you, overachiever."

"You two come inside. It's cold out there and I just made some hot chocolate," Beau called.

Jezzy cast one last look at the stick and Cora before heading to Beau.

"The dog knows what's good," Cora told him before grabbing his cheeks in her hands and giving him a kiss.

"Everything all right?"

"Yes. She's just having trouble letting go so she's using things to get my attention. I just need to keep her on track and to not let her see me react."

He frowned and she nearly coaxed him to share, but she didn't want to have to do that. He'd share—hopefully—when and if he wanted.

"Come on. I put whiskey in your hot chocolate."

She took the hand he held out. "You're perfect."

Beau shook his head. "Cora, it's you who is perfect."

He pulled her close and Jezzy yipped, dancing around as they hugged.

"Give me chocolate and booze. The surest way to make me easy," she teased.

"Always happy to keep you easy when it comes to me."

"In case you haven't noticed, it's really not that difficult to get me naked."

"You have many fine qualities," he said, stealing a kiss.

"You make me laugh," she confessed. "Not as an insult, but a compliment," she added quickly. "Being with you makes me happy."

"That is most definitely a compliment." He put his hands at her waist, and then dragged her up his body.

She wrapped her legs around him, sighing happily when he backed her against the wall and held her there with the weight of his body.

"Just so we're clear, this also makes me happy." She slid her palms all over his shoulders and biceps.

"Handy."

He kissed her then. Slow and sweet. At his feet, Jezzy sighed heavily like she couldn't possibly believe they were kissing again.

Grabbing her by a double handful of her ass, he easily carried them both into the bedroom. They nearly fell when Jezzy got too near Beau's feet, but laughing, they managed to make it to his newly made bed, where they collapsed in a tangle of arms and legs, mouths fused together in a kiss that sent a hot flush through her like wildfire.

Every time. He rocketed her from zero to melting with seemingly little effort. This was what it meant to be a match for another person. That nearly tangible click of recognition and connection.

When Rachel and Maybe had said their men were different from the others, Cora had understood. Or thought she had. But this sort of thing was so much more than she ever could have imagined. How could she have known what this felt like when she simply had nothing to compare it with until that very moment?

And now that she had it, she knew to her toes that living without it would be awful. She tried not to worry about losing it, tried not to think about what would happen if they broke up. She'd survive, no doubt. People did every day. But now that she had this thing with Beau, she knew she'd forever feel its absence.

One armed, she managed to pull her shirt up and off while he got his pants unbuckled and unzipped. Jezzy howled at the door she'd been left on the other side of.

"Jesus," Beau snarled, and sat up.

She snickered as she tossed her pants at him. "Let her in. She's scared to be alone."

"She's just fine but she wants to be in here with us. I don't like being watched having sex," Beau told her once he'd gotten out of bed and went to open the door.

He pointed at a pillow he'd taken off his bed and the dog, knowing this was a good deal, hopped up onto it, circled three times and heaved a doggie sigh when she finally settled, her head on her paws.

Grinning like a hot pirate, he grabbed a condom, ripped it open and rolled it on all as he made his way to the bed. "Now, I think we were in the middle of something," he murmured, his mouth skating over the skin of her throat, down to her collarbone and across. He traced her ink with deft touches of his fingertips as his lips and then the edge of his teeth met her nipple.

Pleasure speared outward from her nipple as she sighed, fingers sliding into his hair to hold him there.

He chuckled in that way, that *I know I'm about to have you* way she found so very sexy.

Rolling, he settled beneath her as she scrambled up to straddle his waist and all she wanted was for him to be in her.

Grabbing him at the root, she held him still as she slowly sank down his cock. Going very still once he was all the way inside.

Once she began to rock, grinding herself against him, Jezzy decided it'd be awesome to jump up onto the bed, but it was a tall bed for a big dude and it took her three times but she made it and marched right up to attempt to sit on Beau's chest.

"Aw, jeez. Way to ruin the moment," she said as Beau twisted to set the dog back on the floor with a gentle admonishment to stay down.

"Stop saying ruined." Beau rolled his hips to emphasize just how in the moment he still was. "Let's just keep this going."

Laughing, she leaned down to kiss him, snarling and groaning as he dragged his short, blunt nails down her back, and then yanked her hips forward.

He held her there, bent over his body as he thrust up into her over and over. Slow at first until she got caught up in the nearly magical rhythm, and then he sped slightly, building the pressure, that need to climax deep in her belly.

And that was before he shifted to slide a hand between them, his fingertips brushing against her clit and sending her nearly hurtling over the edge just from that touch.

More.

She must have said it out loud, though she hadn't intended to.

He gave her more. Thrusting deeper. Harder as he increased the pressure of his fingertips.

There was nothing to do but try not to leave too permanent a mark when she bit into the meat of his pectoral muscles as orgasm slapped into her and then over him as he continued moving for several long moments more.

"Damn. You made me a turkey. Gave our dog a home and made me come all in one afternoon. I feel like I need a daily affirmation about you so I can be partially worthy."

He laughed as he stumbled to the adjoining bathroom for a few minutes. Jezzy had commando crawled from the pillow to the bed and looked up at Cora with pitiful eyes until she patted the bed.

"I can see spoiling is going to be an issue." Beau tossed her sweater and she pulled it on, along with her underpants.

"She was abandoned, Beau. Humans she should have been able to trust have betrayed and harmed her. And then she was all alone. Probably confused. She needs spoiling. Like you do." Cora scratched behind Jezzy's ears.

He'd been abandoned too. Lost people he should have been able to trust to have his best interests at heart. So if a little spoiling helped and made them both feel loved and cared for? She'd damned well do it.

"How lucky then that she and I have you to spoil us," Beau told her with a kiss to her forehead and then to Jezzy's. "We didn't spoil animals when I was growing up. They were for working. My father has a very low opinion of sentiment, especially for beings he doesn't consider to have souls, which is everything but humans. So. This is new. But it seems okay to me. Except for the interrupting sex part. We're going to need to work on that," he told the dog, who licked his face.

Cora was quite sure it was she who was the lucky one in the arrangement.

CHAPTER TWENTY

"FOR REAL, JEZZY, you are the bestest dog in the world," Maybe crooned to the dog in her lap.

"Cutest, for sure," Rachel said.

"Right? Doesn't that sweater look freaking adorable?" Cora asked.

"I guess we're going to ignore the fact that you knitted a sweater for a dog?" Vic asked.

Beau snorted a laugh but said nothing else.

"I had yarn left from the sweater I knitted the baby," she told Vic, who blushed. "I like to knit and she's clearly a shorter-haired terrier mix because once the groomer cleaned her up she gets a little shivery when it's cold. It was easy enough to make in two days. Are you saying she should freeze, Vicktor? Monster." Cora winked at him.

Rachel snatched the dog from her sister and Cora decided not to inform them that Beau had fed Jezzy an entire can of those gross sausages that smelled like dog food. Cute though Jezzy was, she also farted like a demon, and then pretended it wasn't her.

The whole crew was over at Beau's place for a housewarming dinner and they'd settled on the couches in the living room. The fire warmed the space and gave it such a pretty glow. Jezzy had gotten over her initial shyness and the terrier had taken over, sending her to all the new humans in her house, sniffing and charming, getting lots of snuggles and belly rubs.

"You're getting married a week from today. That's bonkers. Everything okay? Can I run any errands or help doing anything else?" Cora asked Rachel and Vic.

"It's all in place. We kept it simple on purpose. Food is handled. Service is handled. Because it's freaking Christmas, there were so many awesome decorations to be grabbed, so we're all good for that and most of it was on sale and we can use it next year." Rachel nodded like everyone had that level of calm when they had barely any time to plan a wedding while they were suffering from morning sickness.

Small. Intimate. Something for only very close friends and family that would be more like a Christmas Eve dinner and party than anything else. And because the Russian Orthodox church didn't celebrate their Christmas until January, Rachel and Vic weren't stepping on anyone's toes or offending anyone with a December 24 ceremony.

"When you're feeling better and once the wedding is in the rearview, Beau and I would love to host a dinner for you two either here or at Luna," Cora said. Beau smiled her way. He'd been so awesome to offer that up. A wonderful, very personal gift from them to her best friend and her husband.

"Oh! I hope you don't think I'll try to refuse such a lovely gift. Because I've come to be very spoiled by your amazing cooking and what has turned out to be a really fantastic pipeline to one of the region's top restaurateurs." Rachel kept her tone deadpan but Beau understood it was a tease and took it as such.

"To be fair, you're my bread pipeline so it's sort of mutual," he said.

"Heading into the kitchen. Anyone want me to bring something back?" Cora asked them as she stood.

"I'll help you bring it all." Maybe popped up. "This house is gorgeous," she said once they began to assemble all the various drinks people had requested.

"Right? I love it. And Jezzy prefers it here to my place. Which I can't really take personally as I prefer it here to my place because it's wide-open and bright and sleek and the view is awesome."

Before he'd moved, they'd slept at her place most of the time. But ever since he closed on the house, they'd spent most of their time there. Her cozy little town house seemed cramped with him and the dog in it. And Jezzy couldn't really run around off leash though she had a small area around her town house she could technically call a yard. But at the house they had a big yard. And very tall ceilings and heated floors. She'd even found a new favorite local grocery store and the wine guy there was awesome.

"You think it's too soon," Cora said, not really that worried her friend would agree.

Maybe scoffed. "Are you fucking kidding me? I think it's perfect because you're both totally into each other. Also? Alexsei pretty much moved into my house a few months after we started dating. He never moved out. Your dog is also perfect. What do you think of his art?"

Cora laughed, delighted that her friend got her so well. "He's got good taste. I mean, thank god, because it might have been a deal breaker. Even better is that he's tasked me with helping him flesh out his collection. It's like my birthday every day."

Beau gave her a puzzled look when she came back with Maybe, giggling up a storm. She just smiled serenely.

"You're all coming to the New Year's Eve party my parents are hosting, right?" Cora asked them.

In addition to the November family dinner, Cora's mom and dad always held a big party on New Year's Eve at the gallery with great food and drinks. Her father's clients and her mother's business associates came and it was quite the evening. This year she'd be going with Beau at her side. The first time she'd ever brought a date.

She'd let her mother have control of the event, even though it was at the gallery. It was her parents' night and it gave her pleasure to help make it successful. In turn, her mother had seen it as the olive branch it was and had eased back some of her manic need to control everything.

As Beau had said, little steps added up over time and all she could do was her best.

"Totally. Your parents throw a great shindig. Plus it's over by ten so we can go watch fireworks from your place."

Another thing they did was to hang out in the courtyard at her town house for the countdown fireworks at the Space Needle. Her porch was perfect and they brought out blankets and booze to bring in the new year.

This time so much was different. She'd taken over at the gallery. She'd met Beau and fallen in love. Jezzy had come into her life and she and Beau were learning how to be better pet owners and to only spoil her in the good ways.

Mainly it worked but those eyes were hard to resist when she wanted just a little taste of whatever Cora or Beau were eating. Then again, Beau thought she hadn't known about the Vienna sausage thing, but for goodness' sake, it wasn't like he ever had them in the pantry before they got a dog. Plus the smell, good god.

But someone he'd known had given them to their dog as a treat and he'd remembered, introducing them to Jezzy, who apparently adored them. Enough for Cora to ignore the gas and find it cute.

The sight of Beau with Jezzy on his lap, blissfully happy with the petting and loving she was getting made Cora pause and only barely withhold a pleased sigh.

Giant and strong but always gentle. Especially with those smaller than he was, or vulnerable.

She handed over his root beer and took her place next to him.

BEAU LOOKED AT his phone and excused himself. "Gotta take this. Come on, Jez. Wanna go outside?"

He knew she'd come out with him. Even though it was chilly, the dog loved the yard. Her kingdom, as she'd come to consider it. She seemed to have an endless love of playing fetch and he had to admit he loved to play along with her.

Once he was out of earshot of the crew in the house, he called Ian. "Tell me exactly what happened," Beau said when his friend answered.

The uppermost yard was large and level. He'd had it fenced off so Jezzy would be safe out there. So he flipped on the main lights so she could see for a game of fetch and tossed the bright green ball she loved so much.

Ian said, "Some dude comes in and leaves an envelope for me. Says it's a contract I need to see. There was a clipboard for a signature but the hostess who signed for it doesn't remember a specific name of a delivery service but it wasn't any of our normal ones. Leaves after a thank-you."

Beau listened while he tossed the ball Jezzy had just dropped at his feet.

"I didn't see it for several hours until my dinner break when I cruised by the back office and it was on my desk. Inside there was another envelope with your name on it. That's where the letter is tucked."

Beau swapped out the slobbery green ball for the pink one and Jezzy barked her excitement. When he turned to look into the house, Cora was laughing, listening to something Wren was saying. In their house. Oh sure, he hadn't asked her to move in just yet because he didn't want to spook her. And the fact was, they spent most nights together anyway.

He had something real. Something he could see lasting. A dog. A group of friends who all had a positive influence on his life.

His old life would not destroy what he was creating in Seattle. It would not touch Cora more than it already had. She deserved laughter and a life full of the things she wanted most. She'd just gotten away from her mother and he wasn't going to drag any more drama into her life.

He had promises to keep. He would continue this search for his children until he found them or he died. He would help when he could. But his past would not own his future.

"Read me the letter," Beau asked.

"'Someone in your family is gravely ill but The Anointed won't grant permission for treatment. Specifics to follow. Don't ignore your phone.'"

Ian sighed. "Nothing else. No signature. It's been printed on generic printer paper."

Beau blew out a breath. "Thanks. I'm sorry this bled into the restaurant."

"Shut up, asshole. I'm in this with you. Always have been. Keep your phone on, I guess. How'd they get your number and why not just call it instead of doing all this cloak-and-dagger shit?"

"My uncle Obie has my old number. I have a phone just for that. The last contact I had used that phone too, but not on the first few contacts. Maybe they're watching me to see how I react or they read spy novels under the covers at night and hope they don't get caught. Perhaps they're jerks who like messing with

me," Beau said. "Since I can't be certain which phone
they might mean, I'll keep them both on me."

Ian said, "Okay. Good idea. Pops says he's having
you and Cora over for lunch. Invited me as well but I
said I'd run that by you first."

"Why would I not want you there? Cora likes you.
I thought you liked her?"

"I do. I just know my grandpa is important to you
and you want to present Cora to him for his approval.
I didn't want to get in the middle of that."

Beau had really good friends.

"Thanks. Yeah, I suppose I am presenting her to
him. Like, hey, look at this beautiful thing I managed
to get right. But you're part of that. Cora knows you're
like my brother. She knows Pops is like a father to me.
She'd probably appreciate your being there because
she'll at least know you. Take a little bit of the pressure off. At least he won't act like a fool at dinner like
her mother did."

Beau was trying really hard to like Walda. He had
no trouble when it came to John and Cora's siblings.
But her mother, while admirable in many ways, was
really fucking entitled when it came to Cora's time
and energy.

Ian made an unhappy sound at the mention. Beau
had shared the details with his friend a few days after
that dinner and he'd been upset on Cora's behalf.

"You want to drive up with us?" Beau asked. "We're
bringing Jezzy. Your grandfather demanded it and who
am I to refuse that?"

"I'll let you know for sure once we get closer to that

day. I'll bring the letter to you tomorrow. I need to get back to work."

They said their goodbyes and Beau tucked his phone into a back pocket before calling the dog. "Come on. It's too cold to be out here any longer. Plus your mom keeps looking out the window at you."

A girl and her dog.

She lit up when he opened the door and Jezzy raced over to her, jumping up into her lap and giving her lots of kisses.

Fortunately she'd given him a happy smile and would let him lick her anywhere he liked when they were alone so he had no reason to be jealous of the dog.

"Everything all right?" Cora asked him after everyone had left.

"It was Ian. Among other things he said to pass on his hello and said he'd be coming to lunch with us when we go up to Pops'."

It wasn't as if he liked not sharing everything with her. But at that point when he really had no new details that she needed to hear, he figured he could spare her any stress. If and when something major happened, he'd share the information then.

"Oh good! It's always nice to see him."

"If you stay over I'll drive you to work in the morning," he said.

"You really don't have to do that. My car is here. I can drive."

"I know. But I like to. I like taking care of you. Ian and I are going produce shopping shortly after you need to be there anyway. So it's not out of my way." Even if it was, he'd have taken her.

With the second contact, he'd been reminded about how much better he felt when she was there with him. In his house that had a top-of-the-line security system. And just a few days prior, they'd finished construction on a gate at the front. Mail and packages could be delivered but it wasn't easy to come into the front yard unless you were supposed to be there.

Her town house didn't have that. And they knew where she was. Sometimes that brought sick dread to his gut.

He couldn't make her totally safe from all dangers but he could do all he could without going overboard. And he did get obsessed fans who inevitably found out where he lived so the gate and security system kept *him* safer too.

"Twist my arm. I suppose I'll make the sacrifice and sleep over where there's awesome sex on tap and a very well-stocked kitchen. Jezzy likes it better here anyway. She barked at The Hugger after he took her stick and he gave me a lecture about noise. *They* listen to Foghat and get drunk in their hot tub! At eleven at night! The. Nerve."

"The guy is a total tool. You know," he said, "you could move in here." He'd planned to say that in February, not the end of December. "The dog is here most of the time anyway. You have your own closet that's just as big as mine. It's not walking distance from the gallery, which is a drawback. But it's fifteen minutes and I'm always happy to drive you. I like having you here.

I like your things in the bathroom and you and your friends watching movies in the living room. I love you, Cora. You're all I never knew I wanted because how could I even have known such a thing existed? I know it's early and you're probably worried. But I'm all in."

She looked at him long enough that he began to wonder if he should try to rein some of it back in. Ease off until she was ready.

"You said you loved me."

He nodded. "I do. Probably should have waited a while. I'd meant to. Like make it romantic, tell you on Valentine's Day and then ask you to move in. But I don't want to wait that long. I want to tell you now and have you live with me now. Jezzy wants that too."

The latter barked when she heard her name.

"I've loved people before. Not romantic love, though until you, I thought the fondness I'd felt was something closer to love than it really was. Because now that I have you and I know what love is capable of being. I love you too. And I have for pretty much a month at least but I've been telling myself it was too fast but." She shrugged. "Whatever the case. I know what's real. And if you're cool with me living here, then okay. I'll need to handle my town house. Maybe I'll rent it out."

It hit him then that he'd just made the biggest commitment in his life. Yes he'd been married in the eyes of the church but he'd been a kid. This was a woman he planned to grow old with. He chose her. Every day, multiple times a day, he chose her and chose what would be best for her or for them.

This was the next step on his journey and now he

had a partner at his side. Now he believed he was worthy of the kind of happiness he'd begun to experience on a regular basis.

"You've done more for my brain than years of therapy," he said as he watched her let the dog out to do her business.

"How so?"

"I'm happy and I'm not sabotaging it. I like it. I want more."

"Probably the therapy loosened you up, like when someone tries to get a jar open and someone else takes it and pops that sucker right away."

When the dog came back inside, he locked up while she got a nighttime yummy for Jezzy and they all headed into the bedroom.

"How do you think your family will react?" he asked her once they'd settled into bed. Jezzy didn't much like the crate they'd bought, but she slept just fine in the bed in the corner of the room near the heater vent.

"Beto will be supportive immediately. He knows me best in my family so I won't get any of that too soon stuff from that direction. Finley will keep a close eye on you. But she'll respect my choice and they both really do like you. My dad likes you too but I'm his youngest kid. He's going to think I'm blinded by lust and jumping the gun. But he'll be supportive overall. It's who he is. My grandparents are like mega super Catholic but I don't see them often because they live in Central California so there's no need to tell them and break my Gigi's heart because I'm living in sin."

"Walda?"

"She's going to find a reason to pick. It's what she does. She does like you."

Beau scoffed.

"No really. She does. Believe me when I tell you that if my mother does not like you, you'll know it. She has never made a secret of her dislike of anyone or anything. Trust me. You're a fucking catch. She knows it. And she can see I am totally into you."

"So what's there to complain about?"

"Well, first, it's more than just the actual subject of the complaint. It's the act of complaining that makes it like a cigarette after sex for her. Or chocolate and a glass of wine. So if I were to guess—and keep in mind she's a wild card so it could be anything—I'd say she'll bring up how I'm no longer within walking distance of the gallery. How I took it away from her but now I'm already tossing it aside for my boyfriend."

He sucked in a breath. "My dad's narcissism is similar. He assumes authority like she does. He'd say something like I should be spending my energy on serving him and through him, God. But really it was a way to get people to fulfill his needs. Emotionally and physically. Will she get over it? Any insight helps."

"Part of this is just who she is. So she's not actually trying to be bitchy and complain. It's just part of how she sees things. She puts so much passion into her music and art. Fire. But in her life she can also be negative. It's her personality. The darkness that balances all the light in her work, I suppose."

"You have a lot of insight," he told her, kissing her shoulder and settling deeper under the blankets.

"You grew up with a personality like hers so you know you learn how to live around it. I don't want you to think I'm complaining. Yes, her behavior can be a total pain in the ass. She can be self-centered and all about herself. But she's also really fun. And interesting. Her work is fantastic. When she's not getting herself into trouble or making people cry, she's the type who will take her kids to picnics in the park. I've eaten bread and sipped wine on the banks of the Seine with her as we had heated debates about what our favorite piece we'd seen in this or that gallery on any given day. She was a super fun mom when she wasn't a super distracted mom. She's not mean. She loves her family. She's just… Yes, she'll get over it. And she'll still complain five years from now, just so you know."

He liked that she saw the two of them together years from then.

"Well. My biological family thinks we'll be going to hell. But if it's any consolation, they already thought that about me when I left. But my friends, especially the ones who know you, will think this is great because they know I wouldn't do this lightly."

"We have a dog now. We need to work and stay together so she doesn't have to suffer through her parents breaking up," Cora told him sleepily. "You love me," she sighed happily.

"I really do, Cora. I really do. And you love a mug like me." Miracles did happen. She was his.

"I do, Beau. I really do."

CHAPTER TWENTY-ONE

We're supposed to love hard.
That's why we're here.
Love like you were born for it

CORA WALKED AN already-leash-trained Jezzy around
Rachel and Maybe's neighborhood with her friends
at her side. She wanted to tell them her good news in
person so it had been agony to wait the three days to
see them.

"Who is the bestest girl?" she called to Jezzy, who
pranced just a little bit more.

"I can't believe someone would just toss her out.
She's such a sweet dog! Who does that?" Maybe said.

"Garbage people, that's who. She's potty trained,
great on a leash, sweet and obedient. Though she tries
to steal my man. Can't really blame her though," Cora
joked. "So. I'm moving into his place. Oh, and he told
me he loved me."

"Wow! Wow, wow." Rachel turned to hug Cora and
Maybe threw her arms around them both.

She told them the story while Jezzy sniffed things,
peed when necessary to leave a calling card.

"I'm assuming you're happy or you'd have told us

differently. Congratulations. I think this is a very good step for you both," Maybe said. "I'm thrilled. Or all three of you since you have Her Majesty now."

"Have you told your parents yet? Your siblings?" Rachel asked as they resumed their walk.

"Not yet. I will but you know how it goes. I want to present it right while letting them know it's my choice and I already made it as an adult. Everyone will be all right, but as usual, Walda is the wild card. I think she likes Beau. And I know she's happy to see me happy even if she has difficulty expressing it. I told Beau if she didn't like him, everyone would know and that's the truth. But that doesn't mean she won't make it into a big deal if the idea appeals to her."

"If you need a big mom type reaction with hugs and excitement, tell Irena. She'll be happy for you," Rachel said of her mother-in-law-to-be.

"I'm holding that in reserve for that very reason," Cora told them both with a laugh. After a bit of silence she added, "Things are wonderful right now I'm trying not to worry about the other shoe dropping."

Rachel took her free hand a moment and squeezed. "I understand. It's okay to be wary. This is your future and your heart and obviously Maybe and I are just fine with your being careful with them. But you deserve this man looking at you like you hung the moon. You deserve to be treated with kindness and respect and also like you're hotter than fire. That's Beau. Let yourself be happy but remember not to lose your head."

"Pregnancy has made her wiser than usual," Maybe said. "But she's right. If he fucks up, we'll descend on him like furies. I think he gets that. I think *you* get that. Love is good, right? Let yourself have it."

"His house is really safe," Rachel told her. "I checked the grounds out and his security system. The gate around the front access point is very wise. I don't like it that the letter to him showed up at your town house. You're far more exposed there. Another plus to moving in with Beau. Do you need help with getting stuff moved?"

"Why? If I do, are you, the woman getting married in just a few days who also happens to be knocked up, going to heft boxes? I'm sure Vic will be just fine with that idea." Cora rolled her eyes at her friend's re-action to his pregnant wife being part of any moving crew at that point.

"Maybe and I know a lot of wild bearded Russians. I was volunteering them," Rachel explained. "Vic barely lets me out of his sight at this point, so no, I don't think I'll be helping you take your bed apart or hefting all your books."

Beau's stuff was a lot nicer than hers so she wasn't that worried about her furniture. But she'd never leave her books behind. In fact, she was thinking about floor-to-ceiling built-in bookcases in what had been a formal living room near the master at the back of the house. They didn't need a formal living room. But a library would be perfect.

"I think I might rent my town house. See if the renters want a lot of the furniture left there. Then I can finish paying my mortgage and have it for my old age. Or if and when I have a kid who needs to go to college. It's not like Beau will take money from me. I offered and he just looked at me before saying, *Why would you do that? I'm rich. I don't need it.* He then sexed me up so hard I forgot to argue with him." Cora smiled at that memory.

"Ugh. You are such a filthy whore," Maybe said with a snicker.

"I'm a flawed individual, absolutely," Cora agreed. "The power of good dick I guess."

After they'd all stopped laughing, Cora added, "I'm so grateful for you two. To have you to share all the good stuff—and the bad stuff too—has been such a great part of my life. I don't know what I'd have done without your support and love."

Rachel's laughter shot into tears and sniffles. "Damn this pregnancy hormone stuff! I cry at everything now. Cotton commercials? Check. The bartender at Whiskey Sharp brought me water with lemon slices because that helps with my nausea and I legit burst into tears. If I'm like this and the wee sprocket is still a tenant in my uterus, what am I going to be like once he or she is born?"

Jezzy turned to cock her head at Rachel before she trotted over to her. Rachel picked her up and they all walked back to Alexsei and Maybe's house.

"For what it's worth, you're going to be fine. You're going to get past this stage at some point," Cora said, hoping it was true. "There'll be a new stage. And come on, let's be real, it's also okay if you do end up being more emotional once you have a kid. I sing songs in the shower while Jezzy howls along on the other side of the enclosure because I don't want her to get lonely. And then I get sniffly when I think what if she doesn't want me to get lonely either and that's why she's singing with me? You're supposed to love hard. That's why we're here."

After hanging out awhile longer, she headed to her town house to grab some clothes and a few boxes of things she needed for the house. Jezzy followed her around, sniffing things when Cora held them out.

"This is what I envisioned when I thought about having a dog," she told Jezzy. "You and me hanging out and shiz. Singing in the shower. Eating stuff and looking adoringly at Beau. It's like we're twins."

Cora got kisses in response and that goofy dog smile. Jezzy's tail got to wagging so hard her whole back end was moving and it made her laugh.

"I have a lot of clothes and shoes," she confessed immediately when she and Jezzy got home an hour or so later.

Home.

"You have a closet twice the size of my first apartment in New York but if you need more room, the house is big enough for you to find it." He bent to scratch Jezzy's ears before straightening and kissing Cora. "I take it you have boxes in the car you need help with?"

"A few, though they're mostly light. I did bring some of my books though."

The closet he'd given her—no, it was her closet in their house—was indeed massive and far larger than she actually needed, but it was hers and theirs and she felt nothing but excitement about the future with him.

She hung her things up. Slid things into the built-in drawers. Lined up some shoes and bags and sighed, satisfied. Jezzy had scampered off to the living room, where Beau let her watch dog television which was an actual real thing. And Jez loved it. They even left it on for her if they went out.

"I told Maybe and Rachel about us moving in together," she said as she dropped onto the couch at Beau's side. "We had one of those squealing happy girl hug moments right there in the middle of the sidewalk. Then Rachel cried about some stuff, and then we all cried about some stuff, and then laughed about crying. Jez was all up in our faces giving kisses though. She's so handy that way. If I wasn't watching her so closely I think one of those Dolan women would steal my dog, and then I'd have to hunt them down."

"*Your* dog? Our dog. I'm glad they were happy for you. I told Ian and Gregori this afternoon so you'll want to tell Wren soon."

"Oh crap, that's right. Hang on." She called Wren. "Hi there!" she said when her friend answered. "I wanted to tell you when we were face-to-face but Gregori knows now because he had lunch with Beau and Ian so I figured I'd call. To tell you Beau and I are moving in together."

"That's awesome," Wren told her. "I can't wait to hear all the details when we see you at the wedding on Saturday."

They chatted a minute or two more before she disconnected and turned her attention back to Beau. "Done. How was your day other than lunch with Gregori and Ian?"

"Pretty excellent. After lunch I returned a call to my agent. I don't even have to go to New York for the show pitch. The notes I sent, along with the cookbook-connected stuff was enough. I have a new series starting filming in the spring. It'll hit the air about three months after that and coincide with the cookbook release. This will be my third so I've got the process down pretty well. I'll spend about a week cooking and photographing all the dishes, and then send it all to my cookbook team and they'll organize it into something awesome."

"Holy shit, that's amazing!" She launched herself into his lap and rained kisses all over his face. "I'm so proud of you." And happy to know he'd be working in Seattle instead of elsewhere. In their home, which would maybe be weird but he said it really wasn't that bad so she'd trust him.

"It's a level of success I really appreciate, that's for sure. I was thinking you should try your hand at doing the photography. I mean if you wanted to. I like your eye. More than that, you have a very what I like to think of as a Northwest perspective. I want that flavor to ring through on every level with this cookbook so I think you'd really capture that through your lens."

"Wow," Cora said as she settled next to him again. Jezzy gave her the *are you finished* look and got back into her place in between them. "I'm wildly flattered but I hate to think of screwing up and tanking your sales. Shouldn't you hire a professional?"

"I want you. You understand what I mean by the feel of the entire project from an artistic standpoint. I've seen your work. It's hard not to when I walk past it all the time." He indicated one of the framed pieces she'd given him. His hands at work, one a blur as he tipped sliced vegetables into a bowl. She'd taken it while kneeling so the perspective was on the implied motion. The elegance of this basic thing he elevated with his own kind of magic.

"You're here with me. You take pictures all the time anyway, why not use them in the book? If they're terrible I'll hire someone else to fix it. Does that make you feel better?"

"You really get me," she said. It did. He wouldn't let his feelings for her mess up his career. He'd fix it rather than be afraid to hurt her feelings and let the mistake go forward.

"Sometimes. Not that I don't find you a total surprise on a regular basis. But you want to do well and you want me to do well. Okay. We can agree that if I feel like your work isn't right I won't use it. Though I will compensate you so don't argue." Beau put a hand up and got his stern face on.

"Then let me pay rent," she countered.

"Why would I do that? I don't have a mortgage so I don't need rent. This is your house too. You don't need to spend money like that."

"People are going to think I'm using you for your money," she said with a frown.

"People who would clearly not know either one of us might. But everyone who matters would know the truth. I don't need you to pay rent. If I did, you would, and that's what's important."

"FINE," SHE SAID in that way that meant it wasn't fine at all. Beau, having known a few women in his day, watched her with wariness.

He wanted her to accept this. Because he wanted to take care of her. Protect her and give her things. A good, safe life where she was adored and spoiled like she should be. He had it and after some years spending it like it was nothing, he realized no amount of retail therapy and bottle service would erase the privations of his childhood.

Now he spent it in ways that pleased him in healthy ways. Cora Silvera was his finest thing. The best gift he'd ever received and he would treat her as such.

"You said *fine* but you meant you were up to something and said it to fool me into relaxing while you plan my imminent demise."

That made her laugh and Jezzy started to wriggle when she wagged her entire butt at the sound.

"You say it doesn't matter and you might be right. But it *feels* like it matters when people make those assumptions about me. You have money, yes, but so do I. I don't want you to ever feel like I'm freeloading. And I don't want Ian to think it either. Or your manager."

In the past there had been men and women he'd dallied with who'd been dazzled by his money and celebrity. Who'd hinted about or outright requested jewelry or other expensive gifts. It hadn't mattered to him because to be honest they hadn't really mattered to him. So what was a bracelet or a designer dress? He got his sex on, played with his partners and moved on to the next one.

"Ian doesn't think that. He's seen us together. Even if he didn't know you and like you, he knows me. I don't need to pay for pussy, for god's sake. You aren't some starfucker."

She threw up her hands, startling the dog in the process.

"But there are starfuckers!"

"Why are you mad about what you aren't? At what no one thinks you are?" He truly didn't understand why it mattered to her. But it clearly did. She was pissed off and defensive and that was no way to leave this between them. "Explain to me if you can," he asked in a softer tone.

"I haven't had a real long-term relationship before. I had a thing a few years ago like I told you about, but really, it has nothing on this." Cora waved a hand between them. "Growing up the way I did, with a famous mom and parents with money, people always blew me off. Like, oh she must have this job because of her family influence. I have had to prove myself over and over and, gah, I don't know. But it pushes my buttons to have anyone think I don't pull my weight. And you buy this umpty-jillion-dollar house and suddenly me and my dog are living here and not paying rent and it looks weird."

"There's no rent to pay. You're not my roommate. You don't need to pay an entry fee to my life, Cora.

What you add isn't something easily quantified. It's everything. It's priceless."

"You're more than your bank account or your face, gorgeous as it is. More than your cooking and your celebrity. I don't think it's an entry fee, I just don't want to be perceived as harming you. Or taking advantage. Because *you* matter to me."

He took her face in his hands long enough to kiss her. "Baby. I am in love with you. I know your heart and there's not a single part of you that would use me. Don't you think I see that? I understand that you see all of me, not just the outside but my heart. It's the reason you're my everything. If you want to fill the house with art, you do all the work finding it. And all the wonderful life and color you carry with you, that's all I require. Love me back. We're actually saying the same things, you know. We just come at them a little differently."

She let out a shaky breath but then she smiled. "Okay, so how about this? Let me pay for whatever job you hire my dad to do. Believe me, he's a great value no matter what he charges. Then I'll feel a little more like this is my house too instead of me living in *your* house. And when I say I want to chip in for something I want you to accept it."

He thought about it and finally agreed because it was fair and he got her point, though he certainly considered this to be her house too.

"Did we just make up?" he asked.

"Were we fighting?"

"A little. I was pissed that you wouldn't just let me do something nice for you and that you placed any importance on what some random person who didn't know you thought. I wasn't seeing why you were being so defensive. I have my own issues I guess," he confessed.

"I'm sorry people treat you like you're just a pretty face. It is a pretty face. But you're so damn much more. I never thought I'd have a happily-ever-after like you."

Naturally, Jezzy chose that moment to fart, sending them both scrambling off the couch with their stinky, flatulent dog running after them, barking her delight.

CHAPTER TWENTY-TWO

My heart is the head of a river
always leading me to you.

RACHEL WAS ABSOLUTELY gorgeous in her wedding dress.
Vic looked at her with so much love and happiness
Cora had to hold back tears more than once, especially
as they started saying their vows.

She'd been there at the start, as Vic and Rachel had
fallen in love. And watched over the last two years as
that love had grown and deepened. They'd both been
such wonderful friends to her, had given her an example of what a committed, working partnership was.

And now they were married and having a baby girl
in six months. By summer there'd be a new friend to
snuggle and love. And she was there when it started.
Well, not *that* part. But their romance and the first steps
into their happily-ever-after.

"May I have this dance?" Beau asked her as he approached.

She took the hand he held out and he drew her close.

"So glad I wore the really high heels or I'd be looking at your chest right now. Wait, that sounded like a
complaint and really it's not. I could happily look at

your chest for hours. But now I can see into your eyes and your lips are close enough to kiss."

He gave her one, slow and sweet, to underline her point.

"You look really beautiful in this dress," he said as he pulled back from the kiss. "I've been to a few weddings but most of the bridesmaid outfits looked like costumes."

"Thank you. As little black dresses go, yes, it's a great cocktail dress. I can wear it to events at the gallery, which is always nice. But you in a tux? I have plans to strip you out of it all James Bond style when we get home tonight."

His laughter tightened things low in her belly.

"License to fuck you?" he asked in an undertone, his breath against her earlobe.

"You qualify for expert rating, that's all I'm saying."

Mrs. Orlova clucked over Rachel several times during the rest of the reception. Making sure she wasn't tired. That she ate. It was so sweet, even if Irena was one of the scariest people on earth when she wanted to be. It made Cora happy to see Rachel spoiled and cared for the way she should be. Made her certain her friend's future was a good one.

"We were all a little lost when we first met. Rachel and Maybe had just moved here to Seattle and we clicked right away. They made me their sister. Made room for me in their lives and have been at my back. Each of us struck out on our own to make a life as grown-ups," she told Beau. "First Maybe found a job and then love with Alexsei and then later, the healthier Rachel's heart and mind got, the closer she and Vic became until it all fell into place like it was supposed to. I was on that plane back here from London, feeling lonely and adrift. Wanting some roots and security and to finally claim the direction I've wanted for years. And there you were."

"Lucky me, right? I show up to make dinner at a friend's house, and then you walked in. I never believed in fate until that moment."

"We're so schmoopy," she told him through a big smile.

"Is that a sex thing?" he asked.

"Do you want it to be?"

He hugged her closer. "I always want it to be a sex thing when it's you."

"Damn, you have some of the best pantie dropper lines ever."

"If I let my game slip I might lose you to some suave younger guy. Gotta keep you buttered up and happy."

As if.

The song ended and he took her back to their table, where Maybe and Alexsei were enjoying a glass of champagne.

"Do you think your aunt could be convinced to try my cabbage rolls? I've been working on a recipe for a few years and Cora tells me she's the one who made the ones we had tonight. She could give lessons," Beau said to Alexsei after handing Cora a glass and clinking his to it.

"She'll be totally flattered. Lead with that line about the lessons and how it took you years and her recipe is still better," Maybe said. "And listen, what person wouldn't be flattered by you telling them that? Irena's a very real person. She'll sense that in you too."

"If not, she'll tell you," Alexsei said, tone dry, though he was totally serious.

"How does she get along with Walda?" Beau asked, thinking that the two very strong women had a lot in common.

Cora choked on her champagne. "They don't. Get along I mean. It's an old story and it has to do with bread. My mom is set in her ways and she didn't take any care when she related her bakery preference to a woman who runs a family bakery. Then she got slapped for it and that was a thing for a while. But now mainly they ignore each other if and when they run into one another, which we try to keep rare."

"Irena was yelling in Russian and Walda was yelling back in Portuguese. It was scary because they're both pretty intense people. But it was also fascinating, and even though I only understood about a third of what was being said, I wanted to just watch and eat some popcorn. Don't tell Irena I said that though." Maybe looked quickly over to where both of Vic's parents stood speaking with the newlyweds.

The wedding and reception that had followed were very much indicative of who Beau had come to know Rachel and Vic to be. Intimate and small. Less than forty people total. He hadn't been lying about wanting to talk to Irena about her cabbage rolls. She and the ladies at the church had put together countless slow cookers full of them. All based on her recipe and from what he understood clearly as her direction. There'd been a really nice dinner from a caterer, but Rachel and Vic loved the cabbage rolls so much she'd made them for the reception.

"Did you know she and Evie, Vic's sister, made the cake at the bakery?" Cora pointed at the beautiful cake, covered in a sea of roses and violets cascading down three tiers. Instead of a bride and groom, birds in flight topped it.

"The birds on top are spun sugar. Evie made those," Maybe said. "My sister loves birds. Vic did it as a surprise. The violets are sugar too. Lots of buttercream because Rachel's not a fan of fondant."

He was so glad Cora had these people in her life. This family she'd made. They were kind to one another. Close-knit and protective. But they could fight too. He'd witnessed a spat between Cora and Maybe and wondered if they were ever going to speak to one another again but a few hours later they were apologizing and moving on.

Glad too, that they'd made room for him in their family. Cora was a package deal. With her, came this group of people. What they thought was important to her and they had very few secrets from what he understood.

Gregori had been part of that too. That he and Beau were close meant a lot to them because they trusted Gregori. His friend was one of their family, both in the sense of biology and of the heart.

Again, he was clearly meant to be there in Gregori's kitchen that day so he could be part of this family. Include Ian when his friend actually took time off.

"That's beautiful. The cake. The story behind it. The cabbage rolls and this venue too. All because people love Rachel and Vic," Beau said. One of Wren's friends had a rental property just north of the city and they gave it to Rachel and Vic for the day. It was one of those houses people often used for family reunions or work retreats so it fit the party perfectly.

Cora's face lit with love and happiness for her friends. "Yeah. All that. The wedding has been as special and unique as they are. And you got to meet Rachel's aunt and uncle. They're really nice too. They deserved a day that fit them both. I think this hit the mark."

Cora was so pretty. All dressed up in a long-sleeved dress. Short enough to show off her legs. Not too snug, but it had a vintage feel to it, which always seemed to work magic on her. Roses with bits of green holly sat just behind her ear. Part of the bun thing she had her hair pinned into. Her lipstick matched the deep velvet red of the roses.

She was a total knockout and all his.

And she was blissed out for her friends.

"Is it weird that I'm worried that Jezzy might need to go out and we're not there and she's so sweet and doesn't want to pee in the house so she's trying and we're not helping," Cora said, just a tiny bit drunk.

"Yes," he told her before he grabbed her bag and helped her into her coat. "Let's go home and save Jezzy from loneliness."

"It's nearly midnight so it will be by the time we get to the house. So we should open presents then because it'll officially be Christmas," she said like it just occurred to her instead of the fact that she'd been pestering him about opening presents early for the last week.

"I'm totally sure you were just making up holidays," he said, one brow up.

"I have no idea what you mean. Let's find Maybe and Rachel and say good-night," she told him while tugging him toward the door.

"Like for instance Day of Delight wasn't part of my religious education."

She snickered. "Look, there very well could be a holiday where you're allowed to open a present or two early. In fact, in the entirety of human existence I refuse to believe there isn't one. And since I didn't know the name of it exactly, I just gave it the name it should have. Because clearly if you have a day where you get to open presents early, it's a fucking delight."

"I really like drunk Cora," he told her as they approached their friends to say goodbye.

Rachel pulled Cora into a hug after kissing her smack on the lips. "You are the best. Vic and I just can't say thank you enough."

Cora had gone to Rachel's aunt and Irena and had gotten photographs from them, together with the ones she'd taken since they'd begun dating, Cora created a custom photo album telling the story of Vic and Rachel.

That's when Beau had really known asking Cora to do the photos for his cookbook was the right thing. She was not only talented, but she knew how to take the resources and create something new with them. Knew how to create a feeling with whatever she did.

"I love you two and I love you as a couple. I'm so glad I got to be part of this day. I'll talk to you later. Call me when you're bored with newlywed sexytimes. Merry Christmas in about forty minutes," he was pretty sure he heard her say as they hugged one another.

Then Maybe came over and there was more with Wren until finally he managed to get her in the car and them back home, where Jezzy had been napping.

He liked this Cora too. A little messy. Tipsy. Silly and not a small amount profanity laced. She'd still put her shoes under the bench in the front entry carefully and neatly.

She got changed while he took the dog out and by the time he came back into the house, she padded out in yoga pants and a snug T-shirt with Santa riding a unicorn on it.

Holiday music played softly in the background and she'd turned on the fireplace and the lights on the tree they'd decorated together not too long after he'd moved in. Now that she'd started living there, new elements had shown up on the tree. Her own ornaments on what was *their* tree.

"I'll be back out shortly. I'm done with tuxedos."

"Until a week from today when you wear one to my parents' New Year's Eve party," she called out.

"Oh joy," he muttered as he headed to their room.

They were headed over to the Silvera's the following afternoon to exchange presents and have dinner. Beto and Finley were going to be there as well, and he liked them both so it'd be easier than if it had just been the four of them.

Back in the living room, she and the dog had settled on the chaise near the fire. Jezzy was on her back, her belly exposed to the warmth and Cora was already under blankets. It wasn't even cold, but he didn't say that because he wasn't stupid and he certainly had no complaints about her wanting to get close enough to soak up his body heat.

Though that often ended up with sex because once they started snuggling, it wasn't too rare that it progressed to naked snuggling, which, given the near-insatiable need to fuck her, wasn't such a surprise.

"It's officially Christmas, let's open presents," she said with a bright smile.

"You're absolutely unrepentant," he told her, thinking about which present he wanted her to open first.

"I have lots to repent for—don't get me wrong. But loving presents isn't on that list," she explained. "Thing is, I love giving presents as much as getting them, so sit and let me choose the first present." She flipped the blanket back and jumped to her feet.

"I love to watch you in action. You never do anything halfway," he told her as she left the room.

"Nothing worth doing is worth doing halfway," she called back. "Okay, so close your eyes."

CORA NEARLY GIGGLED with nervousness and probably also margaritas, which had been the signature drink for everyone who wasn't knocked up.

It was the most important present she'd ever given.

Her first Christmas with Beau. Her first Christmas in love. She wanted to give him something that would tell him she listened. That he was worth listening to.

She brought out the painting and faced it toward him. Cora had already staged it the day before so she knew just how to lean it so it would catch the best light.

Once she'd stepped back she told him to open his eyes.

It was a hyperrealistic painting of an elephant. A close-up of one side of her face. Close enough to see the life in her eyes and the fringe of her lashes. Every wrinkle was done so well. The personality of the elephant just radiated from it.

He sucked in a breath, taking a few steps closer to examine it better. "Cora, this is amazing. I'm stunned. I've never seen anything like it."

"I thought it would look good in the bedroom. On the wall behind the bed. The light would be perfect and because it's grays and blacks it's a good neutral."

"Where did you find it?"

"I saw it last month. Well, not this one but another from the same artist. And I got in contact with her and she had this one. The minute I was able to look at it in person I knew. It's the angle, the emphasis on the individuality of the animal. The intelligence and knowledge in her eyes. There's a story about this particular elephant that came with the painting. She's the matriarch of her herd. Her mom was before that." Cora clamped her lips closed before she babbled anything else.

"It's incredible. You took this thing I love and you

not only found a present for me, but the perfect present. Yes to all that art stuff you said about the angle and perspective. She's so real. You chose this for me a month ago?"

She was so pleased he loved the gift she had to clear her throat before speaking. "Yeah. It's a thing. Okay? I like to spend time finding gifts for people. And I knew you were going to be moving and would have space and so I called the sanctuary and spoke with the director there and he mentioned this husband and wife team who did photography and painting and that's how I found the artist. They live in North Bend of all places so it wasn't that hard to go out to her studio."

"*Wasn't that hard?* Cora, you called an elephant sanctuary halfway across the world to talk with them because I love elephants and you wanted to get ideas about different types of art they might want to recommend? Then you tracked the artist down, drove out to her studio, which is an hour and a half or so from your place to look at a painting in person to be sure you had the exact right one for me. Just another Tuesday for Cora perhaps, but the rest of us are mere mortals and that level of detail is beyond us. You made real effort for me. For no other reason than to please me. Thank you."

He straightened and moved close enough to give her a hug.

She swallowed back her emotion, not wanting to cry and get snot on him. "I'm glad you like it."

"Now, how can I even come close to that?"

"It's not a competition," she said. "But it if was, I win."

That broke the seriousness, making them both laugh as he pulled her out to the back deck. Jezzy raced past them, heading for her ball no doubt. And that's when she saw the new handrails on the steps leading down into the yard.

When she saw her poetry had been written into the wrought iron work.

"Dancing drops of rain light your skin like diamonds." Scrolled down the right side and on the left was "My heart is the head of a river always leading me to you."

"You left me the second one scribbled on the back of our order ticket from that diner. Remember?" he asked.

"I do now. I remember that you looked at me a certain way and it made my heart sort of swell. Left me breathless. This is really beautiful." It added to their home. Gave it her stamp. Made it *theirs*. Which meant he'd listened to her that day they'd had the discussion about whether or not she was going to pay rent. He'd listened to her and shown her just that with the railing.

"Come in now. It's cold and there are more presents, including part two of this one."

Part two, which was the scribbled poem on the back of the order ticket from a greasy spoon. He'd had it framed. "I thought it would be good in our bedroom too. Looks like we have complementary thinking on liking to spend a lot of time in there."

There was some jewelry she should have been embarrassed by loving so much, but she did. Gorgeous dangle earrings with emeralds and diamonds, as well as a watch he'd seen her admiring in a shop window in downtown.

After everything had been unwrapped, and then cleaned up, they headed off to bed sometime after two.

Cora didn't need Santa. She had Beau, who made her dreams come true.

CHAPTER TWENTY-THREE

BEAU LOOKED UP at his painting as he tightened his bow tie. He'd been hoping to get away with a suit instead of a tux for the Silvera's party but unfortunately that didn't work out. Black tie was black tie, he was told.

Though Cora did say he could wear whatever he wanted, it wasn't as if he planned to do that and agitate her parents or make them feel he was disrespecting them. His only consolation was that all his male friends attending would be similarly uncomfortable.

"What do you think?" she asked, coming out of her closet wearing a dress he'd given her for Christmas. One shouldered. Asymmetrical neck. Navy blue, which she wore very well. It showed off her shoulders and some of her ink, as well as her new watch. He loved her legs so the hem skimmed along at midthigh. She looked like a piece of art herself.

"I think that dress was made for you. You're beautiful. Which is true all the time, of course. But right now you're particularly gorgeous."

"You know my feelings about you in a tux. And if you recall we didn't play James Bond after the wedding. Damn."

"That's because you were driven by your ever-present lust to open presents early."

Her smile, damn, he'd give her anything for one of those open, silly, affectionate Cora smiles.

"My priorities were...momentarily different. Plus I wanted to give you your painting. And you can't lie and say it wasn't totally a Day of Delight. Tonight though." She groaned. "Damn. Well, naturally after the party we're headed back here to have people over to watch fireworks. I'm not going to make you wear it for hours longer than you have to just so I can play my dirty games with you after. For damn sure I'm taking these heels off when we get home."

"The difference between you and me there, I guess. See, I'm willing to wear a tux all damned day if it led to sex with you. However, as I own the tux, I'll put it on whenever you feel like being interrogated."

She smiled again. This one was her sex smile and he adored that one too.

"What if I want to be the one interrogating *you*, Mr. Bond?" She slid a hand up the front of his chest.

"Fine with me." He held his hands up in surrender and she hugged him, laughing.

"It's nice that we'll be able to set up with our blankets and stuff and watch the show from the front yard here. I loved that about my town house but my porch wasn't as nice as it is here and it was far more cramped. And the house here is big enough that if everyone wanted to stay over instead of drive home they could quite easily."

Satisfaction settled into his bones as he realized it

was the fact that he'd given her a home she liked and wanted to share with their friends. It still surprised him when that hit. Each time she was pleased by something in that way it appealed to him on some primitive mate level. Sometimes when he made a recipe that she really truly loved, it felt like he was presenting her with gold and jewels. Tribute to his beloved.

Cora took off her shoes and stood on the second step of the staircase to the upper floor. She'd discovered that it brought them face-to-face. "You just had an expression that said you were deep thinking about something. But you were smiling so I figure it was good?"

Another thing he'd still found himself surprised by was the way she checked in with him. Not in a domineering sense, but Cora wasn't one to not ask if he looked upset or puzzled or what have you.

It was still so very intense with her, but it wasn't overwhelming, and better, it was tempered by the way they'd been growing as a couple. He'd never lived with a woman other than his wife and that had been, well, far different than what he and Cora shared.

Cora's energy made him happy. He liked the evenings when she got home from the gallery and he made them dinner. It was blessedly normal and their time to talk about the day. But Cora never made anything boring. She always had a story, or a bit of poetry she'd written, a photo she'd taken while out and about, whatever. She shared herself with him.

"I was just thinking about how being with you made me happy," he told her, leaning in quickly to kiss her.

"Oh well, that is a nice thing for a gal to hear. You make me happy too."

Jezzy barked a few times just to let them know she was happy, as well.

"I need to get back to the gallery just to be sure everything is running smoothly," she said.

Cora had already been to the gallery for a full day's work before closing and getting the crew in to set up for the party.

"All right. I'll drive so you can have as many glasses of champagne as you like," he told her.

Someone needed to take care of her. Walda kept on telling everyone this party was all hers, all her idea and planning, but it was Cora who'd implemented all that Walda cloud talk into solid plans. Cora who'd organized and checked in with all the various caterers, florists and service staff.

And she'd done it while also running the gallery and having a very full social life with him and their friends. She wasn't getting enough sleep and the stress of Walda's demands had worn her a little thin at the edges.

Tomorrow when they finally got up—and having a dog meant they couldn't sleep until two in the afternoon—he planned to make them both brunch, which they'd eat while watching movies and the parade. She needed rest and some spoiling and he would be sure she got it.

She came down the steps and got her shoes on once more. "I mean if you want to drive, thank you and I'll take your offer because then I don't have to walk from my town house. Just be advised the parking tonight is going to be impossible. Between all the clubs and restaurants and people headed into Seattle Center for the fireworks at midnight, it's probably best if you park at the town house when you come back for the party. Go have a drink with everyone over at Whiskey Sharp once you drop me off though. Just come when they do. Otherwise you're stuck at the gallery for another hour and a half while I bark orders at people."

"You totally underestimate how hot it is to watch you bark orders at people. Even when it's me. I have some calls to make. I'll hang out in your office and do that while you do your thing. Don't waste any more of my time by trying to do me a favor by sending me to Whiskey Sharp," he said to forestall her argument.

The truth was, he wasn't entirely sure how Walda would act and he wanted to provide some backup in case it was unpleasant. Yes, Cora could handle it and she did on a regular basis—though not nearly as selfishly enough as she should in his opinion. But his being there would underline that he was *always* going to be at Cora's defense should that be necessary.

Even if it was her mother who needed to hear that point. Jesus, the woman called Cora all the time for the most petty of bullshit. Just to be sure Cora was there. He wanted to tell her that she could assure herself that her kid was there by having lunch with her instead of trying to make her responsible for Walda's entire fucking life. But it would start a mess and Cora didn't need that.

He and Cora's mother would have a set-to at some point. She pushed but he didn't react. So far. But Beau wasn't under any misapprehension that she wasn't just thinking about what *would* get him to dance to her little tune.

NATURALLY BEAU DROPPED her right out front of the gallery before telling her he'd park at the town house and walk from there.

She was still smiling as she walked into the main room that'd been decorated to her mother's precise instructions. Her coat and bag went into the closet in her office, as did her shoes, which she traded for flat slide-on slippers.

Out in the gallery, she quickly intervened in some sort of kerfuffle between the bartender and the caterer and was still untangling it when her mother came in.

"It's very vulgar to have this sort of thing happening in front of party guests," Walda said once Cora had solved the problem.

Cora wasn't going to be goaded into some battle of wills over this petty crap. "There are no guests here yet. It was a basic problem—it took a basic solution. We're good. Would you like me to make you a plate? Get you some tea?"

"Make me a plate with all the appetizers being served tonight," her mother said. "I want to be sure everything is up to my standards."

"I'll do that," Beau said. Cora hadn't even heard him come out of her office, where he'd headed once he'd arrived. "Good evening, Mrs. Silvera. You look lovely tonight," he called out with a wave before he turned to deal with the food.

"He's here early," her mom said.

It had snowed so hard on Christmas Day they'd had to drop out of the day with her family because the roads had been a mess. She still hadn't told them about moving in with Beau, but they most certainly knew she was in a serious relationship with him.

Which was probably why her mom was acting a fool.

"He drove me in to save me trying to find a parking spot. Dropped me right out front."

"There's a spot here at the gallery, why would he have to do that?"

Beau had returned to hear the last part of the interchange so he replied, "The spot your car is in now? Cora wanted to keep it available so you and John could park there and not have to worry about a long walk in your formal wear."

Then he handed her a plate with all the things being served during the party with a flourish and a slight bow.

Cora's heart was still pounding after the way he'd just answered her mom's question but also put her in her place.

"The caterer said to let her know what you think," Beau said as he straightened. "If you need to handle anything else, I've got your mom," he told Cora.

"I don't need handling," her mom said.

Cora looked down at the plate in her mother's hand and then back to her face. Was it simply that her mother had no idea how things showed up in her life? She was so used to being taken care of she didn't even see it as people doing things for her? She never worried about parking spots or food, even the party she was standing in that Cora had done all the work for she didn't see as being handled.

"Go on," Walda said with a wave of her hand. "You need to change out of those ratty slippers before anyone sees them and thinks they're a reflection of the work on my walls."

"So, Mrs. Silvera, how do you like those crab bites?" Beau asked her, snagging her attention.

Cora stood there for another few moments, debating, but in the end, she took the reprieve he'd handed her and moved off to handle other things—including changing into her heels.

Beto came into her office with a smile and a hug. "Hello, my darling. You look gorge. What's happening tonight? Can I help?"

"This old thing?" She indicated her dress. "A present from Beau. Also, you look fantastic, as well. Silvera men do know how to wear tuxedos. As for help? I'm good. We're ready to go. People should be arriving any moment."

He linked arms with her as they headed back out to the gallery.

"By the way," Cora said quietly, "Beau and I have moved in together. I haven't told anyone else in the family yet because it's a face-to-face sort of conversation, but I wanted you to know."

And she understood her brother enough that she was certain his reaction would be pleased and she wasn't disappointed when he stopped to give her a hug and a kiss on her cheek.

"I like this Cora. Happy. Passionate and totally in charge of your future. Dad and I are going to your boyfriend's, uh, your house I suppose, to look over the lot and get some ideas about our design."

"Excellent. Then you can meet Jezzy—that's the dog I keep texting you pictures of—in person. She should know her uncle. You will love her. Or lie about it because she's like my kid and that's part of the sibling rule book."

"I can't tell you if your baby is ugly when you have one? That's some bullshit, Cora," Beto teased.

"You've seen my man. We aren't making any ugly babies."

"But you will be making babies? I mean, moving in is a big step but it seems to me you're doing just fine with that. I've just not seen you so, I don't know, solid in your choices. At ease in a way you haven't been."

Cora had figured she'd have kids one day. She'd hopefully find the right man, but if not, she'd do it on her own if she really wanted to. But being around Beau every day, watching him nurture and protect the people and canine he loved, had convinced her she'd very much be interested in making babies with him.

"Not like tomorrow. Or even this coming year. But yeah, at some point I think I do want to make tiny humans with Beau." After the history he'd had with his sons, she knew the choice to have more children would be one Beau might not make for a while, if ever. But they'd talked lightly of it and he hadn't seemed opposed to the concept. There was time to figure it out.

"This is the real deal. Wow. I'm insanely jealous, but also really truly happy for you. If anyone deserves a happily-ever-after, it's you."

"It's still early days. I'm good with a dog and a house right now as he does his new show and I dig in here at the gallery. It's all I can manage at the moment anyway. I figure I'll get some great practice when Rachel has the baby too," Cora said.

"You're killing this adulting gig," Beto told her.

"Ha! Not so much. But I'm muddling through."

THE PARTY WAS in full swing as their friends and family and favorite clients moved around the gallery, drinks in hand, food in bellies. Walda had calmed down a little once people had begun to arrive, and then sought her out to compliment her and thank her for being invited.

Sure, she acted like she was a queen, which rankled Beau a little. But she also remembered little details about people's lives. Asked about this or that trip they'd taken, how their families were.

She was eccentric and sharp-tongued, entitled too. But she was also generous and warm when she wanted to be. It was why Beau still tipped toward liking her even when she was a bitch to her daughter.

"Tell me, Beau, do you have any contact at all with your family?" Walda asked him.

"Yes, with some cousins who live on the East Coast. I have friends here who are as close as family. A nice bonus to being with Cora is that her friends and mine overlap so my entrance into her social life has been easier, as has hers into mine."

Cora's father nodded. "I can see how that would be true. We quite like Cora's friends, including Gregori and Wren, who we also have known through the art community."

"Gregori's paintings are in huge demand. He's immensely talented." Walda's comments weren't calculated at all. They were genuine admiration for his friend's work and in her way, he realized she was trying to find common ground with him.

Not that he would let his guard down. Walda was jealous of him and that made her dangerous at times. Petulant and impatient, she was quick to complain and very at ease with using emotional manipulation to get what she wanted.

Cora had given her mother all her attention. Now Cora had shifted to the gallery and to him. Walda had to share her daughter and it was hard on a person so used to being catered to.

John was a good influence on her, the laid-back charm to her high-strung eccentricity. He clearly loved her, and to her credit, she clearly loved him too. But it was time for the man to hold to the promises he'd made and take the weight Cora had been carrying since she'd been a teenager.

"I'm happy to say I've got a few of his early paintings. Even happier to say I now live in a house and property that can do justice to one of Gregori's sculptural pieces. Cora is going to have him work with your design plans to create a custom work for us. I don't want to mar the view, but there are several spots in the front and in the back of the house I think would enhance both the landscape design and the sculpture, as well. I'm excited to work with you and Beto on that."

"I hadn't thought about a big piece in your yard, but yes, that does sound like a fantastic idea," John said.

Cora came over to them then. "As always, this is a great party. Happy New Year, *Pai*." She hugged her father and came to sit at Beau's side.

"I was just about to tell your parents that it was your idea to have one of Gregori's sculptural pieces as an outdoor piece of art," Beau explained.

Cora brightened, leaning into his side a moment. "Wait until you see this house. Because it's on one of the highest spots in the neighborhood, it's got absolutely gorgeous water views to the west, north and south with the Space Needle and downtown. We're watching fireworks from that spot later tonight."

"You're very involved with this process, Cora," her mother said. "He said *we* a few times but I hope he realizes the type of services *you're* providing with design and curation are of a type few are fortunate enough to have. You'll be increasing his home value and the value of his collection."

As backhanded compliments went, it was a winner and it landed with a slight flinch he only felt because Cora leaned against his side.

"Beau and I are living together. It's my house too. So naturally I'm involved. He's got great taste, which you'll see when we have you all over for dinner. He already has a fantastic collection but when mine is added and we flesh out the rest, it'll be stunning."

"What did you say? Living together?" Walda narrowed her gaze and her husband put a hand on her arm with a soft murmur.

"Yep. I wanted to tell you when we came over on Christmas but then the snow happened and things got pushed back."

"Your phone hasn't been broken," Walda said.

"No. But I wanted to tell you in person, and today was the first time I've seen you since."

"How long?"

"Officially it's only been two weeks so it's not as if I've been hiding it for months," Cora explained.

"Are you out of your head? Cora, you barely know this man. What are you doing with your town house?" her mother demanded.

"I have a yearlong lease in place. My tenant will move in tomorrow."

"What if things go wrong? You'll be homeless."

"Mom." Cora paused and took a steadying breath. "I am fortunate enough to have resources should things not work out and I need to move. I have several friends and two siblings living nearby. I can easily stay with one of them. I have money, a job and good credit so I will be able to locate alternate housing for myself should the need arise. I appreciate your worry, but I'm a grown woman. I've been taking care of myself—and you—for a long time."

Walda looked to Beau. "So here you are nesting in your new money house and your sweater vest and your art world girlfriend. You swoop in because you were bored with your old life. Cora is a novelty and when you are done? When you get tired of sweater vests? When nesting loses its charms, along with my daughter? When you go back to the life you had before, wallowing in easy sex and too much alcohol?"

"Enough!" Cora said, her tone deadly sharp. "You're being rude and disrespectful to not only me, but Beau."

"I'm trying to figure out what he's doing with you. If that's disrespectful I can't help it. He could just answer my questions," Walda shot back.

"Your questions were rude. And based on the assumption that he couldn't possibly just want to be with me because I am nice and smart and I make him laugh. Based on the assumption that should we break up, like people do from time to time, it would be because he wronged me terribly and I'd be too weak to suck it up and move on like everyone else who deals with heartbreak. He's not a monster. I am not fragile. I am not gullible and I am absolutely awesome enough for someone to love me."

If Beau hadn't already loved her, that impassioned defense of herself and of their relationship would have been the final thing that got him there.

"Stop this before you say something you can't take back," Cora's dad told Walda in a quietly firm tone.

"Ma'am," Beau said, "I believe with all my heart that you love Cora and you want to protect her so I'm going to choose not to be offended and to address some of the things you asked."

Cora turned to him, "You don't have to do this. Her questions were insults."

He kissed her quickly. "It's okay. Really."

Cora sucked in a breath, and then nodded for him to go on.

"I made the decision to move up here before I knew Cora lived in Seattle. I was already working on a new show and cookbook concept with a Northwest flavor. I just signed a contract yesterday for a show—filming here—and the cookbook, which Cora will be doing the photography for. Did she tell you that? It's going to be amazing. I know you both would be proud that Cora's talent was being recognized."

Her father smiled and said something to Walda softly that erased some of the anger on her face.

"Our home is beyond my wildest expectations. I grew up with pretty much nothing, so to have been able to live the way I do and share that life with Cora has been something I am very much grateful for. I have no plans to kick Cora out or dump her. In stark contrast to the idea that I'd get bored, I should tell you she fascinates me multiple times a day, every day. She makes me laugh. She is the kind of partner I never figured I'd have." Or be worthy of. "I won't apologize for my romantic life before I began seeing Cora. It's frankly none of your business. I don't need to explain or get permission for my choices. Not from you. But I will tell you that I am with Cora because I love her. The only secret about it is how on earth I merited such a person."

Walda said nothing as he stared at her, and then he finally shrugged. She'd do what she wanted and he'd stay out of it unless it involved him or it hurt Cora and he could make it better. All he could do was be the kind of person who Cora could love.

Walda would have to let go of this petty need to slap out when she wasn't getting her way, or when she got scared. Cora was patient long past sainthood with her mother, but eventually she would end up distancing herself from them and neither would benefit in the long run from that.

"I have guests to visit with," Cora's mother said before getting up and flouncing away.

John gave his daughter a kiss on the cheek, and then he held his hand out for Beau to shake, which he did. "I apologize on her behalf and I want to congratulate you because my Cora is perfect and you're very lucky to have her. Her mother will come around. She's hurting right now but soon enough she'll realize she's been wrong. She's strong willed but not without integrity."

"What do you say we get out of here early? Go home, change into our warm clothes and get ready for our friends to come over so we can watch fireworks?" Cora asked as she turned to him. "Then I can thank you for everything you said and if I cry it's in private."

"Let me go first. I'll get the car and pick you up out front in ten minutes?" He'd run to the car just to get her the hell out of that place and away from her mother.

"I can walk in heels you know. And I have sneakers in my office too."

"Say your goodbyes and meet me out front in ten minutes." He kissed her and made a quick escape.

CHAPTER TWENTY-FOUR

CORA HAD TO ADMIT—though it wasn't hard—that Pops was as amazing as Beau had made him out to be. He'd met them at their car and had swooped in and grabbed both Ian and Beau up into bear hugs before turning his deep brown eyes Cora's way.

He bowed and took her hand. "You are Cora. I've been hearing all about you from my boys here. I'm going to lord it over Ian's daddy for a minute or two that I got to meet you before they did. Come on inside. I made us some lunch but I figured you might like a tour of the grounds first. Bring that little doggie."

Jezzy jumped from the car and trotted over to sniff around the area. Pops bent down and spoke to the dog quietly before chuckling at the way Jezzy's butt got to moving so much when her tail wagged.

"I'd absolutely love a tour. I hear good things. I ate here once. My oldest sister was visiting from the East Coast and we had a birthday dinner here and it was out of this world," Cora said, meaning every word.

"It's pretty much all Ian's work. I just make sure everyone does what he tells them to."

The house Pops—his name when it came to his kids was Pops, he'd told her when he ordered her to call him that—lived in was perfect. Ian had gone to the effort to have built a single-story residence where his grandfather could continue to thrive but also be able to avoid stairs. The kitchen was astonishing, though she didn't know why it surprised her. He was the source of both Ian's and Beau's love of cooking so it made sense. It smelled like she'd died and gone to food heaven when they came back inside after they'd tromped through fields of winter veggies, checked out the hoop tunnels where they could keep a higher temperature and grow more produce for the restaurant.

Pops insisted on walking with Cora on one side, holding Jezzy's leash loosely enough for her to stop and smell things or bark at birds whenever it appealed to her.

Back at the house, once the muddy boots were left in the mudroom and Jezzy's paws had been cleaned up, Cora headed toward the kitchen, where she knew the others had gone.

Ian and his grandfather were at the stove, one tasting a sauce while the other stirred another pot.

Beau was totally relaxed as he chatted with them and she sat at the stool next to his. "Anything I can do to help other than staying out of the way?" she asked, knowing how Ian and Beau worked in the kitchen. It was usually in everyone's best interest if she kept to the side and watched, reaping the benefits of their hard work when it was time to eat.

"I was just telling Pops about watching fireworks from your house," Ian said. "Nothing for you to do but eat what we serve up and tell us it's all delicious. Even if that's a lie."

Beau snorted.

"Easy to be me right about now, I have to say." Cora laughed and stole a piece of cheese from the plate in front of Beau.

"That cheese is from a creamery just fifteen miles away," Ian said. "Goats and cows, so they have a nice variety. The chèvre there is something we're going to start adding to our cheese plates at the restaurant. What do you think?"

She tried some. "In Maui I had chèvre with lavender from the Surfing Goat Dairy. I know that sounds odd but it was so good. This has that sort of taste, still a little flowery but maybe more smoky. Like Earl Grey tea. I really like it."

"It is Earl Grey. Good catch."

He talked a little about community farming and the work Northstar was doing with different suppliers in the Northwest. He was trying to make his food better, make his community better by being part of it.

It made her like Ian even more.

"Did you tell him about your show?" Cora asked Beau.

Ian gave her a look, a wink. He was pleased she'd brought it up. And she was too when, after Beau gave Pops the details, the older man whooped.

"That's my boy. Good work. I'm proud of you."

The meal was fantastic. Spaghetti and meatballs, which were Pops' specialty, along with a salad with fennel and celery that managed to be sweet and spicy at the same time. They had brought the bread, as Cora had been at the bakery the day before and came home bread laden. As god intended.

"We need to have a big party at the house when the weather gets a little warmer. I think you'd really like the Orlovas, who run the bakery. A lot of their family dinners feel just like this one," Cora said.

Beau told them both about the cabbage rolls from the wedding and how Mrs. Orlova had taken an afternoon to let Beau come over and get a lesson on how she made hers, as well as a taste test of his.

They cleaned up the dishes and got things put away and were getting ready to leave, so Cora headed off to use the bathroom before she was stuck in the car. There were pictures up on the walls. Ian as a kid, maybe six or so, on the Dumbo ride, a huge smile on his face. High school graduation. Several magazine covers featuring a young and relentlessly hot Ian were also framed and she discovered he looked really good with his hair in braids and hoped he might decide that would be a nice hairstyle to return to at some point in the future.

Ian's father, Rian, was featured in many photos too, along with his mom. He'd progressed from hot young stud roles to now smoking hot older man with a little salt at the temples. His mother wasn't a model or an actress but she was no less beautiful.

A nice family with a nice life. That made her happy. So much so, she was still smiling when she came back out to the kitchen where the guys still were.

"So they sent that note and then another to Ian's restaurant and then they called you on New Year's Eve?

What do they want and can you trust anything they say to you?" Pops asked Beau.

Wait. What?

"He said my mother has cancer and she needs treatment. They have no health insurance and no money. Or so they say, and who knows? All the accounts the authorities could find have been frozen. He's on the run with two dozen people and that gets expensive. But even if he's lying about not having money, it's my mother," Beau said. "I can't take that risk."

"But the note they sent to me said your dad won't let her leave to get any treatment. How are you going to deal with that?" Ian asked.

"My uncle—he's the one who called—said he's working on my dad to let her go. Said he'd accompany her. If anyone can convince my father to do something it's Obie. They're close. My dad depends on Obie for a lot, so there is some hope."

"Will they tell you where she is? Or where your kids are? Anything but give me fifty thousand dollars based on trust?"

"Obie says he's been working to get my ex-wife to allow him to speak to my sons. To tell them they're old enough to have contact with me and that I want to have contact with them."

Cora leaned against the wall at her back. Aching for Beau to have to face the potential death of a mother who'd actually rejected him when he was still a damned kid and the distant hope that maybe *this* time would be the one that finally brought his children into his life.

He hadn't told her any of this. Not since the letter

on her door and she'd asked about it more than once. That hurt. But it wasn't about her at that moment. She was in someone else's home. He was clearly still reeling from it and she wasn't going to make a scene.

But it hurt.

She made some noise and heard Ian shush his grandfather.

BEAU HEARD THE rustle as Cora finished up in the bathroom and made the *shut up* motion at them. He needed to talk to her once he knew anything concrete. He certainly didn't want her to find out what was going on by overhearing it.

Just a few scant minutes later, she came into the room with her coat in her hand as she headed to Pops. "Thank you so much for having me today. The best spaghetti and meatballs I've had probably ever."

Pops hugged Cora. "You're welcome up here any old time, darlin'."

"Don't tease me now," she said.

Beau turned to Ian and whispered, "She doesn't know so keep it quiet."

Anger flashed over Ian's face. "You haven't told her yet?"

"No, and I have my reasons. She doesn't need the stress or the drama. When I know something concrete I'll tell her," Beau whispered before he ended the conversation by grabbing his stuff and moving to join her in saying goodbye to Pops.

When she left the kitchen, he turned back to hug Pops hard.

"I like her. You best tell her about this. Let her share this burden," Pops told Beau. "You can't move forward when you carry secrets and if you blow this thing with her, you'll be doing yourself some harm. That girl loves you."

"I know. Every day when she looks at me and I see it in her eyes I just hope to deserve it."

"Keep it up, boy," Pops said. "Both of you." He pointed at Ian.

He was surprised to see Cora in the backseat with Jezzy, but she was on her phone and pointed to Ian to take her place so they rode back to Seattle that way with her getting some work done and he and Ian fleshing out some ideas about Ian's midwinter menu.

At home, she took Jezzy outside and when he went to look for her half an hour later, he found her wrapped in a blanket out on the back deck.

"Hey. I've been looking for you," he said, sitting on the chair next to hers.

"I'm right here. What is it you want?" she asked. But her voice was flatter than usual. Enough that he swung his legs out to angle himself to face her. "Is everything all right?"

"You tell me. *Is* everything all right, Beau?"

Uh-oh.

"You obviously have something to say so just spit it out."

Her head whipped and he knew those words were ill chosen.

"Are you actually kidding me? Or did you have some sort of health issue that destroyed your ability to tell when you've pissed your woman off so much she's about to tell you what's what?" She pressed two fingers over his mouth before he could respond. "I want to be really clear right now that if you fucking lie to me or blow me off this has to be over. Be honest or fuck off."

He had nothing to hide but one thing and he damn sure wasn't going to push her into breaking up with him over it.

"The cult has been back in contact with me," he said at last.

She just looked at him. Waiting.

"I didn't tell you because at first I didn't know what they were going to ask for and it wasn't worth it to get you upset until I knew more."

"You heard from them *twice* more that you never told me about. You told Ian. And you told Pops but you didn't tell me. Even though I asked you more than once."

He saw it then, the hurt in her eyes.

"I didn't know anything more than to have my phone with me at all times. My uncle called on New Year's Eve. When I popped out to get the car to pick you up. You were already upset because of that scene with your mother. I didn't want to make it worse," he tried to explain.

"Tell me why *you* get the satisfaction of defending me to my family but I don't get the same opportunity," she said. "I never hid my crap, even though it can be off-putting. I never hid Walda. But you, after you told me you'd share, you hid this from me. And I found it out because you were discussing it with people you *had* told. And I get that you've known both of them longer but it's some major bullshit and you seriously hurt my feelings."

"At the party, right before the phone call. Your mom, she said I'd get bored with a calm life, that I'd walk off and leave you for something exciting," he said.

Cora nodded that she remembered.

"And then you wanted to leave and the call from my uncle came not two minutes after I left the gallery. I didn't." He stopped, scrubbing his hands over his face. "I didn't want to make her right. I didn't want to bring my damned drama into your life and I didn't want to give your mother any more ammunition against me." He blew out a breath. "I'm sorry. I wasn't hiding it from you because I didn't trust you. I just didn't want her to be right."

Cora sighed and Jezzy poked her head out of the blanket she'd been snuggling under to yip her hello at Beau.

"I'm sorry she made you feel that way. But *I* don't feel that way. This stuff with the cult isn't about you or your character. You're a parent who had his children stolen. A child whose parents abused him. You're a victim and you're trying your best to deal with that. I can help you. Or not. Maybe I don't know shit. But I *am* your person. Right? Even if all I do is listen I'm always on your side," Cora told him quietly. "If you let my mother control that and keep you from doing what you know I'd want you to, you might as well be with her. What I tell you is what's important. What she thinks isn't."

"You're right. Do you want to hear all of it? Inside where it's warm?" Beau held a hand out her way.

She took it and let him pull her to her feet. "Yes, I'd like that a lot."

After he'd given her the whole rundown, he said, "So essentially my mother is dying and my father won't let her get treatment. Treatment that will cost at least fifty thousand dollars if my uncle is to be believed. And if I help, he'll do all he can to get me in contact with my kids."

"Do you believe him?" she asked.

"Does it really matter?" he asked. "Being wrong could truly be a life-or-death type situation."

"Obviously it doesn't matter on that level. But I think the question does. I'm trying to understand the situation as well as I can. Can you believe your uncle? Be honest with yourself at least, so you can keep your expectations where they should be. You're a lot of things, Beau, but you're not a liar. At least you haven't been with me." Cora shrugged from her place in the chair by the fireplace.

A chair big enough for her and Jezzy, but not for him. She was keeping him back and he figured he deserved most of her wariness.

But she hadn't left. Hadn't run off or thrown things. Hadn't broken up with him. She wanted to know all she could to help as best as she could.

"My uncle, though he's my father's right-hand man, has never lied to me. He doesn't usually promise much, says he'll try and from all I've been able to tell, he *has* tried. But really, it's fifty thousand dollars. I have it.

If my mother can be saved because of it, great. Even if she won't speak to me. If not, I've lost some money but not my soul. Maybe it'll make its way to his flock so they can eat better."

"All I want to do is make this happen for you so you can get the outcome you deserve. I want you to find your kids. I want your mother to be all right and I want you to tell me when something like this happens without fear that my mother will use it or that you'll bring me drama. Fuck that and fuck her for making you feel that way. I want you, no I need you to tell me or I'll eventually start to feel like you're holding parts of yourself back. I love you and I don't want to resent you."

Beau got off the couch and moved to kneel in front of her. He took her hands and gave the dog a look when she kept sticking her face into his and her nose into his ear. "Back it up, weirdo."

Cora's laugh seemed to shatter the brittle film of fear and anxiety slowly suffocating him. He sucked in a deep breath and laid his head in her lap.

And she made everything okay once again when her fingers slid into his hair and held him there.

No matter what happened with his uncle and his mother, he had Cora, who loved him to the core.

CHAPTER TWENTY-FIVE

"I THINK YOU should write each one of your kids and your mother letters," Cora told him later. "I know you wrote them before when you dealt with a different person, but this is your uncle. Perhaps he can be trusted at least to deliver the notes."

Beau paced the yard, tossing the ball for Jezzy to run after over and over. Like meditation.

Cora didn't say anything else. She merely watched him pace as she drank her tea. He liked that about her as much as he loved her vibrant energy. When she needed to be quiet, she was.

"That's a good idea." He'd been hoping his uncle would give him a phone number or an address, but he realized that was very unlikely. His uncle had to sneak away from whatever business his father had Obie on to contact Beau, so it might be easier to have the letters with him. So if his uncle took the money and dashed, he'd be able to convince him to at least take a few envelopes. Less risk than exposing the group to Beau's presence.

He'd begun spinning out all the possibilities from the most unlikely to far more realistic. Would Obie bring the twins? Or his mother? Would Beau be able to go and sit at his mother's bedside when she was in treatment? Would Obie be able to convince Beau's dad to even let her get the help she needed? Would his sons even want to have contact after what he knew they must have grown up hearing about him?

"You're going to 'what if' yourself into a heart attack if you don't stop," Cora told him. Of course she knew when to speak up too. Knew when to snap him out of whatever he'd gotten himself tangled up in.

"I know. I'm trying not to. When I spoke to him on New Year's Eve, Obie said he'd call back within two weeks. It's been two weeks today."

"Wanna have sex to distract yourself?" she asked with the same casual tone she'd use offering him coffee or waffles.

Only this was sex, which was far better than coffee or waffles. He turned to her. "You're offering yourself up?"

"I'm sure as hell not offering anyone else up to sex you into distraction," she told him with a mock frown.

Okay then. Sex would most definitely be preferable to pacing back and forth, and Jezzy had been taking longer and longer to bring the ball back so even their fetch-loving dog was getting sick of it.

But instead of going inside, she got up to turn off all the outdoor lights. The standing heater was on because she liked being on the deck even in the cold weather. The glow from within was the only illumination as she tossed her pants on a nearby chair.

"I'm leaving the sweater on because it's too chilly to be out here sexing totally naked," she told him.

"It's okay. I know your tits from memory. I'll just imagine them," he assured her.

With an imperious point of her finger at him, she said, "You should get yourself similarly available."

Amused and definitely interested in making himself *similarly available* to have sex with his woman, he unzipped his jeans and went where she indicated—the chaise she'd been on before.

"I have honestly fantasized about having sex in this chair at least a dozen times," she said, directing him to sit so she could be on his lap facing him.

"Wish fulfillment is something I'm happy to provide."

She took his face in her hands and kissed him before letting go to get a condom on him. Cora knew he wasn't about long and slow. Not when he was worked up the way he'd been.

Instead she sank down onto his cock so fast they both got a little surprised and breathless at the end as body met body.

"So far so good," she murmured into his ear, and began to rock and grind herself against him. Deep and relentless. She was going to take him straight to climax.

No one else had ever read him so well. Knew him the way she did.

That was nearly as sexy as the way she felt, hot and wet while all around them the late afternoon was settling into a brisk night.

"I love you so fucking much," she told him, taking him deep again and again. Her angle meant she was totally in control, which she used to break him down until all there was was sensation. Hot and wet. Tight. Over and over, as her breath caressed the side of his face.

He found her clit, not wanting to go alone. Climax screamed toward him, barreling down, and he wasn't going to be able to resist much longer.

Her moan caught then, shifted into a snarl, the sound so dirty he ended up panting to keep from coming.

"Let go, my beautiful Cora. Come all over me," he urged and her head fell forward to rest on his shoulder as her body obeyed. Groaning as his body followed, his climax swallowed by hers in a feedback loop of sensation until he managed to get them both in the house and onto the couch.

"I'll get your pants in a few minutes," he wheezed as she snuggled against him. He needed to get rid of the condom. Should close the door leading out to the back deck. Should do lots of things and probably would again once he got his breath.

The plus was that he'd forgotten entirely about the phone call he'd been expecting. Until she came barreling into the bathroom an hour later holding his phone up as it rang in her hand. The shower had been pounding down on him hard enough he hadn't even heard.

She shoved it his way along with a towel. "I'll get the water handled. Answer it."

It was Obie.

THE FOLLOWING DAY she stood in front of where he'd been loading things into a messenger bag at the dining room table.

He'd already taken two surprisingly heavy duffel bags with the money to the truck and now he was gathering the letters he'd written and some other stuff like antibiotics that might be helpful to the rest of the group. He and a group of other survivors of religious cults had connections for certain kinds of medication to get to people still inside those groups. Beau had no real idea if they ever reached the people left behind, but he could only control so much. He just had to hope.

Beau knew she wanted to come with him. Wanted to be there to help in any way she could. But though he'd never worried about physical danger in the past toward him, he wasn't going to put her in harm's way if he didn't have to.

"Obie said to come alone and that's what I'm doing," he reassured her, kissing her before she followed him out to the front driveway. Not knowing what he might have to drive over or through, he'd borrowed one of the trucks from her dad's landscaping business. A bonus was the lockbox in the truck's bed where he'd been able to secure the money.

It was a lot of cash to just be rolling around with so he wanted to keep it as low-key as possible.

"Call me when you're done. I mean it, Beau. I'm going to be worried sick until I know you're okay. Don't go off and do something stupid. Please. I know you want to see your kids and your mom but use your head. I know you can do this and I'm hoping and praying this is that final step to finally getting reunited with the twins."

Cora hugged him. He knew she was trying not to cry but she failed. In some weird way it actually helped him stay calm. He kissed her, and then set her back. "I'll be in touch. I promise. And I'll be careful. You and Jez be careful today too."

She lifted a hand. "Love you."

"Love you too," he said before driving away.

Two hours later, he pulled down a dirt road and at the end of it was a small house perched on a river. His uncle sat on the front porch when Beau arrived.

He'd forgotten how alike his father and uncle looked and it brought him to a momentary pause as he thought about the last time he'd seen them both. Remembered his father looking right through Beau, the son he'd beaten and had kept locked up on near starvation rations for asking questions. For wanting the truth. Remembered too, Obie standing next to his brother. His gaze had settled on Beau briefly and he saw pity there before it hardened and Obie had looked right through him.

That had been the last time Beau had seen his father in person. In the intervening years he'd only seen grainy surveillance photographs.

Beau sure couldn't miss how his uncle had aged. He'd lost weight and most of his fiery red hair—same as Beau's and his dad's—had joined the pounds. Life on the run wasn't glamorous.

Beau didn't know what his uncle had planned for their meeting, but Obie came off that porch and pulled him into a hug and the child he'd been a long time ago remembered the connection he'd had to his uncle. "Hey there, boy. How you been?"

"Missing my children grow up. How about you?"

he responded. Whatever that nostalgia, they'd stolen his fucking children and he wasn't about to let it go.

"I surely do feel bad about that. God's honest truth. You made your choice though. You left us and in doing so, you lost your grace."

Beau barely withheld a sneer. He guessed having sex with a fourteen-year-old was so much better than calling it out as abuse. If he'd remained silent at other people's suffering that truly would have stolen his god-given grace.

"Where's my mother now? Were you able to talk him into letting her get help?" Beau asked, rather than get into a pissing match with his uncle. Obie had something he needed. Once that was handled he could be as frank as he wanted. Until then, he'd hold his anger in check.

"She's still with your dad. He's off praying about it. If I can come to him with that money, a clear and free way to get her help, I think he might be convinced to let her go. I was able to secure her a spot somewhere. A private medical facility. No, don't ask where because I'm not telling you. Just know that your money will be a big factor in saving her life."

"Will they know where the money came from?" Beau asked.

"I told your mom I was going to see you when I came back stateside. She'll know. It's best if your dad thinks I got it elsewhere. You look good, Beau. Your mom is real proud of you even though cooking is wom-en's work."

There was a lot there to parse through. Enough

backhanded compliments to give Walda a run for her money.

"What's her outcome if she doesn't get the treatment?" Beau asked. Obie had refused to say exactly what cancer it was his mother had, not wanting to give any more specifics than he had to. Beau wanted to assure him that knowing if his mother had liver cancer or lung cancer wasn't going to help him sic the authorities on his dad.

Beau wished it could. But his dad knew the score. Knew it had been nearly two decades and the authorities had other cases to pursue. George Petty had kept his head down, kept the group in places no one would find them unusual enough to investigate further, and in doing that, he'd stayed under the radar.

He hated all the undercurrent of unsaid things between him and Obie at that moment. Beau knew his uncle still loved him. It was in his manner, even when he was being a judgmental prick. It was in the way he'd come to Beau, knowing he'd help his mother. Obie shouldn't even be talking to anyone who'd been excomm'd from the group. Beau was pretty much Satan's minion as far as the group members were taught. But the hug had been real. And in his own way, Obie was trying to help. At least that was what Beau had decided to believe.

Beau held on to that small thing. It was more than he had before he'd shown up here.

"Even with the treatment she's got a thirty percent chance of survival. Without it she won't make it through the summer."

Beau scrubbed his hands over his face. His mother hadn't been in his life since he was seventeen years old. She'd been the one to refuse contact with him. But that didn't mean he was comfortable with the idea of her death from whatever illness she was suffering through. She was still his mother.

"You do what you need to. Make him understand. If anyone can, it's you." Beau stalked over to the truck and brought the money over, tossing the duffels at Obie's feet. "Here. Now where are my sons?"

"I can't tell you where exactly because it would endanger everyone else. They don't have phones or I'd just give you the number. I promise to work on your dad to get him to let your mom get medical help. And I promise to work on getting your sons to be open to contact."

Beau pulled out the envelopes with the letters he'd written. "One for the boys and one for my mom. Will you give these to them?"

Obie nodded. "I'll have to do it when they're alone, but yes. I promise that too." Obie paused. "I saw you on the TV at the airport. Cooking some kind of French fancy food. Glad to see you successful and happy."

Beau was in so many ways, but there was still that glaring empty spot where his kids should be.

His mother was an adult. She'd made her choice to stay more than once. Beau wanted to give her the opportunity to leave and he had, twice since he'd left, but she'd refused contact with him both times.

His sons, though they were adults now, weren't when the choices for their life were made. And they'd been raised to hate him and think he was out to destroy the group and their lives.

"Tell me if the boys are all right, at least," Beau asked his uncle.

"They're healthy. Handsome like you. Their names." Obie broke off a moment before speaking again. "Their mother changed their names when she took on a new church marriage. Dyed their hair until they got to be teenagers. They never complained. Always helped bring in the harvest if we was farming. Never once shirkers."

"Are they married? Did they get an education? Do they have jobs or are they only working on group land?" Beau asked, hungry for details.

Obie shook his head. "I already said more than I should. They're happy. And faithful members of the flock. I got places to be." He kicked one of the duffel bags. "Gotta get things in motion now that I have the money."

"Will you be in touch?"

Obie shrugged. "If I can. I'll keep my promises. Even if you never hear from me again, know I delivered those letters and did all I could to help your mom. Take care of yourself, Beau. God bless and keep you."

Beau made it home, but once he turned the ignition off he could no longer hold back the shaking of his muscles and the ache in his heart.

CORA HEARD BEAU's truck pull up and waited impatiently for him to come in. But after a few minutes she headed outside, concerned.

And found him, head resting on the arms he had folded on the top of the steering wheel. Worry had her quickening her steps, opening his door, and then the look on his face broke her heart.

"What's wrong?" she asked.

He turned and slipped from the truck's cab, pulling her against him with a barely suppressed sob. Cora's heart began to thunder, worried his mother had already passed or that his children had rejected him somehow.

Worried because, damn it, she loved him so much and seeing him so obviously upset filled her with an urgency to make things better.

She led him inside and into their bedroom, where she took off his shoes and settled against him, her head on his chest as he got himself under control again. Jezzy seemed to know exactly what was best. She laid over his feet at the bottom of the bed, giving him warmth and some weight.

"I gave him the money. He promised to give the letters to my mother and my sons. He said my ex dyed their hair until they were teens. I don't know why that hurts me so much, but it's all I could hear as I was driving back."

These motherfucking people made her so angry. That they did this to him and called it religion really pissed her off.

"A rejection of you? I assume they have red hair too so she erased that connection. She's terrible and I hate her very much. It hurts because they're yours and she's doing all she can to keep them from you."

He didn't say anything else for a time and it wasn't

necessary to. She simply wanted to be there. Wanted him to know she would always support him and listen to him. Would burn shit down on his behalf. All she could do was hope things turned out however was best for him. Knew most likely he'd be hurt again before the end, but hoping for the best anyway.

CHAPTER TWENTY-SIX

CORA LOOKED UP to see the receptionist walking toward her carrying a massive bouquet of flowers. So massive it hid the poor woman's face and part of her upper body.

"Delivery for you," she said from behind the explosion of roses and peonies.

Beau was really pulling out all the stops for their first Valentine's Day together. She'd started the day with an excellent orgasm followed by chocolate chip waffles, and now she had a flower arrangement probably visible from space.

She hoped her own preparations were half as awesome as his had been.

She'd gifted him a massage at this great little spa near the house, along with a haircut and shave at Whiskey Sharp after that so he'd show up that night looking good, smelling good and feeling relaxed.

"Dude, you're killing it in the boyfriend department today," Rachel said as she came in a few minutes later. Maybe was due in shortly as well and the three were going to have some tea and cookies to celebrate their Valentine's Day.

"I know! He just texted to tell me we had dinner plans and to be ready to be picked up here at six to go home and change into whatever is in some swanky box on our bed. He just sent a picture so I don't know what's inside."

Cora hugged Rachel and turned on the kettle to get water boiling for tea.

"He's got good taste. That dress he got you for Christmas that you wore to the New Year's Eve party was perfect for you. Whatever it is, I bet it'll fit perfect and make you look bangin'."

Maybe strolled in at the last comment.

"*Bangin'?* I don't think I've been banging since my teen years."

"Too bad for you. I'm bangin' every damned day," Cora said, giving Maybe a hug.

Rachel laughed and ran a palm over her belly in an unconscious movement. So sweet. Full of love already for a little life that wouldn't even be joining them all until mid-June.

"I almost bought you several novelty pregnancy T-shirts day before yesterday when Maybe, Beau and I were at Pike Place. One of them said Pregnant AF and I still might get it for you because it was perfect and it's not like your boss won't let you wear it. And, in case you hadn't noticed, you totally are pregnant as fuck. I love your baby bump."

"Most of the time I love it too. I'm officially sized out of my nonpregnancy pants. My god, can you even imagine what pregnancy was like before leggings became so easy to buy? I can't say I miss pants with zippers."

Cora curled her lip. "There are pictures of my mom

when she was pregnant with Bee and it was a never-ending nightmare of Peter Pan collars and big ass bows. With fabric that didn't breathe. Blech."

Rachel's nose scrunched up a moment. "I can tell you since we're alone in here that I have been sweating like a whore in church at night. I looked in my pregnancy books and I guess that's going to be a thing now. Along with perhaps too much spit. Can you imagine? Too much spit. Like a Saint Bernard?"

"Like everyone who gets pregnant drools? Because I haven't ever seen that." Cora would have added her thanks for that information, but if Rachel really did end up as a drooler, Cora would only mock her behind her back so as to not upset her. Like a good friend did.

"No. I guess it's more of a *some* pregnant ladies have excess spit," Rachel said as she looked at her phone to confirm.

"Well, good. Let's hope you can avoid that and all other less pleasant pregnancy side effects."

"She's gassy though," Maybe said as she snagged a cookie.

"You need a dog so you can blame it on her. That's what Beau does. Poor Jezzy doesn't even know how quickly he throws her under the bus."

They chatted and laughed, had tea and cookies and complimented one another's boobs. A perfect Valentine's Day so far.

Cora was saying her goodbyes, heading toward the door when her mother came in.

"Hey, Mom. Happy Valentine's Day," Cora called out. Things weren't totally back to normal after the scene on New Year's Eve, but they were speaking once more, which was forward motion.

Walda gave her a kiss and the flowers got a side-eye.

"Aren't they pretty? Beau is killing it in the boyfriend game. You and Dad doing anything special?"

"He's taking me to dinner shortly but we wanted to stop in to say hello and see if my painting had arrived."

Her parents had purchased a gorgeous painting while they'd been in Vancouver and it should be arriving any day now. Shipping to the gallery was far more common sense than to their house.

"Not yet. I can call to check on it tomorrow if you like though," Cora offered.

"Yes, that would be fine." Her mom paused. "Thank you."

A sleek limo pulled up out front and the driver got out and headed to the doors. "Oh! That's my ride. I've got to run. Have a good time tonight, Mom." Cora hugged her on the way out.

Her mother looked long at the limo, but then seemed to break out of whatever she'd been thinking and said, "I love you," instead of complaining or being mean.

Cora paused in the doorway, pleased. "I love you too. Tell Dad the same. I'll get back to you once I hear about the painting."

The driver held her door open. "Mr. Petty will meet you at home. He wanted you to help yourself to the champagne I've laid out," he said.

Indeed, a silver ice bucket held a bottle of champagne and a glass waited to be filled. Never one to pass up a lovely glass of champagne, she enjoyed it as they drove home.

Beau hadn't arrived yet when she went into the house. But he'd left a note that he was taking Jezzy for a walk and would be back shortly.

It gave her time to get ready though, and she really wanted to see what was in that box on the bed so she hurried into their room.

A beautiful green dress with cap sleeves and a heart neckline that showed off her boobs without putting them in jeopardy of loosing their bonds and surging free was nestled into tissue paper. When she pulled it from the box and the material slid over her skin, Cora fell a little more for Beau.

Formfitting without being tight or making her self-conscious. He'd thought of everything, including new shoes and a bag. Damn, he really was winning the boyfriend game.

A week before he'd come into her life she'd been in London, feeling trapped by her life, knowing she had to make some scary changes or get so mired she'd never leave her mother, never shake her life up and run the gallery like she wanted.

Three days after that she'd made the choice for certain. She'd flown back to Seattle filled with conviction about her future, and then there'd been Beau.

He'd never held her back. Never slowed her down or tried to manipulate her to make choices that were the best for him. No. He urged and supported her into making choices that were best for her. Over and over, he put her first. Even when he'd been a dumbass and hadn't told her about some of the communications with the cult, he'd been trying to protect her. Trying to keep her mother from having ammunition against him.

How could she stay mad at him once she knew that? Once she understood he'd done it to protect, not harm. And now he knew not to do that again. Knew her hard lines and he'd respect them.

After years of a life with everyone else put first, here she was in the house she shared with her boyfriend and their dog. Living a life where she made her own choices. And yes, she did put other people first sometimes. When you loved someone, you did that when necessary.

But she didn't do it because she was being manipulated there. And her mother seemed to maybe finally be realizing that sometimes loving someone meant letting go enough for them to breathe.

The front door opened and Jezzy came into the house, nails clicking as she ran toward the bedroom, knowing Cora was home.

Jezzy had been to the groomers and sported a red bow on each ear. She was fluffy and clean and absolutely adorable, as usual. Beau came in holding dog-sized angel wings. "She was supposed to wait so I could put these on but she got one sniff and knew you were home so she bolted," he said, and then stopped, checking her out from head to toe.

"Well, a gal does love to be loved." She bent to pet Jezzy and got some kisses in thanks. "I do love those red bows in your hair. You look very pretty for the holiday."

When she straightened, she caught Beau staring again. He said, "You look fucking gorgeous. Sexy and curvy and damn it I don't want to leave the house now."

"We don't have to." She shrugged. "We're adults. Oh, and I love the hair and beard. Maybe is an artist in her own right. How was the massage?"

"I'm feeling limber so watch out. As much as I'd love to take you up on your offer and stay here, we have reservations. Come on."

When he stopped at the marina, she was sure they were headed to one of the restaurants nearby but they headed away from the noise and toward the boats.

"Okay so we're going on a boat—I get that much." He gave her a look. "You're very insightful."

"Oh, was that sarcasm? Nicely done."

"This way, beautiful." He turned them down a dock and they headed up to what she figured out was the boat he'd arranged for them. Fairy lights had been strung all around and music played softly in the background.

At the gangplank, a server met them and escorted them on board, pausing while Cora toed out of her shoes before handing she and Beau both a glass of champagne.

"We'll be leaving the dock shortly. Your table has been set with appetizers and the chef will join you shortly to update you on the evening's menu," their server told them as he led them to the lavish saloon.

"You're getting so lucky when we get home," she told him as they pulled away from the marina and headed toward the lake and a leisurely cruise away from the noise and traffic.

"I'm already lucky, Cora. I've been lucky every day of my life because everything brought me to Gregori and Wren's kitchen in October when you came back into my life."

She swallowed and leaned against his side. "And they say I'm the poet? I think you have a poet within you, Beau Petty."

"It's just proximity to you. I've had a lot of Valentine's Days and I'll be totally honest. They mostly were about cooking dinner for other people to get out of having to deal with a date that night. You can't go on a casual Valentine's date. So I mainly avoided it or made money from it. But now that I have you, it's a whole new world. Yes, yes, I know it's a corporate holiday, blah blah. But you're my Valentine, Cora. Every day is Valentine's Day because you're the best thing that's ever happened to me."

"For winging it, flowers, a designer dress, bag and shoes and a private yacht with a fantastic chef-made dinner is pretty A-plus work. Thanks for being my Valentine too."

"You inspire me. This love gig is unexpectedly awesome. I'm glad you like it all."

The private chef turned out to be Len, which made the meal all the better because he knew them both and created a dinner she'd probably remember for the rest of her days. All her favorites. Things Beau had made for her in the past and he'd given the idea to Len so he could craft a menu that would be pleasing on every level.

Yet another way Beau showed her how much he listened. Every detail told her he paid attention and wanted to make her life happy and better and what on earth was better than being loved like that?

They ate dessert and had some port before going out on deck while the yacht headed back to the marina.

The stars wheeled overhead as they drove home. Their first Valentine's Day had been a huge success in her book. It wasn't the flowers or the yacht, it was the way he knew her. The way he put her first that she never ceased to be touched by.

When they got home and out of their fancy clothes, Jezzy followed her around with her stuffed pig in her mouth. It was lovely. Normal. Sweet even.

And when they made love that night, Cora drew closer to him, wanting as much contact as she could get. That touch of skin to skin sending warm waves of pleasure through her. It was long and slow and full of unspoken words.

She didn't need him to say he loved her when he held her face tenderly, when he kissed the hollow of her throat and hummed his delight. At each touch, something in her leaped up to greet that something in him. It was connection and homecoming even as it was passionate and hot.

It was love because love was all that and then some, and for she and Beau to have found each other twice and fallen in love, that felt like the best kind of magic she'd ever experienced. Once in a lifetime, struck by lightning while eating a cinnamon roll sort of magic that was so many things at once.

And afterward, he made her a grilled cheese sandwich at two in the morning because her life truly was awesome.

THE NEXT MORNING Beau dropped Cora off at the gallery and headed to Luna, where he and Ian had plans to do some cooking. He wanted to firm up the last few recipes and Ian was always a great taster and sous-chef.

It also gave him the opportunity to talk with Ian and let him know how the evening before had gone. Len cruised through at one point so Beau was able to thank him again for giving up an evening to come cook for them.

By one-thirty he'd finished up and called Cora, asking her if she wanted him to bring her some lunch, which she did. So he got to serve up some food to his woman to make sure she was well taken care of. Always a pleasure. Also a pleasure to watch her eat his food because she never held back on the moans of appreciation.

The receptionist knocked on Cora's office door and brought in an envelope. She glanced at it but continued with her lunch. Once they'd finished up and Beau was about to be on his way, she opened it.

And inside was another envelope. Addressed to Beau.

"Uh, I guess your family knows about the gallery." She handed it over.

"I'll apologize for that," he said.

"If you do I'll kick you in the taint."

"Um. Well, all right then. I take it back." With shaking hands, Beau pulled the note free. It was from Obie. "He convinced my father to let my mom get treatment. Still doesn't say exactly what cancer she's being treated for, but at least she's getting medical help. He says she's doing better already but they're still guarded."

Beau paused as he read the last paragraph a few times. Trying to wrestle his hope back a little. "He got the letters to my sons."

Cora pulled him back to where they'd been sitting to eat lunch. "Tell me."

Beau said, "One of them says to never contact him again because I'm damning his soul as an excommunicant. That means I was kicked out of the cult and my father told them to never speak to me again because I was poison. Standard treatment for anyone who questioned him or his methods."

"What about the other?" she asked, keeping her tone carefully neutral, but he saw the flash of anger in her eyes.

"Obie says his heart is not as hardened toward me as his brother. He's not interested in contacting me now, but he might be open to it in the future."

She knelt in front of him and took his hands. Love flooded him.

He told her, "I'm not even sad. I mean, that's not entirely true. I'm sad, but it's not the crushing desolation I used to feel when I thought about them. And then I think what a terrible person I must be not to be devastated right now."

"Or, maybe you're sad, but you've done all you can do. You've never stopped looking for them. You told them both that. You love them enough that you never gave up and now that they've expressed their wishes, you need to love them and yourself enough to let it lie for a bit. Hope the son who isn't totally cutting you out of his life comes around and opens his life to you. They know you're real. They know you want to see them and have a relationship with them. You can't get them to reject this cult they've been raised in. They're adults and make their own choices. For what it's worth I think you will be able to reunite with at least one of your sons. When he's a little older and better able to question what he might have been told. But what I know for certain is that you have consistently done all you could. And how can you do more than that? You are not bad or wrong for being where you are right now."

"I don't know how you always manage to say exactly the right thing at exactly the moment I need to hear it. But you do. And I'm so glad for it. I don't know how I'd have gotten through these last months without your support."

Knowing she loved him, that she believed in him, had helped him realize he deserved to be loved like that. Helped him see he deserved to see his kids, even if they didn't want to see him. He'd get through this time of sadness. Hope his mom got better and that one day he'd be able to hug his children once again.

But he didn't need to wish for real love because he had it. Right there in front of him. Filling his life with all the things that made life worth living.

"Come on, I'm the boss and I say I should leave early so I can go home and get schmoopy with my dude."

"You sure? I'm fine. I'll see you when you get off in a few hours," he said, but damn he hoped she didn't listen.

"I'm totally sure."

She held a hand out and he took it.

Beau knew then he'd always take that hand. Always walk into his future with her at his side. He came to her torn and not a little bit broken and she'd smoothed some of those rough edges, leaving the love behind.

Always bringing love. And understanding. Recognition and a sense of connection he'd never thought possible. And now knew he never wanted to be without.

* * * * *

ACKNOWLEDGMENTS

To all those who participate in the transformation from the weird thoughts in my head to a finished book: Everyone at HQN and Carina, the art department, marketing, promotion, sales, editorial from the most awesome Angela James to copyediting and proofreaders, audio, formatting—and anyone I may have left out—thank you all so much!

You've met Gregori and Wren in the
WHISKEY SHARP *books.*

Now read their romance in the standalone novella

CAKE

Available now from Harlequin and Lauren Dane.

CHAPTER ONE

SHE HEARD THE music as she ascended the stairs and knew he'd be working. Her heart sped as she hastened her pace. Watching Gregori Ivanov work was a sensual treat. He tended to fall deeply into his work. The building could fall down around him and he wouldn't notice.

There was something incredibly sexy about that. His intensity was a little overwhelming, but in the best sort of way.

Once she got to his floor, she didn't bother ringing the bell—Gary Clark, Jr. was playing so loud Gregori wouldn't have heard it anyway.

She let herself into the front entry of the massive space Gregori occupied. Three stories of windows washed the place in light. He took up a corner of the old building in Pioneer Square. Depending on where you stood, you could see Puget Sound or the redbrick buildings lining First Avenue.

She dropped the envelopes and the box she'd been delivering on the counter and wandered into his studio, leaning against one of his worktables to watch him.

Pale winter sun gleamed against his bare back. Ink trailed along his spine, over lean muscle. Lines of poetry, mainly in Cyrillic, wrapped around his forearms. Barbed wire marked his ribs, interspersed with more words. When he went shirtless, she'd discovered both his nipples bore silver hoops. He wore fingerless leather gloves, one hand grasping some sort of tool as he prowled around a large metal sculpture he'd been creating for the better part of the past three weeks.

His hair, currently scarlet red, stood up in liberty spikes, but other days he didn't bother with the full Mohawk effect and he put it in a ponytail to keep it from his eyes. On many it would have looked ridiculous. But on Gregori? It worked. Like really, *really* worked.

He wore eye protection, but she knew beneath the goggles his eyes were hazel, fringed with sooty lashes usually at half-mast like he was thinking of something particularly dirty.

He worked in jeans so old they bore threadbare spots in all the right places and, though he often went barefoot around the loft, today he wore work boots.

In short, he was a visual buffet. And she was really hungry.

He stalked and paused. Bending to tug on something. Or to grab more tools and sharpen a piece. Wren just watched. Fascinated by the way he created.

It went on this way for another twenty minutes until he finally looked up and noticed her there.

He slid the goggles up, a smile marking his mouth. "Wren. How long have you been here?"

His accent was jagged. Like he was. He spoke in staccato bursts, the sharp twists of his words sliding through the air between them.

"I don't know. Twenty minutes maybe. Half an

hour? I brought some paperwork by and a box. Kelsey says you need to sign the papers in the red envelope and get them back to her." Kelsey was Wren's cousin and Gregori's personal assistant.

He often proclaimed to hate signing things and attending to the business side of his art so she wasn't surprised when he sighed, taking the goggles and gloves off.

Ignoring the sigh, she stepped closer. "Can I?" Wren tipped her chin toward the sculpture.

He shrugged, pleasure mixing through his annoyance. "Sure."

She took it in. A man, crouched in the grip of briars and something else she couldn't make out. The metal was polished in some places, hammered in others. Sharp edges fanned out here and there. "Like flames," she murmured.

"Yes. Exactly." He moved closer and his scent caught her attention. Sweat, soap, the product he used in his hair. The fuel from the welding stuff he used. It all married together and became essentially Gregori.

"This is brilliant." Wren wasn't flattering. It wasn't a lie. He was a genius. One of those rare few who not only made a living at what he did, but had ascended to art celebrity.

He made a sound. A growl of sorts. "It's missing something." They both looked at it for some time longer until he sighed. "Come have tea with me."

He issued the invitation like a command. He tended to be imperious at times. But she rarely took him seriously, so she let it wash over her and perhaps might even have liked it. A little bit.

"While the water is boiling, sign that stuff or Kelsey will only send me back here."

They'd known each other for a year or so by that point, she having met him by bringing things to his loft several times a week. Over that time they'd developed a flirty back-and-forth and the more often she came to his place, the deeper the sexual undertones began to dig.

He looked up from where he'd been spooning the loose tea into a pot. "Do you have other things to do instead?"

"Are you asking if I have anything else but bringing papers, checks and doodads to Gregori Ivanov in my life?"

He laughed. "Do you?"

"I do. Shocking, I know, to imagine a world outside running errands for an eccentric artist, but there it is."

He sniffed, his lids falling as he took in the scent of the tea. "Bergamot. I love it." His eyes snapped open, gaze homing in on Wren, who'd perched at the nearby table. "What's a doodad?"

"Little bits of this and that." At his puzzled look, she got up and moved into the main room. He had a collection of what looked like gears scattered across a shelf. She pointed. "Like this. A generic term for bits of stuff. One of my moms says doohickey or thingamabob."

"Hmm. I like those terms. I do suppose you bring me all manner of little bits on a regular basis." The tea-

pot whistled and he turned to deal with it. "There may
be something to eat in the fridge."

She moved to the sleek, stainless-steel work of art
that filled her with refrigerator envy every time she
saw it, peeking inside. For a supposed wild bachelor,
he had a lot of really good things to eat. "Cheese, honey
and nuts?"

"Hmm, yes. There are crackers in the cabinet."

She began to pull things out, pouring nuts into small
bowls, hunting down the honey.

"How's school?"

Wren was going to art school at Palomar, an arts college. Her messenger job paid part of her bills and had
the benefit of being flexible around her classes. She
was also working on her newest graphic novel and a
few digital side projects. It kept her ridiculously busy,
but she was never bored.

"Fine. I'm really digging my autobiographical com-
ics course. I've got a digital-imaging class I'm learning
a lot from." She shrugged.

"You should bring more for me to look at. You
haven't in a while."

It made her uncomfortable. Not to seek his opinion.
She respected him as an artist. But she knew others
took advantage and she never wanted him to think of
her that way.

He had a hot button about it. Being used. It was
part of the reason he always wore his reputation as the
chain-smoking, hard-drinking, inked-up wild man in
bed to keep people back. He shared part of himself
with others, but he controlled just how much. She'd

rather have this connection, sitting, drinking tea and eating cheese and crackers, than the bored celebrity with the big dick.

"Maybe next time."

He took the tea to the breakfast nook and sat. She joined him, nibbling on the cheese and crackers while her tea cooled.

"What's this piece for anyway?"

"A commissioned piece. Rich guy wants it for the front of his office building." He shrugged.

He always acted like it wasn't a big deal.

"Nice. That piece will absolutely make the front of any building look amazing."

He ducked his head a moment, sipping his tea until he looked up again, gaze locking on hers. "Tell me about *your* work. You don't only do what you're told to in class. You had a graphic novel. What's the status with that?" His tone, to an outsider, would have been imperious. An order given to an underling. Even a slight emphasis on the *what you're told to* that made it clear what he thought of her need for school. It was partly the Russian in him, partly the artist thing and partly because he was one of the most supremely self-assured people she'd ever met.

At first, when she'd started delivering things to him and he'd addressed her in such a way she'd thought he hated her. Or that he was a rude asshole. Or both. But after a while she realized it was just his delivery.

When it came to his perception of art school he was most definitely abrupt. He was old school and in his opinion you had it or you didn't so why waste time in classes? Given his path—self-taught, sold his first piece at fifteen and now routinely sold pieces for six figures—it would have been a waste of time.

But she'd been exposed to so many things in her program. So many paths she could take. She'd learned about types of art and design totally out of her major, but that would serve her anyway. What she did was different from what he did. How she took in information was part of her process.

"I'm still working on it. I'll have it finished in a few weeks I think."

"I want to see it. You're very stingy with it, Wren. Didn't I just show you mine?"

"Are you offering to show me yours if I show you mine?"

He paused, thinking over what she'd said until his mouth curved into a slow grin. "Ahh, well." He shrugged but managed to make it dirty and suggestive. "But I did show you mine, didn't I? Unless there's something else you'd like to see?"

She blushed straight down to her toes. Flirting with him was big league. "Maybe so. I'll bring it by sometime."

"Bring it next time you come. Kelsey always has something else to make me sign so it will be soon enough."

"All right." She finished her tea and dusted her hands off. She didn't want to rush off, but she'd been there nearly an hour and she had work to do. He kept getting a faraway look on his face and she knew he was thinking about his own work.

She carried the dishes back to his kitchen. "Thanks for the tea." She moved to the entry counter and indicated the envelopes. "I need to run and you need to sign these papers."

He frowned. "Always with the signing."

"Poor you."

"You have no sympathy. A hard, hard woman." One of his brows rose as she snorted.

"Kelsey will kill me if I don't return with these. And, if I have to come back, you have to pay a delivery fee the second time. You sign the papers, she takes care of things and makes your life easier. Seems to me, buster, you need to stop crying and pick up a pen."

"Other people are nice to me." He read through the papers, signing where he was supposed to.

"Meh. Stop pretending you're not business savvy. I know you and your game. As for other people?" She rolled her eyes. "Other people want things from you. I just want your tea."

"I have better things to offer besides tea, you know." He waggled his brows and she laughed, though she couldn't fight the flush building through her belly.

"Yeah? You offering any of that up?"

He signed the last sheet, tucked all the papers back into the envelope and turned to face her. "I'm not sure you have enough time for all I have to offer."

She stepped close enough to touch the envelopes, which put her just an inch or two away from his body. "Try me."

The moment stretched taut between them, heating slowly, deliciously. Until he stepped back with a raised brow and a harrumph. "Go on then, Wren. Bring me something more fun next time."

She took the envelope, tucking it into her bag. "I already bring myself. Nothing is more fun than that."

One corner of his mouth rose. "I bet."

She turned, heading out, but paused at the door. "One of these days, you should see for yourself."

CHAPTER TWO

IT WASN'T UNTIL she'd gone that he realized he'd forgotten to give her the tickets for his show. Or even let her know he had a show coming up.

He stalked back to his workroom, pausing for a cigarette after he was sure all his welding supplies were shut off.

French. One of his small indulgences. He slid one from the pack and the scent of the Turkish tobacco rose. Distinctive. Connected to his work.

He loved the act of tapping the edge against his lighter. The ritual of putting it between his lips, the flick of the lighter and that first rush of nicotine into his system.

Yes. He knew they were bad for him. His dentist told him so every six months. His doctor told him so. He'd cut back to two or three a day. Almost always while he worked.

The light was good, he thought as he smoked, looking at the flames of metal. The color was also just right. Nearly bronze in places.

He smiled as he thought of how Wren had understood nearly immediately that he'd been creating flames. Intuitive, that one.

He really didn't need to have tea. He'd known exactly what needed to be done next. But more and more often as their friendship had grown, he found himself delaying her departure to spend time with her.

Gregori picked up one of his hammers and moved to his worktable where several sheets of metal he'd cut earlier that day sat. He worked, still thinking of her, of the way she'd teased him and of how he'd teased her back.

It wasn't that he never flirted. He was rather shameless about flirting, as it happened. He loved women. Came by that love honestly as he got it from his father. He flirted as easily as he breathed.

But with her it was different. She wasn't world-weary. Wasn't a social climber. She flirted back but it was…not pure, no, he was quite sure Wren Davis knew what she was doing. It lacked artifice. Which made her dangerous.

The artist, named after a bird, who delivered packages and envelopes to pay for art school. He stubbed the cigarette out, exhaling the last of the smoke from his body as he thought of her.

Long and tall. She moved as if she knew exactly where she was going and what she planned to do once she arrived. She often had her hair braided, held back from her face, exposing that beauty so easily.

Freckles danced over the bridge of her nose. Her eyes, bold and bright blue, took in the world all around her. Gregori always got the feeling she weighed, accepted, approved or rejected things as she went.

She wore jeans a lot, though in the summer she'd

worn shorts. She had lovely legs. Powerful, probably from bicycling up and down the hills in downtown. He liked the warm days because she wore T-shirts and tank tops, exposing the outline of some seriously gorgeous breasts.

Glasses often perched on her nose. He wondered why she hadn't gotten the surgery to fix her eyesight. Glasses worked for her in any case, though he wondered how they affected her when she worked on her animation for long hours at a time.

Art school. He scoffed as he began to pound the metal, shaping it, giving it texture. He'd gotten a few peeks at her work. She had a lot of talent. She didn't need art school.

Wren was vibrant and clever and certainly one of the best parts of his day when she stopped in. A constant in a world he knew was filled with mostly temporary people and experiences.

He blew out a breath and fell back into his work. He'd deal with the tickets the next day.

WREN FOUND HER friends already seated in a booth near the back windows of the tavern. They waved, calling her name as she made her way through the already burgeoning Friday night crowd.

The music was loud, but not so loud she couldn't hear Kelsey tell her they'd just ordered her a margarita.

"Yay." She shimmied from her coat and ordered tacos when the server came back with her margarita. She sipped it happily, leaning forward to listen to Kelsey talk about her new boyfriend—apparently now ex-boyfriend—and the way he'd sprung on her that he lived in his mom's garage.

"He tried to say it was all right because it has its own entrance. I wasn't impressed because she came in to do laundry when we were about two minutes away from pants being off."

"Well, at least when you smell Tide the next time, you'll have happy thoughts."

Kelsey took a drink. "Not only does he live in his mom's basement, but he tried to get me to see if Gregori could get us into Fixe."

Fixe was Seattle's hottest nightclub. Gregori knew the owner so he hung out there from time to time.

"Well, this is the guy who used a coupon to pay for dinner on your first date."

Wren had nothing against coupons. After all, they were all at the tavern just then because it was happy hour. Half-price drinks and four-buck appetizers were a great deal. But coupons for dinner were a long-term couple thing. Or a high school thing. And you didn't use your girlfriend to see if her boss could get you into nightclubs.

"I know." Kelsey nodded. "You told me he was bad news."

"But he has a great ass. And good hair. Did you dump him?"

"Yes. When his mom opened the door to the house and yelled down at him to change the laundry over when the buzzer sounded, I made my escape. He had the nerve to call me today to ask about Fixe. You know, since we're still friends and all."

"Get out!"

"I wish. Anyway, I managed to find it in me to laugh as I hung up on him."

Zoe, Wren's roommate, raised her glass. "Good riddance."

They all joined her in the toast.

"So now that we've heard Kelsey's news—" Zoe leaned closer "—what's today's hot Russian artist update?"

"Working shirtless when I went to his loft. Sweaty, but in the right way if you know what I mean. Man." Wren fanned her face. "He gets so intense when he's working. All that focus on what he's doing. It's so sexy. Makes me wonder—" *like every twenty minutes*

"—if he's that intense in the sack."

That got a laugh, but plenty of quiet moments afterward as they all totally went there.

"He made me tea. Flirted as usual. But he didn't pull the trigger. He flirts with everyone, though. I don't read anything into it. Though I'd like to."

"He *does* flirt with everyone. But he talks about you differently than the scores of chicks he's got on his speed dial." Kelsey shrugged. "He's got you in the employee camp. So you're safe to flirt with because he tells himself nothing is going to happen."

"I'm *not* his employee." Though she'd be lying if she denied the image of some naughty boss fantasies hadn't just run through her head.

"Nope. Just keep at it. He'll see it eventually. I mean, maybe. He's…well, you know. He's not a permanent type of guy. He's one of those live-in-the-moment people."

Sure, sure, Wren knew that. Knew he'd tried marriage once, years before and that it had ended up a smoldering pile of rubble. Knew that ex of his had meant his distrust of people had grown.

But she wasn't his ex. She wasn't his employee. She liked him. Wanted to know him better and it wasn't the worst thing in the world to imagine that he wanted to know her, too.

"I'd tell you not to go getting hurt, but you're not a dummy. Still, he's sort of…magical. Alluring with all those pheromones of his rushing around when you're near him." Kelsey shrugged. "He's a total handful. I like him. He gives great holiday presents and he pays me well. But I would not want to manage a man like him."

"Gregori is not a man to be managed. He's the one who likes to be in charge." Wren waggled her brows as they all laughed. "That's okay, I don't mind a man in charge. Well, in bed I mean. I can pay my own bills and order my own dinner. Anyway, he's an interesting, titillating part of my week. He's in a totally different world with models and hipster girls and jet-set travel." He was fun and sexy, but she knew reality from fantasy. Flirting was great, but Kelsey was right and Wren had no intention of getting serious about a dude who was a fun crush.

The conversation shifted to Zoe's new job at a design firm in town. Wren and Zoe shared a two-bedroom apartment just a few blocks away from the school where, up until a few months ago, both of them had attended.

CHAPTER THREE

JUST A FEW weeks after that girls' night out, Wren was in the student lounge, working on her sketch pad when her phone rang with Kelsey's number on the screen. She put aside her pad and answered.

"Wanna make Gregori your last stop of the day? I just got some contracts he should probably see this week. If not, I can take them by."

"I can do it. I'm done anyway. I was just hanging out and working on some sketches. I'll stop by his place on my way home."

"Great. I'll call it in for you."

But when Wren arrived at Kelsey's apartment, which also served as her office, she interrupted a hostile phone call.

Kelsey made the wrap it up move with her hand to whoever it was she was talking to on the phone. "We've covered that. No."

Wren sat across from her cousin, watching the interplay.

"If he wanted you to know his new cell number, he'd have given it to you."

Kelsey paused, holding the phone away from her ear. The yelling from the other side was audible.

"I'm his wife! I need to talk to him." Oh, her.

Kelsey rolled her eyes and, the genius was, it sounded in her voice, too. "You're his *ex*-wife and if you have a message you'd like me to pass on, I'm happy to do so."

Kelsey examined her nails as the yelling continued. Finally she'd reached her limit after a particularly vicious spate of epithets was hurled her way. "Nice. You kiss your mother with that mouth? Classy. This call is done now. I'll let him know you're looking for him. Don't call back." She hung up.

Kelsey snorted. "The last thing he needs is that crazy bitch back in his life. Ugh."

The crazy bitch was Prentiss Ivanov, Gregori's ex-wife. Wren was biased, of course, but she thought the way Prentiss kept pulling Gregori back into her life when she got bored was selfish and petty. Every time they reconciled he devolved into too much everything and yet not enough. Too much partying, too much anger and public scene making. Not enough work on his art, not enough happiness or stability.

"I thought they were done for good. Why's she calling you?"

"After the last time they had one of their *reconciliations*, he cut her off. He changed his number, had the building owner change the codes and locks on the outer door at his place. He's done, thank god. Anyway, she's getting his message and she doesn't like it. I think she truly thinks if she can get him face-to-face, she can pull him back in."

Wren took the envelope and a few other packages.

"I hope she's wrong. I don't think it's good for either of them. I have one other delivery to make and then I'll go to his place. Call me if anything changes."

It was an hour or so later when Wren buzzed up from downstairs as the main door to the street was locked. He didn't respond so she used her key and let herself in. Her arms were full so she took the elevator, hearing the music before the doors even slid open on his floor.

It was a guess that he was working. He often didn't come to the door when he was. She had a key but the last thing Wren wanted was to let herself in and interrupt some makeup sex if the crazy ex had gotten past Gregori's protests and back into his bed.

She kicked the door because her hands were full. No answer. There was only one other tenant on his floor and the building had good security, so it wasn't a risk to leave stuff. She scribbled a quick note and then texted him, informing him there were deliveries on his doorstep.

As she headed back to the elevator she heard his voice, raised, arguing in Russian with someone. His door opened and he stormed into the hall. His face... she froze at the anger on his features. But then it was chased away as he recognized her.

"Wren!"

Standing, her hand on the doorknob of the stairwell, she was able to tear her gaze from his face to find him, barefoot, in threadbare jeans and a snug T-shirt, his hair in a ponytail, eyes ablaze with emotion. The intensity of the entire package continued to freeze her in place.

"Yeah?"

He lifted a shoulder and she saw beneath the hard outer shell, into the vulnerability beneath. "Why are you running off? Why didn't you let yourself in?"

She blew out a breath. "I didn't know if you were working or if you...had a visitor."

He snorted and jerked his head toward his door. "Come."

"I really should go."

He put a hand on his hip. "Why?"

"I have a job. Other deliveries to make."

"Your hands are empty."

She sighed, annoyed. "Of course they are. I delivered your things."

"Do you really have another delivery to make right now? Or can you come in for a bit? I need a break and you're good company."

She should have said she did. But instead, she narrowed her eyes. "Sounds like you already have company."

"Me? No. I'm alone."

She took a few steps closer. "I just heard you yelling."

He shrugged. "I do that. It was a phone call." He turned, bending to pick his things up. "Stop hovering five feet away as if I'm going to gobble you up. Come in. I have baked goods. Is your bicycle all right? Do you need to go bring it up?"

She'd left her bike in the lobby. It was locked in a

rack. Everything was fine. He was her last delivery of the day. Not that he needed to know that.

"It's fine. It's locked up downstairs."

"Why are you hesitating? Do you think I'm going to pounce on you?"

She wished.

"What sort of baked goods?"

"Macarons."

"Well, you should have said." She moved inside, closing the door in her wake. The place was a disordered mess. Not his usual.

"My mother came over this morning with them. Had I known it would take so little to lure you inside, I would have ordered them straight from Paris."

She rolled her eyes. "Who were you yelling at?"

Wren followed him into the kitchen.

"I have coffee instead of tea. Would you prefer I make tea?"

"You're awful accommodating today."

"I'm accommodating every day."

She barked a laugh. "You're *imperious* every day. Two days ago you took the envelope from me, snorted and closed the door."

"I did?"

She simply raised a brow and waited.

"I'm sorry. I get wrapped up in work."

"Apology accepted. Coffee is fine. I have work to do tonight anyway."

"Night deliveries?" He frowned. "Is that safe?"

"No, I'm done working for the day. I have schoolwork to do. I'm meeting someone I'm doing a group project with. I have time to eat cookies, but I need to bike back home in a bit."

"I'll give you a ride. It's raining."

"It's Seattle—it's always raining."

"What is this project?"

"It's a short animated film. Shane, my partner, is doing all the edits so I'm going to his apartment to see the progress."

Gregori glowered a moment.

"Why are you grumpy? Grumpier than usual, I mean." She grabbed milk from his fridge for the coffee.

"What makes you think I'm grumpy?"

"I have eyes. Milk?"

He nodded and she poured him a dollop before putting the carton away.

"You're frowning at me. Excessively."

"Did you bring your art to show me?"

She sipped her coffee. "I might have some in my bag. If you, say, wanted to tell me why you're grumpy."

"Oh, so it's like that?"

She laughed. "Yes, yes I think it is. Maybe I don't want to show it to you when you're testy. What if you hate it and then you frown at me over it? I could get a complex. And wouldn't that be a shame?"

CAKE by Lauren Dane
Available now wherever Harlequin ebooks are sold.

New York Times bestselling author

LAUREN DANE

brings you a stunningly sexy, emotional and intense
new series set in and around Whiskey Sharp, Seattle's
sexy vintage-style barbershop and whiskey bar.

"A romance that is utterly captivating, seductive and full of the
kind of raw emotion and sensuality that has made this series
such a winner." —*RT Book Reviews* on *Back to You*

www.HQNBooks.com

PHLDWS18

New York Times Bestselling Author

LAUREN DANE

An impromptu road trip makes for the honeymoon
Gregori and Wren didn't know they wanted

Bad-boy artist Gregori Ivanov wants nothing more than
to marry Wren Davis. Now that the time is finally right,
Gregori has one hell of a celebration in mind—until
their flight to NYC is grounded in Idaho.

Forced to skip the romantic getaway and instead
improvise a road trip back to Seattle—complete with
roadside potato museums, funky galleries in towns with
little more than two stoplights and some seriously great
diner food—Gregori and Wren find a honeymoon as
unique and memorable as their love.

Don't miss *Sugar* by Lauren Dane,
available June 2018 wherever ebooks are sold.

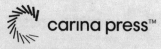

CARLD0718

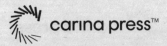

Get 4 FREE REWARDS!

We'll send you 2 FREE Books plus 2 FREE Mystery Gifts.

FREE
Value Over
$20

Both the **Romance** and **Suspense** collections feature compelling novels written by many of today's best-selling authors.